PRAISE FOR *BODY OF WATER*

"Adam Godfrey's *Body of Water* grips like a vise. Mystery piles on mystery. Horrors upon horrors. When you think the story is going one way, it veers another, keeping you unsettled and unable to put the story down. Written with an aching level of sympathy and pathos, while tackling what it means to survive trauma and grief, this is far more than a simple tale of watery monsters in the night. It is a tour de force about what it means to be human in the face of tragedy."

—James Rollins, #1 *New York Times* bestselling author of *Arkangel*

"In *Body of Water*, Adam Godfrey creates a terrifying, claustrophobic, and unique horror...and then throws you in at the deep end. Painfully tense, occasionally gruesome, it also plucks the heartstrings. Brilliant!"

—Tim Lebbon, author of *Secret Lives of the Dead*

"Just when you thought it was safe to go back in the water... the water gets into you. Adam Godfrey goes for the guts with *Body of Water*—then the heart—and floods them all, every last chamber."

—Clay McLeod Chapman, author of *Wake Up and Open Your Eyes*

BODY
OF
WATER

a novel

ADAM GODFREY

sourcebooks
landmark

For my wife, Heather, and our three daughters,
McKenna, Elise, and Teagan, whose boundaries aren't
determined by the world in which they live.

Published by Sourcebooks Landmark, an imprint of Sourcebooks
1935 Brookdale RD, Naperville, IL 60563-2773
(630) 961-3900
sourcebooks.com

Cataloging-in-Publication Data is on file with the Library of Congress.

Printed and bound in the United States of America.
VP 10 9 8 7 6 5 4 3 2 1

Happiness is beneficial for the body, but it is grief that develops the powers of the mind.

—Marcel Proust

PROLOGUE

STERILE, WHITE LIGHT.

Voices came in on the wind. They spoke his name, their echoes mingling with the screaming gulls that seemed to hover at the farthest reaches of his mind.

"Glen," a woman said. "His eyes are open." Again, his name. "Glen."

It took a moment for the brilliance of his sight to calm, diluted just enough to let the details trickle through, slowly inking themselves across the empty page.

He was lying down. The bare earth was gone. A bed stretched out beneath his back and head. His mind felt like a bowl of static, turning over like a restless ghost inside his skull. Understanding of the world around him broke apart like deconstruction of a jigsaw puzzle, thrown back into its box, shaken hard, its picture irrevocably dismembered. The artificial glow bled out and filled his thoughts, and swimming in its alabaster pool, the shapes of his environment began to come together.

A person. No, two people. On one side was a woman, by the sound of her voice alone. The other, indistinguishable. Glen was at a loss for where he was, *when* he was, sense of place and time abolished from his mind. He forced a swallow, going down like shards of glass, and tried to make out details of the space around him.

There seemed to be a door ahead, nothing but a vague rectangularity, its boundary but a dash of black sketched out across the powder coat of white that bloomed around it.

Other objects hinted at their presence. Smaller forms against a wall. Tables, carts. A square of light caught fire at the backside of his eyes, causing him to wince on contact. He closed his eyes to cool the white-hot irons laid against his optic nerves.

"Glen." The woman's voice was in his ears, his head. Someone touched his face, his hair, tending it in rows across his scalp with long and gentle nails.

CHAPTER
ONE

THE MOUNTAINS FLEXED AGAINST THE sky ahead, arched across the red horizon. It looked as if the low-slung scrim of clouds was bleeding out, their crimson underbellies opened up along the edge of day. The scent of the passing forest entered through the partially open driver's window, smells of leaves and soil, dampness, an occasional touch of smoke a constant presence as it circulated through the cabin of the truck.

The hills were loud with color, burning red and orange and yellow underneath the setting sun. The seasonal kaleidoscope had turned across the landscape as predictably as ever, yet the visual contrasted sharply with a slow, unseasonably brutal heat wave that had moved across the Eastern Seaboard for the past two weeks. With it had come rain. Torrents of it. Fortunately, it had moved out two days prior to their trip, as had the heat. In seeming rebound, the temperature had plunged deep into the upper forties. Left behind were scattered limbs and clumps of leaves littering the roadway.

Lauren wrenched her hoodie lower on her arms, hands knotting inside the stretched-out cuffs. She laid her head against the glass and watched it all go by. A clover-shaped birthmark revealed itself behind her left ear.

"Seriously. Can we be done with the open window? It's freezing."

"I don't know about freezing. Maybe cool," said Glen, "but a good kind, right? Better than last week's heat."

Lauren reached back for her hood and yanked it forward.

"Okay," breathed Glen. "You win." He hit the button on the door, sending the window up. The static windsong faded out, replaced with instant, rigid silence.

Glen had been looking forward to this. Just he and Lauren on an early October road trip out into the middle of nowhere. He wanted to bring her back to the mountains where they'd fished together when she was younger, popped their first tent, returning so many times across the countless seasons before the hard years came, back when they could still be called a family unit.

Uncut adolescence marked his daughter's face, her absolute disinterest in the whole affair apparent. In her lap, both thumbs dueled across the surface of her phone.

The nostalgia he had hoped for, the kind he'd fooled himself into believing they could summon, had been a no-show so far. Regret was knocking. Hard. Enough to make him want to wheel the truck around and head back home, wasted gas be damned. World's longest lunch run, why the hell not? They could head back to their zones of comfort—computers, phones, TV, work: the many vices of the modern family as we've come to know it.

But Glen's optimism flickered in the darkness still. It hadn't died completely.

His eyes cut several times between the road ahead and Lauren's screen. "Who's that?"

"Allie."

Lines of text notched upward. Glen strained to read it, but the messages were small, too fast to capture from his vantage point.

"What?" said Lauren irritably. She tilted the screen toward Glen and back again, flashed quickly like a fake ID. "It's just Allie. Don't worry."

There was plenty to worry about. He'd received a call a week before. Lauren's principal, who'd asked Glen if he'd been aware of Lauren's whereabouts. Asked him why he'd not returned their emails. Asked him if a conference would be necessary. Of course, Glen had been confused, but over the course of the thirty minutes following, he'd learned that Lauren had been absent three days in the past two weeks. Three times emails had been sent to inform him of the high school's unexcused absence policy. Glen had seen no emails. Not to say they weren't there. Just, he'd never *seen* them. He'd been fully unaware his daughter had been skipping school. That there was a boy. That they'd *both* been skipping.

Together.

"Let's put the phone away," said Glen. "Have a little device-free time here."

Lauren made a sound and pushed the phone into her pocket.

If Glen had needed some reminder of the ticking clock between him and his child, that call had done the trick just fine. It was an unveiling of the lie. The lie he told himself that she was fine. That he was fine. That their *life* was fine. And the big one: the lie that there was plenty of time, that she'd always be young, always be there, that there would always be a later. Always time to fix the things that needed fixing, to make things right again. It made him question if he really even knew her anymore. *Really* knew her. If he had the slightest clue what she was actually thinking, feeling, dealing with behind the curtain of her private being. Beyond the surface-level pleasantries of everyday existence. At least what pleasantries lay in between the layers of adolescent conflict.

He knew he'd been a good dad once. They'd had a bond. Not the kind of bond that Claire had shared with Lauren. The bond between a mother and her child is something different entirely. Claire and Lauren were two parts of a whole. It seemed to Glen there is no stronger force in nature.

Claire had been his heart, the most vital part of his existence. When she died, everything good about him seemed to die off with her. He'd been there through those past six years since Claire had passed, a functional provider and guardian for Lauren, but at the same time he'd not really been there at all. Not in ways that truly counted. With the call from the school, Glen was shaken into realizing that he needed to be present. He needed to be alive again. For Lauren.

He'd do better. There was still time for them to fix things, to make things right. He'd make sure of it.

This trip was going to be their start. Glen had taken time from work. Lord knows he had the leave stacked up to do it. Plenty. He'd also pulled Lauren out of school for several days, something that she'd treated like a punishment. She hated missing school. More accurately, missing out on time with friends. This only reinforced the necessity of this trip. A baby step toward finding *their* relationship again. It was small and relatively meaningless when held up against the vacant years before, but a step forward nonetheless.

They'd ventured nearly four hours from their coastal Virginia homeland and the area's featureless flats, watching the rapid evolution of terrain through city and crop and hill, the ever-arching earth at their front as they pierced the Appalachians. For the last full hour of that drive, Lauren sat there wincing as she pressed her shoulder to the door, stacking palms against a bladder whose alarm had tripped a good while back.

"Cross your legs. It helps," said Glen.

Lauren slipped him a look. A cut of eyes that somehow met her father without having called upon the pivot of her head, still angled toward the window at her right.

"What? What is it?"

"That doesn't work on girls, Dad." She groaned.

"Can't hurt, right?" Glen's eyes flicked from road to child and back again. He packed his lungs with air and let it go. "Lauren, we'll find a spot. Any minute. Road can't run on like this forever."

"Sure about that?" Lauren twisted in her seat and shot a cloud of breath across the passenger window.

A lump of fur came into sight along the roadside, growing larger over several seconds till it whisked past on their right. A large black bear, dead and crumpled up along the limestone edge. One of many carcasses they'd sped past.

Glen pulled a bottle of Lurasidone from the center console and unscrewed the cap. He looked inside and shook the bottle, rattling the last three pills. He dropped one into his palm and laid it on his tongue. They'd only be away two days, so two pills left was fine. Perfect. He'd place a refill when they got back from their trip. In any case, he'd wondered if they were even necessary anymore. The PTSD and the voices that came with it hadn't shown in two whole years. Of all the areas subject to improvement, things had actually gotten better on that end.

"Check out all those colors," said Glen, swallowing the pill and leaning forward with an outstretched pointer. He gestured toward the forest through the windshield. "Remember what those yellows and reds are?"

Silence.

"Sugar maples," said Glen finally. "Sugar maples. Remember? Used to come through here all the time with Mom. Remember that?"

Silence.

"And that right there. Those rusty-looking sections of the leaves. What's that? You remember?"

Lauren blew another shot of air across the window. With

the phone now in her pocket, her thumbs had gone to work along a pencil's edge, stripped down to the grain beneath her restless nails. Flecks of yellow paint had gathered on her leg.

"Verticillium wilt," he said. "Fungal infection." He let out a breath. "Well, anyway, lots of maples here. Pretty trees. Rest are oaks, white pines."

The route was thread thin, an acrophobic hell that gripped the edge of ridge and tree for miles, sparing opportunity for roadside relief. Some scenic pull-off with a single-serving of brush or stony outcrop to offer cover. It wouldn't have taken much. They'd been up into those narrow roads for more than twenty, thirty minutes. Roads that only seemed to grow more slender, more treacherous as they climbed.

Strangely, they'd not seen another car in more than thirty, forty minutes. It almost seemed they were alone up here, having missed out on some crucial bit of information that had redirected any other travelers to another route.

Glen cast the thought away.

On the side of the road, the diminished body of a large dog came and went, shrinking to a pinprick in the rearview. Lauren hadn't seemed to notice. She hadn't seemed to notice *any* of the carrion they'd crossed. For that, Glen was thankful. She could do without the distaste it would add to a trip for which she had no appetite to start with.

"Crazy. Looks like half the leaves have already dropped," said Glen, almost a whisper, speaking more to himself than Lauren. He squinted through the windshield.

"It's fall," said Lauren.

"No, I know," said Glen. "What I mean is it's kind of early in the fall."

"Can't the heat speed things up sometimes? Make the leaves drop sooner?"

"Check this out. A moment to remember." Glen laughed. "She *does* remember some of what her old man taught her." He reached across and poked her in the shoulder.

"I take it back," said Lauren. She readjusted in her seat, twisting her body closer to the door.

"You're right, though," said Glen. "I mean that would typically be the case, but..." He glanced at Lauren, then trailed off with the realization he had already lost her.

Lauren watched the sweeping landscape through the passenger window. A blur of rock and leaf streaked past, dashed with fleeting bursts of spring and river in between, reminders of the ever-unmanageable pressure that had pitched her up above her seat on rigid legs. She switched her sights onto the sky above, at least attempted to, catching glimpses of the open air and daylight only through the passing voids between the thinning treetops. Like a shutter, they opened, closed, opened. Several buzzards circled in the distance, high above the forest. The shutter action of the passing boughs reduced their flight path to a staggered circle, dotted lines of movement over something dead or dying somewhere deep inside that lush and hidden landscape.

Along these higher regions of the lonesome stretch, roadside dwellings had now thinned to just a fraction of what had occupied the lower elevations of the route. They'd dwindled down to maybe one for every several miles, with only every other structure suitable for more than wildlife seeking refuge. It seemed owners by and large had moved off the main drag some years back, now residing on the narrow lanes that snaked upward into higher ground, leading off into the rocky forest at preposterous, suicidal angles. At the bottom of these lanes, mailboxes could be seen, usually huddled in a nest of vegetation on a single post, four or five at a time. An abandoned shack came into view along their right, its neglect in keeping with the majority of others they'd encountered on this route. Whoever had resided there had sacrificed it to the wilderness no less than several decades prior. Its roof slouched sickly toward the roadway, what once was shingled now replaced by rot and foliage. Small trees sprouted from the soft exterior and chimney. The windows and the door lay open to the world, broken in and black. In the yard lay children's toys, a rusted kennel, and the carcass of a pickup truck, swallowed whole by weeds that stitched them firmly to the wild terrain. Suspended from an outstretched branch, a stethoscope with seashells dangling from it twisted in a subtle breeze. Between the metal arms were runs of twine or wire, crisscrossed, offering the impression of a strange and hastily constructed dream catcher. All these details came and went inside a moment, flashing past and down the endless asphalt throat behind them.

Glen yawned and worked his grip against the wheel, focusing on the pinch and sting inside his palms. The dream had come to him again the night before. It moved his sleep like time-lapse magic as it always did, rushing him up against the morning with those awful visions whirling in the wake. Compression of a full night's rest down to a fleeting wink. Sleep pleaded at the backside of his eyes. Claire's voice still lingered in the shadows of his mind, crisp and present, her breath almost at his ear with every indecipherable word.

He closed his eyes, a lingering blink, and opened up his mouth to fill his lungs.

The diner sprung with little warning. Glen shoved his foot against the brake and jerked the truck into a hard right, rolling past a signpost jutting from a concrete slab that rested at the corner of the property. Across the sun-washed board read OCEAN DINER, the edges of the once-smooth scrawl of letters notched and chipped away in places like some kind of old and unkempt Cheshire grin.

The diner was an antique venue, long and squat, primarily composed of painted cinder block and plate glass windows. A railless wooden porch, no more than a foot and a half off the ground, two at the most, ran along the front with timber columns posted here and there to hold a sagging overhang aloft.

The window running end-to-end offered sprawling views of asphalt and gas pumps, the line of roof above them topped with what Glen could tell had once been one of those spherical orange 76 gas station logos, since painted royal blue, one wave swirling round and over. Bird shit striped the blue, white tears running from the nest that capped it like a crown of grass and sticks.

Adjacent to the diner sat another cinder block construction. It looked to be abandoned, windows broken out and throwing kudzu from the gawping voids, the vines erupting out along the walls like tentacles of some great creature fighting for escape. Imprinted on the white exterior were medic crosses, equally as washed out as the restaurant's sign protruding from the roadside.

The very presence of the diner seemed to run the clock down on her bladder to its last second, propelling Lauren out the door of the still-moving vehicle as they drifted in between the yellow lines. Glen turned the engine off and fell back in the driver's seat, looking after Lauren as she bolted up the wooden porch and through the front door of the diner.

"Sure, sweetheart," said Glen, unbuckling his seat belt. He gave his head a shake, opened up the F-150's door, and planted one foot on the broken asphalt. "Be right behind you."

CHAPTER TWO

WHEN LAUREN CAME BACK FROM the restroom fifteen minutes later, phone in hand, Glen was seated in a booth, shouldered up against the diner's face. Two booths down, an elderly couple softly spoke to one another. He held the one-sheet menu in his hands, frowning at its laminated surface.

OCEAN DINER

The name's peculiarity for its location wasn't missed by Glen, who eyed the common theme of specials lined up on a wall-mounted neon board.

Coastal Crispers
Beach BBQ
Sandcastle Salad

Below those was a Minnows Only children's menu.

Nearby, a portion of the drop tile was removed, exposing the jointed union of a metal water line. A large glass jar sat on the countertop underneath it. Inside it was a scant amount of water, several inches deep. If there had been a leak, the jar had evidently caught the last of it.

An agreeable-looking man with balding head had just left the table's edge as Lauren approached and swung into the open seat. She squinted, eyeing the drink and basket full of chicken tenders sitting at the ready.

"You already ordered for me?" she asked.

"You were in there long enough to send us into dinner specials if I didn't," said Glen.

She poked through the pile of strips as if the real food lay beneath and this had been a clever prank.

"Coastal Crispers."

"What?"

"Never mind," waved Glen. "We don't have long, so this is just a quick stop. Go on and eat so we can get back on the road. We want to make it to the rental before dark." He raised his cup and pulled a sip of soda from its edge. "Anyway, you like chicken tenders."

"Maybe when I was like eight," she grimaced. Lauren folded her arms and flopped back in her seat. "I could've just had a salad."

Glen's expression fell. He pushed a hand across the right side of his neck and breathed, the smile he'd worn dissolving with the action.

Lauren stared into her lap without response, oblivious to the impact of her words. She moved her thumbs around the screen. She steamed and pushed the phone into her pocket.

"We are totally off the map, Dad. There's no cell reception."

"Exactly." Glen winked and managed another smile, weaker now. "That's kind of the point."

She slouched and scraped the edges from a patch of orange polish on her thumbnail.

"You'll thank me when we get there."

Lauren raised her brow, looking up at Glen. "Sure," she said.

The balding man clapped the side of the old-school television craning downward from the wall behind the counter. Glen and Lauren turned to face the sound. The snowstorm on the screen intensified. The bald man cursed beneath his breath and threw his hands up in defeat. "Damn storm. First the pipes, now the TV." He reached up and switched it off.

Sitting at the counter, a large bearded man of around fifty didn't seem to notice. Beside his plate of food, he read the daily paper as he sipped his coffee.

Glen turned back to Lauren. "Can't believe you don't remember," he said, pushing the contents of his meal around the plate. "You and Mom used to tag along with me and my class back in the day on eco trips. Several times. Fishing eels out of the streams, lifting rocks, catching salamanders. Telling you, you couldn't get enough of it. You always had a blast. We all did."

Lauren picked a chicken tender from her basket, turned it in her hands, then let it fall.

"Just you and I came only several years ago," he continued. "Remember that? The river tubing?"

Lauren's face was blank, the memory clearly unregistered.

"Got caught out in the rain?"

Nothing.

Glen frowned. "You really don't remember that? It was only three, maybe four years ago."

"You don't have to do this, you know," said Lauren.

"What exactly am I doing?"

"You know," said Lauren. "The whole involved dad thing. The bonding stuff. It's a little cringe."

"Well, thank you. Good to know," said Glen. A laugh of disbelief escaped him. "Appreciate you letting me off the hook like that."

"It's not too late to turn back, y'know," said Lauren, leaning toward him. She sent her lips into a canted grin. "We have movies, TV, you have your writing or whatever. We have our things. You know, our own *system*. Right? We didn't need to come all the way out here to stickville."

"When we get to the cabin," said Glen, moving past her feeble plea, "what do you think we should do first?"

Lauren slumped and fell back in her seat. "Maybe we could hang ourselves?"

"Cute," said Glen. "I'm serious."

"So am I," huffed Lauren. She tossed her phone down, then sat up straight and flopped her elbows out across the table. She watched her father pin the steak against his plate and play the edge of the knife across its grain. Her face dropped out in some involuntary shape of irritation and revulsion. She looked away and brought her drink up to her lips, drawing a sip to quell the rise of acid in her throat. Diet Coke. At least he'd gotten that part right. She lifted the cup again and pulled another sip, this one longer.

Suddenly two men spilled into the diner through its double doors. Lauren tracked their movement over the rim of her cup. She stared and swallowed, then raked her father's leg beneath the table, the toothy rubber of her Doc Martens biting his shin a little harder than intended.

Glen winced, still working the cheap cut of beef in his jaws. "What was that for?"

Lauren gestured in the direction of the counter, toward the two men who appeared to be rambling on to the balding man about something up the road. "Those men. Something's going on."

Glen turned and glanced across his shoulder, then shrugged. "Yeah, well…" He carved another section from the scrawny cut of New York strip. "They don't seem to be bothering anyone. Just a little worked up. Maybe having a day." Glen leaned forward, taking the piece of steak into his mouth. "It happens to the best of us, no?"

Lauren missed the jab, her attention elsewhere. She leaned forward, an incredulous expression on her face. "Dad, for real. You don't think they look a little…*off*? I mean, they're really going at it."

He turned and looked again. The two men paced back and forth along the cashier desk's abbreviated length, pointing up the road beyond the windows as they railed on. Fragments of discussion found their ears.

Water.

Phone.

People.

Drunk.

"I'll tell you," said Glen, still chewing, "one lesson I've learned in life." Glen chased the steak down his throat with a splash of Coke. "Whatever they have going on, it's best for it to remain between them and that gentleman at the front. Their affair, not ours. Sometimes we do best to mind our own business."

Lauren openly eyed the men. "Yeah, I don't know. Maybe we should just head out anyway. Just get it to go or something."

She looked around. At the counter, the bearded man seemed half attentive to the muffled commotion, half to his coffee and paper. Reba McEntire's "If I Had Only Known" leaked from the speakers overhead. The song was padded with a sheet of static that moved in and out of notes. Two booths up, the elderly couple scraped at their plates, sipped their drinks, overt efforts to remain disengaged from whatever was taking place up front.

More words trickled over. They came louder now.

Crazy.

Kidding.

Serious.

Lauren took her phone from the table and thumbed the screen to life again. No signal. She pocketed the device and turned her eyes back to her father.

"Dad, for real. Let's just go. C'mon. Go on and pay. I'll box the food. We'll just finish on the road." Lauren started shuffling plates and busying hands. Glen knew she was already in motion, gaining momentum, her mother's clone. There would be no stopping her.

"Ah, hell." He finished chewing, sinking the last of his bite with another sip of Coke. "All right. Okay. Let's go." He scrubbed his lips and tossed the napkin to his plate. "Never mind the steak. Can't do much with that in the truck. Like a strip of retread anyway. We'll save the fries though." He slid his way across the bench and stood, working loose the bunch of denim at his thighs. He approached the counter, standing now alongside one of the men, who was still engaged in whispered combat with the man behind the register. The other stood aside, flanking the doors with hands on knees, doubled over, head wagging like a solar window figurine.

The man behind the counter shook his head. He kept his volume low, aiming for discretion. "You've been drinkin', smokin', something. The both of you. It's all over you. Look around you. I got customers, for Chrissake. You're messing with my livelihood. Go on, take yourselves elsewhere, Hank. You're welcome back when you've sobered." He looked to the other man beside the door. "You too, Jesse. Goes for the both of you."

"Gimme the fuckin' phone, Tony. I ain't gonna say it again." Hank spoke with deliberation, slightly louder now, discretion clearly not a matter of concern. His face was sweaty, with a cold and sickly pallor. Glen wondered what he was on. He knew the look, having contended with the chemically altered on more than one occasion over the years in his high school biology class.

"You need to make a call, use your cell."

"Ain't no signal up this hill. You know damn well." Hank straightened, a slow precision to his angle like a snake about to strike, and he stared down at the man behind the counter. "Either you gonna give me that cordless I know you got stashed behind that counter, or—"

"Hey, guys? Not trying to get up in your business here, but we're going to go ahead and pay now, get on our way," interrupted Glen. He pulled his wallet, flipped it open. "Go on and pass me the damage, if you could."

The man behind the counter, presumably Tony, opened his mouth to speak but was cut off by Hank.

"Y'all ain't going nowhere. It ain't safe out there."

Hank's face looked like a well-worn catcher's mitt, rutted deep and prematurely aged. He turned it just enough to address Glen without looking directly at him. Its angle caused the artificial light to glance across its peaks in such a way that it left the hardened trenches shadowed, exaggerated.

"Yeah, well," said Glen, thumbing through the sheaf of bills. "We're just on our way through. Stopped for the toilet and some food. Whatever business you all are working through is just that. Your business, not mine."

"You ain't hearin' me. It ain't safe. You're gonna go on back over there, have a seat with your daughter. Feel me?" His words came slow and steady, a verbal warning shot. The man had moved his hand up to his hip and laid his palm across the butt of a revolver that protruded from his waistband.

Tony took a step back. "Hank, Christ—"

"Fuck you, Tony. Nobody's leavin'."

Glen stopped and slowly closed his wallet, pressing it between his palms. A chill ran through his body, lifting every hair along his neck. The next words from his mouth came low and soft. "Look, we're all adults here." Glen tried to form a smile, a gesture unreciprocated by the man before him. "We all have off days, right?"

"Sport, don't tell me about *off* days. You ain't got a damn clue." Hank turned, for the first time fixing his eyes on Glen. The words spilled from his lips with false tranquility, circuits clearly shorted somewhere underneath those matted locks still sweat-pressed to the shape of the mesh-backed trucker cap now dangling from his left hand. "Like I done told Tony here, there's some fucked-up, otherworldly shit going on down the road there. I'm telling you it ain't safe to leave. I know I sound like some tinfoil hat sportin' asshole right about now, but I don't care. I don't give a damn."

"All right, look, take it easy, man. Nobody said that. By the way, I'm Glen." He held a shaking hand outright.

"Dad?" Twenty feet behind Glen, Lauren called out from the booth, sliding toward the bench's edge.

Hank stared back at Glen, ignoring the outstretched hand.

"It's all right, hon." Slowly, Glen retrieved his arm and held it up behind him, palm upright to Lauren. "Stay there. Just having a talk, that's all. Just a talk." Glen nodded at the gunman, a gesture of reassurance.

Lauren did as she was told, frozen to the seat.

Hank pressed a shaking wrist across his brow to clear a track of sweat, then tugged the cap onto his head. "That lady," he said. "She was screaming, man. Screaming. I mean to tell you she was losin' her blessed shit." He looked to be on the verge of tears. "That water was all over her. I—I ain't never seen nothin' like that before. Not ever in my life."

"Water?" Glen frowned.

Jesse paced, cracking knuckles. "Go on, Hank. Go on. Tell'm what we seen." He was panting now, breathless, trapped in the bluster of his recollection. "Tell'm!"

"The water!" Hank shouted. "It—it covered her. It was coming through the window of her car, all up in her mouth, her eyes."

Glen stared at him. "Raining, you mean?"

"No, goddammit!" snapped Hank. "I know what fuckin' rain looks like, man. I ain't some kinda dipshit."

"Flash flood, maybe." Glen fought to keep a level face, a losing battle as he felt his features shape themselves into a mask of disbelief.

"Ain't no damn floodwater," said Hank. "That won't it. Ain't no way." He shook his head like a pit bull with a chew toy. "No way. No way."

"Why don't you just have a seat? Right here. You too. Jesse, is it? Come on." He gestured in the direction of the adjacent booth, motioning Jesse from the door. "Take a minute, catch your breath."

"I ain't takin' no fuckin' seat, sport!" Hank took a step back, his hand still on his waistline. "And Jesse ain't, neither." Hank threw a glance behind him. "Ain't that right, Jess? Not after what we just seen. Not so we can get blindsided by these fuckheads, put us all at risk."

Jesse came up to his feet, still wrapped up in a self-embrace. Absently, he nodded, eyes downcast.

Glen's palms went up. "All right, look, no worries. Just a thought, a suggestion." He felt the eyes upon his back, the others in the diner watching him like some obscure actor in one of those awful safety videos the city made his class watch each year. "Just trying to understand what's going on, why you're doing this. That's all."

"Your understanding ain't required! I don't need it. But I'm a patriot, and it's my duty to protect my own. And believe me when I tell you I'd jus's soon sling a bullet through any asshole try and head out that door, end up leading that shit this way. Hell, least that'd only be one lost, not more. Now, like I done told you, get on back to your kid."

Glen let the issue lie and did as he was told. He backed his way along the stretch between the counter and the booths. He sat down on the cushion next to Lauren. He could feel the motion of her hyperventilation in the cushion's springs. Her eyes had taken on a nervous, empty look.

Please, God.

Silently, he prayed to a god he wasn't sure existed.

Not now. Not today. Just let this pass.

He moved to speak. Instead, he shook his head with a helplessness he instantly regretted. Beneath the table, Glen took her hand in his. He gripped it firmly.

A vintage Coppertone Sunscreen wall clock read 5:36 p.m. A seagull moved around its edges on the second hand. Had they kept on driving, never stopped here, they'd be almost to their rental now.

Outside, the trees hissed, their tops abrading cold, blue sky that pressed them from above. There were no cars on the road, nobody to happen upon the scene unfolding inside, their private nightmare in the midst of rock and forest.

The place was quiet now, music stopped. A fly buzzed somewhere.

The elderly couple rested at the window, four hands wadded in a bond of prayer, nature at their backs. The bearded man at the counter stared into the cooling coffee in his mug. He chewed a mouthful of food.

"Man wants to use the phone, let him use it." The bearded man spoke through the mash of burger in his mouth, then pulled a swig of coffee, swallowed. "Man wants to call the damn cops, don't quite see what the issue is with that."

Hank stared at him a moment, and for a fleeting instant, Glen wondered if he was going to shoot the brown-skinned man off the stool. Then, Hank nodded, a slithering deliberation to the motion of his head and neck. "Yeah. Yeah, thank you. Yes." He turned back to Tony, still frowning across from him. "Least someone got some goddamn sense around here. C'mon, man. Hand it over."

Slowly, Tony reached beneath the counter and withdrew the cordless handset. He held it out to Hank, who snatched the unit from his hand and flipped it over, fingers tripping over buttons. The intermittent drone of a busy signal could be heard from all ends of the diner as he dialed out again and again.

"Shit. How the hell's 911 busy?" Hank paced, stopped, dialed again.

Busy, then static.

Hank tried again. The dial tone was gone. The phone was silent. "Shit." He shoved his thumb between his teeth and gnawed an edge of nail.

"Maybe some kind of natural emergency. Flooding, maybe," said Glen, regurgitating his suggestion from before. He spoke into the silence that engulfed them all. "Commonplace around here, isn't it? Precipitation's high. Streams and rivers swell, flood the roads."

Hank was no longer listening. He and Jesse now stood at the front door with their faces to the pane, eyes fixed somewhere far beyond the borders of the asphalt lot.

Glen came up to his knee and turned against the window at their booth. Lauren was already there, face to glass.

"There." She tapped the pane. "Dad, at the road."

At a glance, the blacktop seemed to move, to pulse. The surface shimmered in the daylight, moving out across the roadway from the direction Hank and Jesse had come not long ago.

"Just some water. I'm telling you." Glen's unconvincing words ran up against the glass. "Flash flooding."

"Ain't flooding," muttered Hank. Hank moved his face along the pane, twitching right, then left again, the way a bird might challenge its reflection in a mirror.

27

Glen didn't bother answering.

"Dad?"

"Yeah."

"It's coming this way."

"Just a little water, Lauren. That's all."

"Water doesn't flow uphill, Dad."

CHAPTER THREE

OUT ON THE QUIET HIGHWAY, rivulets of water climbed the slope of asphalt. Their movement was erratic, nonlinear, defying laws of gravity which, by every rightful form of human logic, should have reversed their natural course, cast them back downslope.

But there was plainly nothing natural about the situation.

The water pulsed and threw itself across the earth, sprawling out with lengths that moved across the blacktop, thin and long and eager, not as floodwaters might encroach en masse as one single, devastating unit, but almost smartly, tactically.

Faces lined the plate glass window of the diner. They shared a look of disbelief as the roadway was consumed in systematic fashion, water merely inches deep and swiftly turning. The common thought among the group was nearly audible.

We could just drive right through that. It's not too deep yet.

"We told you," muttered Hank. "Told you what we seen. We *knew* it was coming." Hank turned and faced the group. "All them people lined up in traffic back where we was. They're dead now. I know they're dead. If we go out there, we'll be dead too." He turned and looked at Tony.

The stocky man wore a stupid expression, naked in the spotlight of the moment. "What? It just don't make a lick of sense, Hank. You can't blame me for not—"

"We *told* you, asshole!" Hank leapt back toward the counter and throttled Tony by the shirt, snatching him close. "We ain't no fuckin' liars!"

"Jesus Christ!" panted Tony, bowed up against the man's two fists, squirming in his grip. "Jesus, man! It's just water! Ain't the first time the lot's flooded, man!"

From the counter, the bearded man spoke, eyeing them both. "Maybe you'd both like to take it out to the lot." He glared at Hank and threw a nod out toward the seething convergence at the outer reaches of the property. Tony dangled, grunting, still ensnared beneath Hank's fists.

"Ain't. Just. Water," growled Hank, articulating each word carefully as he stared at Tony.

Jesse cowered by the window, arms crossing one another like a straitjacket, wrapped around his torso past the range of natural reach. Hank released Tony, fell back two steps, then turned to find his place by Jesse along front door once again. "Water don't move like that. Not on its own."

"Tell us more," said Glen. "Tell us what else you saw."

"Ain't a whole lot to the story, sport," spewed Hank, one

shoulder driven hard against the jamb. "Anything y'all still having trouble grasping, that ain't on me."

"There has to be some explanation," said Glen, almost pleading with himself at this point. "That's just water out there, and it's not moving uphill. Can't be. Just looks that way from our vantage point. Trick of the eyes."

"All our eyes must've gotten pretty fuckin' clever all of a sudden," quipped Hank.

Glen shook his head but didn't say another word.

Another spill of water turned 45 degrees and crossed into the parking lot. It collected in a low point that was full of stagnant rain, rising up to meet surrounding asphalt, then moved out, resolute, intent, lacking the natural malaise of water succumbing to the laws of physics. It moved with predatorial stealth and purpose, acquainting itself with the terrain. As it did, its volume had already increased, the liquid sprawl now larger than before, in some sections deeper by several inches or more. Glen watched it, doubtful of the reassuring words that had crossed his very lips a moment prior, though the alternative simply made no sense.

The old man reached across his wife and rapped the glass with his finger, punctuating every word. "That right there ain't nothin' more than water. Here we all huddled up against the window like a buncha goddamn fools, talking like it's some kinda living thing, come to eat us up." He tossed both hands into the air, squeezing his body through the narrow slot of bench and table toward the open aisle. His wife reached out and dragged her hand along his arm, a gesture that he shook away with irritation. "You had to come and drag your crazy in here. You wanna tell stories of killer water, bloodsuckin' butterflies, haunted porta potties, you and your buddy there tell'm to each other. We're gettin' the hell outta here. I've had enough. C'mon, Helen."

The woman looked up at her husband, worry in her eyes. "Sit down, Fred. Just give it some time. I don't like the look—"

"See? Look what you done!" Fred cut her statement down the middle, left her sitting in the booth. "You gone and got my wife's head all tossed up in your stupid bullshit now." Fred took a step in Hank's direction. "I'll tell you this right here and now. You ain't keepin' us here." He turned around, addressing his wife again. "Helen, I said get up. It's time to go. It's enough."

The woman edged her way along the bench and took her husband's outstretched hand, coming to her feet.

Hank stepped back from the door and pulled the handgun from his waistline. "Siddown."

"What're you gonna do, big man? Huh? Shoot me? Shoot me and my wife?" Fred glanced around the diner, then spun 360 degrees, open-handed in rotation. "You're damn crazy, you know that? Either that or just plain stupid. Having a right hard time telling which." Anger shook his jaw, a microseism of emotion running high. His breaths moved long and heavy like a tug-of-war waged with the space surrounding.

In that moment, something seemed to pass behind Hank's eyes. The first of many looks they'd come to see again. It was as if his mind had slipped, dropping down into another gear. His words came flat and low. They held the steady pacing of a teleprompter feed. "I don't give a healthy damn what you think of me. You ain't seen what we seen. Now have yourself a seat." Hank let the weapon dangle at his side. He drew the hammer back. The steely resolution of the click appeared to disengage Fred's belligerence, sending him scuffling back into the booth beside his wife. He clenched his teeth at Hank, but this time kept his silence.

Hank rolled back his steps, returning to his post beside the door. He wedged his shoulder up against the jamb and turned his face into the glass again. "We gone be sittin' tight for a little bit."

Lauren leaned in closer to her father. She hung her head and whispered to the table to conceal her mouth, her words. "Dad, something's wrong with him. He's crazy." Her voice had thinned, emerging like a punctured raft whistling at the seam. "We have to get out of here. We have to get away from him."

Glen watched the sweat bead up and dribble down Hank's brow, the pallor of its low and waxen slope now tinged with yellow, like formaldehyde in action.

"He's coming down from something. No telling what," Glen whispered. "Hallucinations, anger, it's only going to get worse. Keep it calm. Nothing sudden, nothing loud. We'll be all right." He rubbed her back, somehow feeling the last time he'd done that had been a veritable lifetime ago, recalling the delicate curvature of her small spine, maybe age seven, eight. Maybe at the zoo, watching the animals. Maybe watching TV at home, perhaps the beach. He wished he'd paid a little more attention, savored those moments, held them closer. It all seemed such a washed-out haze. And maybe it was only in that moment's stress, the entirety of his mind surrendered to the navigation of their circumstances, working free the knot in which they found themselves.

"Jess!" Hank reached up and raked the stretch between his chest and shoulder. "Check the back, will you? Gotta be something more than tea and goddamn Yoo-hoo to drink around here. Shit." Hank stopped midstride and screwed his brow at Glen. "The hell you two lookin' at?"

"Nothing, Hank. Nobody's looking at anyone." The words came tumbling off Glen's lips like a legal disclaimer in a radio ad. "Right, hon?"

Lauren didn't answer, eyes firmly planted on the table.

"Yeah." Hank bobbed his head, folding lips between his teeth, ingesting portions of a salt-and-pepper mask of facial hair. He leaned over, hands on knees. "Right. Well...I *know* what you both thinkin'. What you *all* thinkin'. I ain't stupid, sport. You done implied that more than once already with your condescending questions. Your little comments."

"Certainly don't think you are."

"Certainly? Right." Hank snuffed. "Well." He paused and sucked his teeth, moving his eyes between them. "*Certainly,* you think I ain't quite all there." Hank lifted the revolver and knocked the barrel's tip against his skull. It made a flat and wooden sound. A dead sound. "That's what you're thinking." He smiled. "That we come up in here like one of them idiots on late-night reruns of *Unsolved Mysteries.* On some crazy bullshit about UFOs, maybe upright chimps out jogging in the woods."

"Listen, just think about it, okay? That water out there, it's only water." Glen frowned, his reasoning interlocked against the story that his own eyes recently had told him. Still, he continued. "What else could it be? Look, I'm not saying you didn't see something. I *know* you did. Something that has you and your friend understandably worked up. Something like we all saw with that water out there in the lot. Look, I get it. But sometimes things, you know, they just don't make sense at first, and then we find out later it was something purely logical the whole time."

"That so?" Hank righted himself. "Understandably worked up? Mhm. Shit. You ain't got a clue. You don't *understand* shit. Ain't a one of you even tried. Just sat back, looked down your damn noses at the both of us. But you'll see. Trust me on that." There was something broken in his eyes, a quick and vicious edge like shards of glass. "And when you do, I'll gladly take your thanks." Hank held his arms out straight and turned himself around. "The whole damn lot of you."

Jesse reappeared from the back. Two full handles of Jack Daniel's, a fifth three-quarters full, and an unopened fifth of Smirnoff dangled from his arms, and on his face he wore a simple man's delight. "Hank, looks like we caught us a little luck, buddy."

The interruption lodged itself between the gears of conversation, stopping it cold. Hank took several steps toward Jesse as the handgun winked beneath the fixtures overhead, splashing light across the angles of the polished cylinder. Across his lips, a wolfish smile emerged.

"Now, that's what I'm talkin' about. Here, lemme hold one of them bottles." Hank sidled to the counter, pushing himself onto a stool. He took the handle of Jack, still sealed, and cradled it like an infant underneath his arm. He seemed to whisper to it, speaking soothing words of reassurance as he worked to free the cap inside his gunless palm.

"Damn straight." Hank's breaths had picked up like he'd run a lap around the building. It whistled like a hissing fire log. "That's right."

He lifted it and downed a heavy swig, disconnecting from the bottle's mouthpiece with a snap.

"We gonna be heroes, me and Jesse." Hank held a wrist against his lips, nodding. He winced and seemed to give the burning embers in his chest a moment to extinguish. "Hell yeah...they gonna, gonna give us one of them *keys*...one of them keys to the city for savin' all you self-righteous assholes from that watery shit out there."

He laughed and held the bottle out, pointing it across the range of parking lot. Out beyond, the floodwaters coming from the front had already tethered to another pool that poured in from the building's rear, its surface wind split, like a work of ruptured safety glass.

"Ain't that right, buddy?"

Jesse moved his head in passive agreement. It was the look of some small creature in survival mode.

"What's up with you? All sulky like you dropped your fuckin' ice cream cone," said Hank.

"After what we seen today, and now all this," said Jesse,

gesturing toward the gun, the others in the diner, "how exactly you think I should be acting right now, Hank?"

Hank grunted. He watched his friend for several long and curious seconds before he moved along and sank another mouthful of Jack.

Outside, the landscape surrendered its color as the sky went gray, lifeless. The blackened cinders of the forest's edge burned cold, hateful on the backlight of a setting sun that clawed its way through limb and trunk, the death throes of the retreating day. A flock of blackbirds lifted from the treetops, staining the sky as they bled south. A cacophony of screams trailed out behind them.

In the settling night, Glen acutely felt the press of nothingness around them. Utter desolation. A veil of fog had formed, loitering just above the earth.

Next door, the abandoned medic building almost seemed to glow amid the falling night. On all sides, once-red crosses had now faded to an orangey pink. Any hope of healing had clearly fled the premises, turned its back on better days.

CHAPTER FOUR

LAUREN'S HEAD WAS NESTLED UNDER Glen's right arm. How she'd managed to fall asleep, he didn't know. For a while, he hadn't even realized. Adrenal burnout could work some cryptic magic on a person though. That much he knew firsthand, and it likely wouldn't be too long before it got him too, ready or not. Her sleep was shallow, troubled by the random twitch of nerve and muscle. Glen couldn't remember the last time they'd been so close to one another. They'd lived life at arm's length for the past six years since Claire had gone. It was his fault. He'd kept…busy. Anything to keep the grief from taking over. Anything to shut it out. Teaching biology by day, cultivating a failing writing career by night and, if being completely honest with himself, using every other exploitable moment to shit mediocre words to paper.

When the starry-eyed delusion of authorship eventually cleared, he'd found himself primarily alone, manuscript perpetually half-finished and no real relationship with Lauren to speak of. Those past six years, he'd not been there when she'd needed him the most and in those times her own survival skills had surfaced and developed, largely more effective than his own. At least she'd never let on otherwise, had they not been.

Glen leaned over, breathing in the scent of Lauren's hair, oily from the day's long drive, mixed with floral notes of shampoo and perfume. It slightly eased the storm inside him, leveling out the fear and panic cultivated by their circumstances.

On the window, condensation had begun to freckle. A single bead of water fell. Its course appeared to match the action of his nerves, lurching down the pane from one point to the next. The scent of Lauren lingered. A memory rushed up fast against the trigger.

"Is she sleeping?"

Glen opened up his eyes, interrupted at the fractured crossways of an unintentional sleep. He turned them toward the silhouette inside the strip of light that split the darkness of the tiny bedroom. Hinges creaked, and the vertical beam widened, spilling a chalk-white strip across the covers. Claire edged through the opening, closing the door behind her, bringing the room to blackness once again.

Lauren moved against his side, yawned, burrowed down into the sheets. She pulled a long and filling breath and settled out again into a measured puff of air.

"I think so," he said.

"What about you?" Glen could sense her smiling in the darkness.

"Not anymore."

His wife leaned forward, crossed him in the darkness, pressed her lips against their daughter's cheek. Claire's hair, long and fine, moved across his face, groomed beneath its sweep. The billow of her nightgown draped itself across him, carrying with it the sugared sweetness of her perfume.

He turned and did the same, finding Lauren's forehead in the darkness. He picked up scents of nighttime rituals, baby shampoo and powder on her skin, soft and smooth against his lips. Lauren shifted at the subtle gestures of her parents.

"Come on," said Claire. "Let's go before we wake her."

Glen reached up and moved his hand across her arm, her shoulder, feeling pills of cotton on her nightgown at his palm.

From the darkness, a hand came down and moved along his cheek, his neck, resting on his chest.

"Come on," she patted. "Before I lose you again."

The drop had staggered lower on the pane. It had led him to his own reflection. Exhausted eyes stared back. His shallow rest the night before was catching up, despite the chaos of the situation. Beyond the mess of sleepless nerves reflected in the window, the night had thickened with the settling fog.

Opposite the property, a stag meandered at the far edge of the road, its finer features nearly rubbed out by the whitewashed stretch of night between, though its form was unmistakable. It paused and turned its massive head, its steamy shots of breath discharged against the dripping blackness of the forest just beyond.

Glen's eyes rested in the lingering serenity that lulled his tired and overprocessed mind. From the diner, through the glass and fog, the visual transmission of what he was seeing seemed to take the back roads in its journey to the cerebral cortex. It hit him like a slug some seconds after the deer keeled forward on the asphalt, flailing in the shallow water.

Glen flinched and came up from the seat, his daughter slipping through the void he'd opened up in arm's departure.

"What?" She squinted, true consciousness a technicality as she loitered at the edge of sleep and searched the foreign surroundings of the diner for some anchor of recognition.

"The deer."

"What?" Lauren said again. The word transitioned to a yawn. She looked up at Glen, peering through reluctant lids. "What deer?"

Glen pointed. "Over there. It just went down. Just dropped." He stood, unable to look away from the creature.

Against the window now, Glen pressed his finger to the glass. "Right there. Across the lot. On the ground." He turned around and searched surrounding faces for some sign of recognition. "Jesus, right there. Something's going on with it. You don't see that?"

The others strained their eyes against the falling darkness, now having spotted the great animal wallowing on the wet concrete. It thrashed in place, raking its massive crown of antlers against the asphalt. The muted clack of bone on rock was hardly audible, barely loud enough to cross the lot, the glass, to find their ears inside the diner.

The large bearded man stepped closer to the window. "What's it doing?" He leaned near, palms cupped against the window's glare. "What's going on with it?"

"Just dropped. Hard to see, but it just fell right over." Glen turned to the man and back again. "Right into the water. That shallow water right there. Couldn't be more than several inches deep, at most."

The creature now lay still, save the lingering kick or lunge that fled its failing nervous system.

Lauren was awake in full now, lifted on a single knee that speared the vinyl cushion, her hands laid flat against the glass. "Dad, I want to go home. When are we going home?"

"I know, Lauren," he said. He glanced back at Hank. "Hang in there. We will."

She stared into the night. "What's wrong with it?" Her words were choked by fear, coming thin and short.

"It's fuckin' dead."

They turned around to face the slab of words that hit them from across the room.

Hank raised the bottle to his lips again and sucked another mouthful. He disconnected with a wince like he'd been hit with something nasty as the liquid burrowed south down his esophagus.

"Hank—" started Glen.

"Oh, what? You wanna try and rationalize this too?" He opened his lips and leaked a dry hiss of a laugh between his teeth, eyes pinched to slits like two strategic knife wounds on his face. "C'mon, man. We're all *fucked*, Glenny."

"Hank," repeated Glen, "I want to hear about what you saw again."

"Already told you." Hank stared at the floor, nodding. "Told you we ain't crazy. Told you what we seen."

"That lady you saw," said Glen. "Tell us more about what happened to her."

Hank let his head fall back and sighed. His eyes were wet and empty underneath the fluorescent lights. "Me and Jesse, we was stuck in traffic down the road. Hit a backup of cars that ran about as far as we could see. Must've been there, what, twenty minutes, maybe more, me and him just sittin' there shootin' shit when the lady in front of us come up out her seat, come across the back row, pressed her face up flat against the rear window."

"Dad," said Lauren. Her voice was choked into a whisper.

"And the water," said Glen. "Where'd it come from?"

"It's like I said before. The water won't just comin' through the window. Not *rain* or *floodwater* or no simple shit like that. It was runnin' *up* through the window. *Up*. From ground to door to window, covering her. She screamed till she couldn't no more. Hands, face mashed up against that glass. Lady screamed right up until that water filled her mouth, went inside, filled her lungs. Just kept comin' and comin' and…"

"Please. I don't want to hear this. I just want to leave," said Lauren. "We can just go." She was gripping the table's edge. "Can't we just go now?" Tears filled her eyes.

"And then the blood come," continued Hank. His eyes had taken on a disassociated haze. "Come when it left her face, crawled back out the way it got in, ways it didn't too. Back through her eyes, her skin, mouth, ears. God, Jesus…" Hank's shaking head fell forward and he clapped it in between both fists, one still holding the revolver, the other a bottle. "That's when me and Jesse left. Turned the truck around and got the fuck out of there."

Glen put a hand on Lauren's leg. She leaned into him.

"Must've hit seventy uphill. Came straight here to use the fuckin' phone." Hank looked at Tony. "Y'all know how well that went."

Tony didn't meet Hank's stare.

Silence fell on them. Nobody spoke for several minutes.

"You called yourself a patriot earlier," said Glen. "What does being a patriot have to do with anything here?"

Hank turned his eyes to Glen. They seemed to look right through him.

"You know what this is all about, don't you?" asked Hank. "Where it come from?"

"Do you?" asked Glen.

"You damn straight I do." Hank nodded, a deep and lolling motion. He pulled another mouthful from the bottle, raising a fist to blot the whiskey's remnants from his lips. He winced and paused as if to let the fire burn out in his mouth before he gave his answer. "Government."

"Aw, Jesus H. Christ." Fred rolled his eyes across the ceiling.

"You scoff all you want, old man," barked Hank. He leveled a finger at Fred. "Go on, scoff. It's the fuckin' government and that experimental shit we always readin' about. That's where it come from. You wait. You'll see." Hank let out a sound, some cross between a word and a breath, then turned his head and stared at his captive audience.

Glen couldn't hold his tongue, slinging loose the words

against his better judgment. "You really think the government's out there screwing with us? Out here in the middle of nowhere, in a diner. You seriously believe that?"

"You damn right I do. Ain't exactly like they short on giving us reasons to. Shady assholes."

"And you keeping us locked up in here makes you some kind of *patriot*? Saving all these folks from what? From who? *The man*? C'mon, Hank. You know our own government isn't going to do something like this to their own people, in their own country. Think about that. It makes no sense, Hank."

Lauren nudged her father. "Dad, don't argue with him."

Glen wagged his head. He knew she was right.

"Oh, but wouldn't they?" Hank stood, keeling back against the counter, propped on elbows. The bottle of Jack swung from his left hand like a bell. "C'mon. You think about that, Glen." Several fingers sprung out from the bottle's neck, tagged one by one across the weapon's barrel as he spoke. "Remember MK-Ultra? CIA mind control? Hm? All right? Midnight Climax, all that shit? Then you got the damn Tuskegee experiments. Right? What else..." Hank snapped in realization, jabbing his finger at Glen. "Operation Seaspray. That's another one. That shit they pulled off the coast of California—"

Fred broke in. "The hell you talking about, Seaspray?"

Hank screwed his brow at the old man. "Kiddin' me. You of all us folks old enough to remember that shit. Damn Navy dosed us with them orgasms—"

"Organisms," said Glen.

"What?" Hank lurched his head back, forehead bunched up like a kitchen rug.

"Organisms."

"Ain't that what I said?"

Glen didn't answer.

"Anyway," continued Hank. "Organisms, bacteria, whatever. Sprayed that nasty shit all over the Bay Area back in the 1950s just to see how vulnerable a city like San Francisco might be to a bioweapon attack."

"You're just batshit crazy, boy." Fred started from his booth again. Helen shook her head in disapproval as she reached for his arm. "It's a deer. Just a deer, boy. That's it. Ain't no magic water out there. Ain't no government shit."

Hank didn't budge. He propped himself against the counter, a loose and strawless scarecrow of a man. "Yeah, well, maybe you right, old man. Maybe that buck out there done got hisself into the damn Jack, had a wee too much, passed out on the concrete and jus' gave up the ghost." Hank turned his laughter inward, let it ring around inside his framework. It shook his torso like a piece of farm equipment on a winter morning. He grinned and held the bottle up as if to toast the man, revolver dangling in his right hand from the counter's edge.

Fred glared back at the drunk man on the stool, unbudged from his stance. The others watched him, their collective minds tuned to the same channel, entertaining the notion that he just might roll the dice on Hank. The place had fallen still, Fred's whistling breath the only sound as he panted his fury into the air. After several moments, better judgment seemed to triumph, and the old man succumbed to the direction of his pleading wife, her outstretched hand, and he eased himself back down onto the vinyl cushion. Hank blinked twice and flashed a smile that disappeared as quickly as it came.

Outside, the wind transitioned to an angry drone that buzzed the diner's face. It played the angles of the overhang and wooden posts that hoisted it above the line of deck planks at its base, warped and lifted here and there in ways that sometimes changed the notes of wind with shifts of course. And then, just as suddenly, the wind returned to nothing, and all was still again.

The fog was heavy, like a shroud of airborne wool, nearly impenetrable, and the fallen deer was hardly even there now. Beneath the jaundiced hue of sodium vapor bulbs that hovered overhead, the water shimmered and pulsed like a cinematic dream sequence, a seemingly innocuous flow that moved and filled and deepened with the passing moments.

Where roughly an hour or two earlier the water had kept largely to the asphalt lot and, farther out, the blackened roadway running up against the mountain slope, it now had reached the lampposts at the farthest edges left and right. It wrapped the timber pillars now, no greater than an inch or two in depth as best as they could tell. Toward the middle of the lot, the depth was difficult to read, though judging by the tiny island of two gas pumps stationed in the center of the property, it had risen maybe five or six inches to where it now was resting level with the concrete platform.

The bearded man slid from his stool and stood upright.

Glen could plainly see now how imposing this man was, towering what had to have been six and a half feet or more, bones stocked with rolling knots of muscle, his buttoned shirt drawn taut across his torso as he moved toward Hank.

"What exactly is your plan there, little man?"

Hank rustled to life, nearly spilling from the edge of his seat in his effort to stand, a newborn fawn on unstable limbs.

"Go on, now. Tell us. You got all us folks trapped up in here like a gang of crickets in a bait cage. What's that plan you got knockin' around inside your little drunken head?" The man came to a stop about six feet out from Hank, whose face now bore the crimson heat of an angry blister on the brink of losing its integrity. "Or ain't you even got one yet?"

"What happens now is we stay right where we are. We keep our asses put, where it's safe." The barrel of the gun swung back and forth along his side like a divining rod in search of water, downturned in his palm.

"Assuming you ain't just crazier than a run-over dog, that you somehow right about what's out there, this living water or whatever the hell it is you claim you saw," said the man, his voice the low and soothing baritone of country lullabies, "it ever cross your mind this place ain't waterproof?"

Hank stood slack-jawed, ungreased wheels of contemplation turning stiffly in his head.

"Suppose that water rises door-level. Don't you reckon it'll run right up underneath, maybe in between, right through them cracks?" He struck his finger through the air, gesturing toward the unprotected seam along the entryway. "Seeing as how we already gonna be stuck in here together, don't it make some kind of sense to work together, fortify them openings? Living water or not, we don't need no flooding, and it ain't gonna be long till that happens from the looks of things out there. Whatever the reason, the levels are rising."

Hank turned, eyeing the gaps of door and threshold. The man was right. The base of the door was parted roughly half an inch above the ground, one of those bearded draft guards stuffing the divide. Directly up the middle was a narrow split, large enough for additional seepage, same for the remaining perimeter.

"All right, then. Ain't gonna argue that." He raked the corner of his mouth with the barrel of his gun. Anger dribbled from his punctured ego like blood from bullet wounds. Hank's face grew red, not only from the fury rising from the forced agreement with the man who'd just insulted him but also the humiliation at not having not arrived at the same conclusion first. "You got a point. But you got any ideas might come with it?" Hank alternated leg to leg, left to right, not unlike the defiant fidgeting of a scolded child. "Better yet, you got yourself a name?"

"Laj."

Hank grimaced. "Lodge?"

"Laj." The large man packed his lungs with air, chest doubling with the load. "Short for Lajpal."

"That some Arab shit? You Arab?" Hank squared off, head tipped sideways.

"It's Muslim."

"Yeah, that's what I thought," Hank said. "Hmh."

Laj shifted on his feet, fists tucked up like two rocks at his sides.

Glen and Lauren didn't make a sound, eyes wide as they anticipated the worst. The room had fallen still, the silence bearing a certain mass that filled the space like some unknown malevolence.

"And what exactly *did* you think, Hank?" Laj raised his chin and stepped toward Hank, to where the man now stared a foot or more up into the downcast eyes that gored him where he stood.

"Nothin', nothin' brother. I got nothin' but love for my people *and* yours." Hank winked, forcing a grin. "Don't need no *jee-hod* shit between us. We can all get along. Just know you ain't gonna disrespect me in my own country. Like I told y'all, I'm a fuckin' patriot, son. You be civil with me, I'll be nothin' but civil back."

"I can do civil. But you call me *son* again, we gonna be revisiting negotiations." Laj held his eyes on Hank, a gaze that seemed to cut straight through this so-called *patriot*, seeing nothing but the disrespectful, small-town bigot at his core. Laj flicked his eyes to the gun, as if considering just how fast he'd have to move to snatch the weapon from Hank's hands and turn the barrel back into Hank's ignorant mouth.

"So be it," Hank said, wetting his lips. "Now, if you got a plan, let's hear it."

CHAPTER FIVE

Tony returned from the supply closet with a can of expandable foam and half a roll of duct tape. "Leftovers from the range hood install a couple months back. Meant to seal off all the gaps, never did." He handed the materials to Laj. "Fair warning. It ain't the good stuff. Went generic, cheap as hell."

Laj took the items. "Should be fine. Let's work it out, see what we can't do." Laj walked away, turning back again on second thought. "Might want to see if we got some Windex or something somewhere around here. Gonna want to wipe this edge down, help that tape stay put, especially on that cold steel."

"On it," Tony said, disappearing into the back.

Laj turned. "Hank, seein's how this seems to be your show, you plan on lending a hand here, or you feeling comfortable over there?"

"I'm supervising," said Hank. His eyes didn't settle for a moment, skitting from the windows to the room, from face to face, back to the lot, the water, then repeating through the cycle. "Y'all ain't gonna get over on me. Blindside me when I ain't looking. No thanks. We good right where we at, me and Jesse." Hank looked to his friend. "Ain't that right, Jess?"

Stooping at the base of the doors, Laj spoke into Glen's ear.

"We all play it easy, let him calm, drop his guard a bit, we'll ride this out nice and safe. Let your girl know we all gonna be all right."

Glen gave a subtle nod. "Right there with you."

"He keep nippin' on that drink like that, we ain't gonna have too long before it's lights out," whispered Laj. "Give us a chance to pick that burner off him, then get our asses out of here."

"And the water out there," said Glen. "You suspect it's anything more than that?"

"I suspect our boy is off his goddamn rocker," said Laj. "That's about all I suspect. All we doing with this nonsense here is playing along."

"And the stag?"

"Heart attack. Stroke. Could be anything," Laj whispered. "Don't let this guy pull a fast one on your head, Glen."

Jesse stood off to the side, tall and lanky, an observant fixture in the corner, positioned like an unassuming coatrack. He worked his way across his fingers, cracking knuckles in sequential order, throwing his eyes toward the doors, the others already in motion, then back to Hank again. "Probably should be helping out, giving 'em a hand. Thinking you or me maybe take care of the back door while they handle the front."

"That right?" Hank stared at Jesse, sucking at his teeth. "I'm thinkin' you should *probably* follow my damn lead, chief."

Jesse sniffed and swiped a hand across his upper lip. He moved his eyes again between the others and his friend, pressing on his knuckles, alternating four at a time between both fists. "Look, suit yourself, Hank. I ain't gonna just stand around doing nothin.'" He motioned to Laj. "Here, gimme that can. Save the tape. We might need it later. Foam's enough to kill the gaps on its own for now."

Hank squinted. "Well, you go on ahead then. Sheep or shepherd. Your choice." Hank fell back in his seat, clawing at an itch along the left side of his neck. He glanced behind him, then turned his eyes back to the lot outside, now a veritable lake. "I don't trust none of 'em."

Laj passed the can to Jesse and stepped back from the door.

"This ain't no power play, Hank," said Jesse. "We need to work as a team. We ain't here to take hostages. Least I ain't."

Hank sat up straight, licked his lips. "And what the fuck's *that* supposed to mean?"

"Nothin'. Forget about it." Jesse stepped to the door.

"Well, naw," said Hank. "Naw. Come on now, brother. You got something you lookin' to get off your chest, then come on out with it. Words already done crossed your lips, hoss. Just ain't so sure I know exactly what it is you're gettin' at. I didn't know no better, I might be inclined to think you suggesting my intentions ain't completely on the up-and-up." Hank came up from the stool, taking a step toward Jesse. "But I know you wouldn't go and say nothin' offensive like that."

Jesse simply stood there, staring back at his friend. He had a hard time making eye contact in the same way an abused dog evades his master's gaze.

"Man, something tells me you could start an argument in an empty house," said Laj.

Hank turned sideways on a heel, loosely facing Laj. "Oh, what, you got something to say again?"

"How 'bout we focus on the task at hand instead of y'all running your mouths back and forth," said Laj.

Hank shimmied the weapon back and forth against the denim of his jeans. He moved his eyes between Laj and Jesse till he'd been abandoned, left to bicker with himself. He stood there in the center of the floor, the two others having already gotten back to work.

Fred and Helen watched them from their booth, Lauren standing to the left of them.

"Doesn't this mean we can't leave?" asked Lauren. There was panic in her voice. "If we seal the doors, we can't get out. Why would we do that?"

"Just stay there," said Glen. "It's going to be fine. It's just for now, okay? It's nothing permanent."

Hank nodded, a slow roll, then leaned back against the front desk. "Well, don't y'all let me hold you up there, team players."

"Found the Windex. Towels too." Tony slipped an arm between Laj and Glen, passing off the items in his hands.

"Let's hold on to those for now." Laj threw a nod in Jesse's direction. "Gonna' try this spray foam first."

Jesse shoved the straw into the split between the doors. Starting at the floor and moving up, he laced the gap with sealant, watched it bloom to fill the void, rising like a batch of yeast along the seam. When that was finished, he worked the gap that ran between the door and floor, followed by the farthest sides.

Glen came over and knelt beside him, running his eyes along the weld of insulation. He tried a section with his finger, packed tight in its hold.

Jesse swiped the beads of sweat across his upper lip. He laid his forearms on his knees and double-checked his work. "Should hold up. Least for a little bit. Gonna hit the back doors just the same."

In the pooling darkness out beyond the threshold, the entirety of the lot now shimmered underneath the thoughtless glow of lamps that roosted high. Its depths remained concealed beneath the night and threads of light that wriggled on its surface, though logic told them it was fairly shallow still. Just outside the door and windows, the water was well below the wooden porch that lined the building's front, nine or ten inches at least, offering up some small degree of reassurance that their post was still secure, its resilience to the threat not put to task just yet.

As Glen stood in contemplation of these things, a slap of foolishness struck him, and his face went hot with shame for having succumbed to the lunacy of their armed host. Laj was right. The entire prospect was completely absurd. He knew this. But the image of the stag throbbed in his mind as if some truthful splinter. He couldn't shake the vision of the animal's demise there at the water's edge. They'd all seen it, though it couldn't have possibly been the water itself at fault.

Surely, something else.

Illness, a bad heart, something. Anything. Literally a million other possibilities other than the insane yarn that unraveled from the mouth of the gun-wielding drunkard, food for the gullible conspiracy theorists, chemically altered, readily devoured without question.

And then there was Lauren. His child would look to him for reassurance, a voice of reason, intelligent analysis.

Lauren.

Glen realized at that moment she had disappeared. He turned right, then left, then saw her reappear around the edge of the counter from the back room, several bags of rice laid out across the crossing of her arms like the body of a sleeping infant.

"Here," she called, nodding toward the cradled heap. "For the floor crack." She came up on her toes and dumped the bags onto the countertop. "I thought maybe it would help."

"Smart thinking," said Laj. "Can sandbag the openings with those." She passed them off and clipped the fingers of her left hand in her right, watching him a moment before she doubled back for more. Laj grabbed three bags and stooped, packing them end to end against the bottom of the doors.

She appeared again with several more stacked in her arms.

"There we go." Laj waved her over. "Bring 'em around here. We'll take as many as we got."

Lauren met Laj at the doors and passed the bags into his waiting hands.

Glen met her at her side and laid a hand on her shoulder. Lauren slipped away and moved into a nearby booth.

Hank snuffed and sucked another gulp from the bottle.

When they'd wrapped their task, the door had been foam welded at all seams, a messy arrangement in combination with the sacks of rice at its base, but one which helped to shield them from the rising tide, should it come to that.

Over the next hour, Tony prepped some food, though food was just about the farthest thing from any of their minds. For Tony though, cooking was more therapeutic than anything else. It beat the mindless pacing that his nervous system begged for. That or outright breaking down.

"How long you reckon this is going to go on?" whispered Glen. Laj checked the room across his shoulder. In a far-off corner, Hank was slouched behind his bottle, disinterested in the food. Disinterested in the others, oblivious to their discussion. Any hunger that Hank might've felt was likely decimated by the toxic burn of whiskey in his gut.

Laj turned to Glen. "No telling," he whispered back. "Man's got an iron tolerance, I'll tell you that much. And I ain't seen him lift a finger off that pistol this entire time."

"What the hell is our plan?" said Glen. "Just sit here?"

"Bout all we can do right now," said Laj.

"To what end?" asked Glen.

"Till others come along, help us out of this," said Laj. "Maybe till that water out there drains off, takes our man here down a paranoic notch or two."

"What if it's not just water?" whispered Lauren. "What if it's like they said. What if—"

Glen laid a hand on Lauren's leg, giving it a pat, bringing her to silence. "And if neither happens?"

"Then we take control of the situation ourselves," said Laj. "If it comes to that." He glanced across the room again. Jesse sat across from Hank, staring out the plate glass window. Fred and Helen whispered back and forth to one another, about what he couldn't tell.

Though Hank had been their epicenter of concern, all still remained aware of the surging tide outside the diner. Twenty feet beneath the futile reach of lamplights, the sprawl of water shivered. Its surface glinted like electric veins beneath the hazy cataract of night.

After those who managed to eat had finished what they could, Lauren tucked herself into an intersection of the bench and window. She leaned her head against the glass, peering out into the oily haze of the Appalachian night.

When the unexpected mass first emerged from deep inside the silvered mist, all but indistinguishable at its distance, she pressed her fingers to her eyelids, holding for a moment.

She dropped her hands and looked again. The mass drew nearer, roving on the water's surface, slowly coming into focus. Lauren didn't raise alarm at once. At first a state of curious disbelief had seemed to stall her as she squinted, leaning closer to the window. Only when the human body floated into full, complex view did she draw a breath and return it to their quarters in the form of a scream.

CHAPTER
SIX

THE DINER'S INSIDE BUZZED BENEATH the stir of feet and voices. Lauren's mind had seemingly become a weightless thing that floated in between two dueling layers of consciousness. Some rushed to the aid of the girl's sagging body as it spilled across the table's edge. Others filed out along the glass with hands cupped tight against the glare to gain a better point of view.

"Jesus," said Tony. He leaned into the window, squinting. "That looks like Lindy Sowers. She was working the Sunoco just this morning. I just saw her."

"The hell happened to that girl?" said Fred. He pushed his face against the glass for better visibility. "Her face. Look at it. Her whole damn body."

The corpse now drifted close and nudged the porch's edge, pivoting on its head to swing its lifeless limbs from west to east, face yawning as it turned beneath the mist. The desiccated mask of flesh was drawn up tight, sucked deep, vacuum sealed against the mouth and sockets. Its bobbing head was wreathed by a mane of blond that flared like sunlight, wild and serpentine amid the gentle current. The woman's jeans had fallen low and crumpled on her legs, the frame of muscle shrunken down and liberated from the touch of cloth that rang about her body like a cotton bell. Beneath the sallow wash of downcast light, the diminished casing of the woman shimmied on the water.

"Must've drowned," said Glen. "Swept up in the current." He put both hands on the glass, leaning right to gain a better vantage point of the water flowing from the roadway. No more bodies could be seen.

"Ain't no way. Not Lindy," said Jesse. "Girl was a damn hustler. Used to own the swim hole growin' up. Embarrassed damn near every boy fool enough to take her on, and robbed 'em stupid in the process. Ain't no way she drowned."

Lauren was sitting now, arms wrapped around her stomach. Glen sat beside her on the bench, his arm around her back.

"Dad, it's real, isn't it? What that man's been saying. That water. There's something wrong with it."

Glen looked at Lauren, his jaw half-cocked in preparation as he grappled with the logic knot that wedged itself inside his mind, his throat.

"It's just water," said Glen. "Just flooding. Sometimes terrible things happen. Things we have a hard time understanding, but it's only water." He cringed inside, knowing better. It wasn't only water. Water doesn't dehydrate its victims, and that body was essentially mummified. But what it was, what could actually do what they had seen, he didn't know, and he refused to lay out dangerous speculation. And so for now, for his child, for the preservation of her peace, her sense of safety, it was only water, nothing more.

"It can't be. You saw that lady. You saw her body. It's something else out there." A tear released itself, riding the downward slope of her cheek before she turned to face the glass again.

"Lauren, just because there was a body..." Glen stopped short.

"What, Dad? Tell me you weren't about to say that lady just drowned again."

Glen didn't speak, couldn't speak.

"I *know* what that looks like," hissed Lauren. "So do you."

A flush of cold moved through him. A memory surfaced, rifling toward him uninvited from the archive of his life in four, vivid dimensions.

At the base of Glen's skull, the heavy thump of helicopter blades, turning over orange and white. The chaos of the EMT's surrounding Claire, surrounding him.

His bare back against the sand.

Stinging salt.

Aching lungs.

Lauren screaming.

Twisting from the searing daylight overhead, coughing, purging water. The push of someone's hands, at his shoulder.

Claire beside him, cold, sodden, pale. Sightless eyes, fixed above. Her body shaking on the hard-packed sand with each violent, numbered thrust.

One.

Two.

Three.

Darkness.

"So don't even say that."

Lauren's voice returned him to the present.

"That lady we just saw," continued Lauren. "She didn't drown."

"We can't say what happened to her, okay?" said Glen finally, his voice reduced to little more than breath, now against his daughter's ear. "We just don't know. Don't let that man's story get to you. He's not well."

"You *saw* what she looked like," spat Lauren. "Normal water didn't do that to her. It looked like something sucked the life out of her. Dried her out."

Glen could only sit there listening. She was right. By God, she was right, and there was no way he could argue with her.

"We're stuck. We're stuck in here with all these people. These *strangers*. We're sealed in here. I just want to *leave*. I want to go *home*."

Glen opened his mouth, prepared another explanation. Then, he closed it. Pulling a breath, he tried again, reducing his words to basics they could both agree upon.

"I know you're scared, Lauren. I know," said Glen. "I get it. I do. Trust me, I want to go home too. And…and we *will*." He took a moment, dipping his head to catch her eyes, her attention. "But know this. We're safe in here, okay? Let's just try and focus on that right now." Glen tucked an arm around her shoulders, pulling her to his side. "We're safe right here, where we are right now." He squeezed her tight, holding her there beside him. "You trust me?"

Lauren hesitated, then nodded.

They sat in silence for a moment.

"And there's your appointment, Dad," said Lauren. "What if we don't get out of here in time? You go back to the doctor Wednesday. You can't miss it. You promised."

"I know," Glen said, staring out into the darkness of the flooded lot. "One thing at a time, okay? It's going to be fine."

"It's your health," whispered Lauren. "Your life. Even if *you* don't care. It's not just for you. You can't just keep blowing it off. You're not the only one affected."

Glen's face recoiled and he disconnected from his point of focus, turning toward her. "Why would you say that? Of *course* I care." He pulled her closer. "It's why I wanted to head out here with you in the first place. I thought this would be a chance for us to spend a little time together, do something we haven't done in such a long time. It's not like this part was planned."

"Did you take your pill?" asked Lauren.

"Yes, I took it," Glen lied.

He thought about the voices, shuddered at the thought of their return.

"I'm fine. We'll both be fine."

The old woman muttered something from the other end of the diner, a breezy whimper not designed for understanding, a primal code of mounting terror. Fred rose up beside her, his eyes looking to the farthest reaches of the lot.

Glen and Lauren broke from their discussion, turning their attention in the same direction.

Two more masses spilled down from the western incline on a sudden flume. The forms careened into the open, spinning like two broken compass needles. They appeared to catch an edge of current somewhere in the center of the open space, an easy flow that carried them around the edge of the lot and swept them back along the diner's front, rounding near.

Lauren slid back from the glass, pressing her back against her father, lifted on a single knee behind her. Her body locked itself in place, bracing for the inbound horror.

Fred spoke into the glass, clouded by the shots of breath. He peered between his hands, cupped against the window. "Jesus Lord," he muttered. "What is this?"

The body of a man spun into view, facedown in the water as it drifted toward them, lofty on the water's skin. The flesh was puckered over scalp and neck like something left to wither in the desert heat. The remainder of his body was clothed in full, save the absence of his shoes, one sock half removed, an ivory serpent slithering on the blackened surface.

Laj pressed himself against the window, hands cupped against the glare of the fluorescent lights inside. "Who are they?"

Tony shook his head, a blankness in his eyes.

"Anyone recognize these two, know where they came from?" asked Laj again.

Jesse chewed his thumbnail, staring out into the water. "Don't really matter where they come from."

Laj looked to Jesse, then back to the parking lot. A nervous tic began to tug the corner of his mouth.

"Told you there was people dying out there," said Hank. His words came flat and low. "That it wasn't safe to leave. Ain't you glad we came along now?"

By the time a third form came to greet them, Helen had already lost her breath behind wet palms, beginning to fill the air with broken whispers of the Lord's Prayer. A small boy floated past, his body turned upright, head cocked left. His withered sockets landed on them as the body slowed and rode the current past the line of viewers like some kind of morbid float on its parade route. The lips had thinned and puckered over tiny teeth that lined up like two rows of baby corn. His fist still clutched a stuffed giraffe, its cotton body flailing in the wake of death that tucked and swirled behind, though the corpse was drifting opposite the water's flow. Glen's skin gathered on the backside of his neck, and his insides reeled at the physical impossibility. No wake should trail an object which yields itself completely to the current.

The vision thrust him back to childhood.

Summer of '91 in Kitty Hawk, North Carolina, along that vacationer-stuffed stretch of the Outer Banks. He'd been bored, milling around the rental cottage's stilted foundation, wandering along the dunes that backed the oceanfront dwelling. He'd snatched up broken strips of erosion fencing, slashing through the troops of sea oats springing out along the ridge like waves of hair, green and tan and hissing in the salty wind. He'd wandered out beyond the dune along the surf line where he came upon a small shark's corpse, its head crushed by a wedge of brick that lay nearby, half-submerged beneath the wash of sand. That dead fish became his first toy of the summer stay. He'd used the strip of fence to shove it opposite the current, guiding it through the shallows. He recalled the spill of water over the dorsal fin and tail, the way it cut against the flow and mimicked actions of its larger kin in *Jaws*. God, how he'd loved that movie.

Glen recalled the way the coarse flesh pitted underneath his fingers when he reached to grab it, guide it to the shore. The fish's body fell apart, disintegrating in the salty froth, slipping through his fingers. He recoiled, smelled his hand, inhaled the rancid scent of sunbaked decay. That trip, that moment, it had been so pivotal for him. Such grotesquerie that would have turned most stomachs had actually done the opposite. It had absolutely fascinated him, setting into motion a lifelong love of science. Of living things and what exactly made them tick or perish.

Standing at the diner's window, Glen could almost envision that strip of fencing prodding at the small boy's chest, urging him against the current's will as the cadaver moved along the length of porch. Inevitably, he also envisioned the child's flesh falling from his bones in pluming sediment, scattered out into the black.

The unexpected vision slipped into his mind so fast, so heavy, that it seemed to slide into his gut, throwing him back down onto the seat before the meager remnants of his meal resurfaced.

"Where are they coming from?" panted Lauren.

Glen felt as if the air had thinned, slipping in and out of his lungs with little purchase or delivery.

"We're trapped here. Nobody knows we're here. Nobody's coming," she said, digging her nails into the vinyl cushion.

Glen hushed her, reaching for her back. Every sound around him reverberated in his skull. The room had warped, tilting left. He closed his eyes, could sense the bloodless mask his face had become. His mind ached and reeled from what was happening, the impossibilities, and in its fevered state had instantly begun to map out all the possibilities and risks of their escape.

CHAPTER
SEVEN

"It's the end."

The words came sharp and absolute. Glen and Lauren turned toward the voice. The bluntness of the statement wrenched their thoughts from underfoot, a momentary blankness rushing in to take their place.

Helen rocked forward and back again, seemingly entranced by the motion of her own reflection in the pane.

"This is it," she said.

Glen felt a chill run through his body. He thought he almost saw a smile beginning to develop on her lips, but then it faded, probably some trick of her reflection as it rippled in its movement over imperfections of the windowpane. Also possibly a symptom of his fevered mind, a concern he shoved away before it had a chance to root itself.

"Ma'am?" said Glen, straightening on his seat. His vertigo held fast, though slightly less severe now. His own voice seemed to hit him from the far end of a tunnel.

"It's the second coming of our Lord. Flood and plague. This is it. There's nothing we can do but pray. Pray for our salvation."

I'm fine, Glen thought to himself. *This will all be fine. We're going to be fine.* He felt the room begin to lift around him, and he closed his eyes again, willing it to settle. The beating of his heart had found its way into his ears. Glen breathed.

Helen turned to face the group. Their frantic eyes passed undecidedly between the window and the agitated woman, the floating corpses and Helen's deconstructing sanity.

"Pray with me. Will you all pray, ask for forgiveness?" She glanced around the room, drifting face to face. Her confusion and panic slowly mounted as her pleas fell flat. "It's not too late!"

"Ma'am, please calm down," Glen said. His head, by some miracle, finally had begun to clear a little. His voice had reconnected with him now, not so far away as it had been.

"You!" Her body thrusted forward with the word. "You and the girl. It's not too late. Come pray with me!"

"Please. My daughter is already scared enough," said Glen. "This isn't helpful or necessary."

The whole of Lauren's body had begun to shake against her father.

"You're not listening!" barked the woman.

Fred laid a hand across his wife's shoulder. "Helen."

She twisted in her seat, suddenly impatient, almost angry, scanning the faces starting back at her. "This could be your last chance! All of you!"

No one made a sound, momentarily stricken mute, whether by the corpses floating in the lot, their raw bewilderment at what the woman was suggesting, or perhaps the circumstances as a whole. Several turned to one another, back to the woman, their eyes engaged in silent conversation.

For the first time since all this had started, Hank no longer simply looked unhinged. Fear began to show itself, seeping through the hard exterior, hovering around him like a sickness. His eyes were blunt and distant, subdued by the alcohol despite the fast-unraveling reality surrounding them. Jesse paced beside him, still very present in the moment, shuffling to and from the window like an anxious dog.

Laj stood, his aura strangely calm, and walked over to the woman. He knelt beside her, taking her hand in his. "Ma'am, we're going to be okay. All right? Let's try and calm down, take it easy."

"You don't even know Jesus." She jerked her slender hand from his. It slipped out like a startled fish, seeking refuge in between her thighs. "How *could* you know him?"

Laj drew a breath and shook the words off.

"If you've not made your peace with the Lord, you're going to go to hell." Pity tinged with revelation overcame her face, and she leaned toward him. "But it's not too late for you. It's never too late. It can still happen."

"Ma'am. You've made *your* peace, right?" asked Laj. "You and your husband?"

She nodded, something wild still pacing in her eyes. At her side, her husband shook, whether from fear or fury unclear, though he didn't dispute Laj's efforts to reassemble his deconstructing spouse.

"Then you rest in the comfort of that right now. Nothing more. Find comfort in that."

Somewhere overhead, a fluorescent tube was humming one long note inside its socket. The tone bore a slight resemblance to some vibratory Buddhist mantra, an underlying thread of zen that seemed to penetrate and trim the tension from the space. She sat, mulling his words over, finally nodding her acceptance.

"Good. Breathe." Laj retrieved his hand from Helen's leg, coming to his feet. "Everyone, just take a breath. We're safe enough inside for now. We have food, we have shelter. It won't be long before help comes. Someone's going to come and get us out of this. It's going to be okay."

Glen felt his own pulse slow at Laj's empty words of reassurance. Lauren's shaking body also seemed to temper some, her breathing calmed.

A sudden wind rose up and pressed the doors. Their insulated seams emitted shrieks like rabid field mice as the foam compressed and twisted under pressure.

Laj came back to his seat. "For now, we ain't going nowhere no time soon." He came down on a single breath and pulled a calloused palm across his face, dropping his hand into his lap. The tic that pulled the corner of his mouth had seemed to follow it, momentarily gone.

"Damn straight we ain't." Hank's head bobbed in a manner that could've equally been the dizzied sway of overindulgence as much as it could've been a gesture of agreeability. He glared through drunken slits, open portals to the shaky borders of his sanity. Jesse had at long last settled, standing at the double doors, simply watching, waiting. His face was hidden by his angle, doubtless just as empty, as rigid as the very posture of his body.

Glen mentally detached himself, ignoring them all: the peacekeeper, the zealots, the drunken gunman. Instead, he focused on Lauren, now curled up at his side, head against his chest and yielding to a six-year culmination of suppressed emotion. The walls were down. For the second time now, life's constants that had propped her up, kept her going, had suddenly abandoned her. In a wink, Lauren had careened into the barrens where existence knew no rules. She felt defenseless, terrified of what they were facing, willing for the first time in a long, long while to lean on her father for guidance, where to go, what to do.

Glen had wondered if or when this day would come. When she'd open up again, forgive and trust in him, trust in life again so they could both rebuild and carry on together. And now that those walls had seemed to fall, he wasn't quite so sure how he should handle it, wasn't quite so sure if he was *ready*.

Though the necessary words evaded him, he held his daughter close. And what he failed to communicate in words, he would do in his presence. He would be there for her. She was his and he was hers, and they'd get through this together, one way or another.

He refused to let her down again.

Eventually, the commotion in the diner dwindled from short-circuit bursts of nerves, to a depleted murmur, to an eventual standstill. The air around them was spiked with fear, a drug they all consumed, exchanged with one another through their breaths. Tony killed the lights, their only illumination now emanating from the tired glow of the security lamps, humming their electric lullabies against the night. With removal of the inside lights, outside visibility was enhanced. The fog outside was thicker yet, having dashed what little light there was by half as it embraced the lot. It wrapped the building like a sheet of silk, blinding visibility beyond the porch's edge, though the occasional glint of water pierced the haze and spoke to Glen as he explored the night for signs of movement.

Added to the angst he felt already, something else began to gnaw his insides. He tried to beat the thought away. Still, it clung to him, an aching paranoia. It seemed the water level was increasing still.

Was it?

Adrenaline, cutting through his system, had eventually pushed his mind too far. That had to be it. Delirium had come as an exhaustion far past common fare, prodding him unwillingly against the edge of sleep. He teetered there, resisting, yielding, resisting…then falling.

Memories of Claire, of Lauren, flickered at the backside of his mind. Disembodied images without context came to him, snapping on and off. Something else was there, moving through the recollections, hidden in the darkness in between the visions. Prodded by the broken sleep, Glen's muscles tightened. Fear stalked the ruins of his memories. The same fear stalked him in the present moment, governed by the threat outside, just beyond the diner's walls.

CHAPTER
EIGHT

WAKE UP.

Glen woke with a start, chilled, back aching as the world rushed up to greet him.

"Claire?"

He pushed his hands against the seat and looked around, confused. A bead of sweat ran down his temple. She had been there, somewhere. He'd heard her voice. Glen frowned, unsure if he'd actually called her name aloud.

There were tables, people.

Something pressed itself against his side. He looked down.

Lauren.

His surroundings held the vague familiarity of a stranger whose face he knew but somehow couldn't place. And then the memories rushed in all at once, filling him completely, too much, too soon, stomach sickened with the hefty recollection.

The diner. The gunman. The water. The dead.

He screwed his brow and peered into the murky shadows. A wall clock read 3:42 a.m.

Something had awakened him.

Several tables down, two figures moved against the pale light spilling through the farthest wall. At first assumption, Glen mistook the shadowed figures for Hank and Jesse. But then he spotted them on the floor, backed up against the counter's wainscoting trim, open bottles cradled in their hands. It was then that Glen began to register that the constant buzz that filled his ears was emanating from Hank's gawping mouth. Glen squeezed his lids down tight to clear the gossamer of sleep from his mind.

The shapes maneuvered toward the doors, pausing once in front of a sleeping Hank and Jesse, then stepped past with cautious strides. As Glen's eyes adjusted to the creamy light that smudged out all the finer details, he began to make out certain features of the shapes: a crown of soft curls topping one, the other cut to the shape of a mesh-backed ball cap, its brim protruding outward, somehow catching light across its stitch in winking flecks that spoke like codes of Morse with every movement of the old man's head beneath it.

The couple turned to one another as they shifted at the door, their whispers little more than serpents' hisses to Glen's ears. He didn't move, hardly breathing, watching. Glen looked to Hank, found him still unmoved, the gun resting on his lap beneath his hand.

Then Fred pinched the lock and twisted.

The bolt snapped back, silence penetrated by the clack of steel.

The couple froze, waited. The snoring stopped and all fell flat and mute beneath that moment's weight. Slowly, Fred turned and moved his eyes across the diner, inspecting it for signs of resurrection. Glen kept his face concealed, head slung low. His heart was banging in his chest, and his mind was telling him to say something, do something to stop them. Still, he kept quiet, kept still. Despite everything they'd seen, everything they'd been told, Glen struggled to convince himself that Hank's tales of killer water had been nothing more than tales, and the real threat was still Hank himself. He wanted to see the couple make their way to safety, moving through the water, beyond the misty lot, away from where they were. They'd escape. They'd find help. They'd prove that what was out there was nothing more than simple water. That the bodies they had seen were victims of a flash flood. Of drowning.

Fred turned to the door and pushed, Helen at his back. An obnoxious snap burst from the makeshift seal as strips of insulation split and dropped a lengthy segment to the floor.

Again, they froze.

Hank gagged and shifted. He chewed and smacked a wad of phlegm between his lips. He drew his knees up high against his chest and sank his face into the pocket in between. Jesse hadn't moved a muscle. The diner held itself in utter silence, save the whistling night that huffed and moaned between the steel divide, now exposed. And then, as if a dying engine kicked to life, Hank began to snore again.

Fred pressed onward through the door, the remaining insulation sloughing off and binding at the hinges, emitting no more than a spongy squeal in its compression. Lauren moved against Glen's chest. A narrow edge of shoulder shifted to a space between his ribs, prying deep, its angle like a shim inside the divot. Glen winced and turned to let her slide down to his lap. He felt the room's warmth flee beneath encroachment of the mountain air. If they didn't move out quickly, the chill would make no haste in rousing others.

The two stepped out onto the porch, coaxing groans from wooden planks that fought against their stride, moving up and down on loosened nails. The door came to a rest at Helen's back.

Through the glass, Glen watched the couple drift along the length of porch, mindful of the water coursing only inches from the underside of its construction. A wind kicked up and rolled gray bales of fog across the liquid plane, driving Fred and Helen up against each other as they burrowed down and shielded one another from the cold.

They'd wade into the night, find help, send it back. Just a matter of time now.

Fred stepped down from the porch's ledge and out into the churning blackness of the water, rising to the middle of his calf.

Glen watched in utter stillness. At first, he wasn't quite sure what he was seeing.

It all happened so fast.

The water took Fred in a single upward shot. It rushed up his leg, connecting with his face in seconds. Helen was still holding her husband's hand when the first convulsion hit him. Fred bucked against the reach of liquid driving down his throat, through his nose, his ears.

She snatched her hand free of his grip, jumped back two steps, and screamed into the treetops. The sound cut through the glass like a sharpened tool, snatching half a dozen comatose humans from their dreams and toward the living nightmare taking place out front as Fred thrashed face-first underneath the filthy water.

Hank snapped backward at the sound and jammed his spine against an angle of the countertop. He shouted out a curse as the gun fell from his hand and clattered out across the vinyl tiles below. He snatched the weapon from the floor and leapt to his feet, then fell against the front desk, reeling with vertigo, fighting to establish bearings under blindness of the drink and night.

Still sitting on the floor, Jesse sat up on his crisscrossed legs, frowning with confusion.

"Jesus, Hank," Jesse said, half asleep. "What the hell is wrong with you?"

Out front, Fred turned in place, mouth agape, bound beneath the surface, rolling over and over again as the water wrapped his body like spun sugar to a paper cone, forming a chrysalis of liquid, gathering on itself with each rotation. His face became a smear of features as it passed in their direction, turning in the depths.

Laj lunged for the door, but Hank had beat him to it and with a twist of the lock, turned and jammed the barrel of his weapon up against the big man's throat.

Outside, Helen dropped her body flat across the wooden planks and stretched her arms out for her husband. Reaching from the porch's edge, the upper end of Helen's torso was suspended only several inches above the water. Her fingertips were no more than a foot from the aquatic cocoon that smothered Fred and wrenched his body in its depths. His eyes had been washed white, iris and pupil turned against the backside of his skull. She moaned and shook her head in blind denial, reaching outward, straining toward the living liquid.

Inside, Laj regarded Hank with downturned hatred, nostrils flaring. "Get that fuckin' burner off me."

"Try and move past me and that door and I'll blow your goddamned head off, you anti-'merican, God-hatin' motherfucker." Hank pulled the hammer back and watched the cylinder haul a round into position.

The others moved their eyes between the altercation at the front door and Helen out in front, on the brink of being summoned to her death beside her husband.

Laj moved, a desperate blur that dodged and swatted the revolver from his neck. The gun erupted, turning loose a slug which ripped a path across the foam-tiled drop ceiling. The bullet split the power to a square of fluorescent lighting, raining sparks. The air went heavy with the searing whine of stunned eardrums and, as Laj crushed Hank's nose beneath his massive forehead, even Hank appeared confused as to what had just happened in the sudden chaos of those fast and fleeting seconds.

CHAPTER NINE

LAJ THRUST THE DOORS OUT wide, throwing orphaned insulation fragments to the wind and water. The liquid dashed and spun the pieces, stealing them away into the black and gray. Helen lurched and turned to Laj, eyes wild and tear-burnt. She turned back to the water, straining toward her husband with an outstretched hand. In that moment, something came to her. Words, a thought, a mere suggestion that seemed to come from deep inside, but at the same time didn't.

Reach for him. Touch him.

Helen shook her head, sobbing. "No, please…" she cried. "Please."

Close enough to touch.

Laj grabbed her ankles, hauling her body toward him over wooden planks, dragging her across the porch's rough-hewn ledge and the coursing threat below. Fred was gone now, dispatched beneath a plow of water that had disappeared across the flooded lot in seconds.

Laj raised Helen from the porch and pulled her to his chest. He hoisted her across the threshold, her legs like folding reeds along the ground.

"Make a hole!" He snatched her up again, reinforcing his hold beneath her arms. Helen's head lolled back and round, no one at the wheel as consciousness abandoned post. "Clear a seat!"

Laj brought the woman to the booth and laid her out, legs up and stretched across the cushion, back pitched flat against the window. He came back to the doors, turned the locks again, then spotted Hank. The man was knocked out cold, laid out across the floor against the baseboard of the front desk. His shirt was saturated from the crimson channel gushing from his broken nose. Jesse worked a dampened towel across his face, having smeared the fluids out like greasepaint, turning cheeks and mouth a rusty shade of pink.

Laj scoped the floor, turning left and right, running his eyes around the room.

"Right here. Take it." Jesse held the handgun out by the barrel, its wooden grip turned toward Laj.

Laj hesitated, questioning Jesse with his eyes.

"It's what you're lookin' for, right?" said Jesse. "Go on, man. Take it. Here." He gestured at the handgun hanging backward in his fingers.

"Thanks," nodded Laj, a jagged stutter of a movement. "'Preciate that, Jesse." He accepted the revolver, holding it a moment in his palm as if he wasn't quite sure what to do with it.

"Yeah, well." Jesse dipped his head and shoved the bloody towel into a plastic takeout bag, spinning the top and tossing it to the floor. He pressed his hands along his jeans, tops and bottoms. "I'd appreciate it if you wouldn't say nothin' to Hank about that." He looked up at Laj. "Do me that favor?"

"That ain't no favor, brother. Far's I'm concerned, that's just good common sense." He reached around and slipped the handgun underneath the waistband at his lower back.

Jesse came up to his feet as Tony rounded the corner of the counter with a blanket and a glass of water.

"I...I don't know what she needs," said Tony. "It's something, though."

"No, you good, man," said Laj. He took the items from the bald man's shaking hands. "Thank you."

Tony gave the man a subtle nod, lips pressed into a nervous line.

Laj shook the blanket out and leaned across the woman, tucking the edges up around her neck and shoulders, draping the rest across her outstretched body. Helen's face was granite, unresponsive to his aid. Her eyes were blank like empty vessels, wide and windblown.

"See if we can't get that heat cranked up in here," called Laj across his shoulder. He ran his palms along her arms and legs. "Need to warm her up. She's in shock."

"Do my best," said Tony. "Unit's good for throwing fits, so I try not to ask too much of her." He shuffled off behind the counter, dialing the wheel on the antiquated thermostat with caution. Tony leaned in close and listened like a safecracker, mindful of the unit's temper as it kicked to life and started piping warm air through the ductwork overhead.

Several booths away, Lauren remained in her seat, still pressed against the window, her mind trying to make sense of the horrors lurking out there beyond the diner walls.

"Everything he said." Her voice emerged like leaves, soft and tainted with vibration of her body. "It's all real. Nobody believed him." Lauren shook her head in disbelief. "He tried to tell us. Tried to warn us and nobody believed him."

Glen took her hand in his, squeezing it tightly.

"Yeah," Glen whispered. "It is. It's real." There wasn't much else he could say. He wanted to argue the absurdity of it all. That's what dads were supposed to do. Make it better, make the world safer for their children, even if it sometimes came at the expense of lying to them. She was right though. They'd both seen it. They'd *all* seen it. Whatever was out there, it was something living, hidden in the water, biding its time. And if it hadn't known they were in there before, it did now.

While the rest of the group was tending to the woman, Glen and Lauren simply sat, watching the water shine like volcanic glass beneath the night.

Something caught Glen's eye. A movement out of place, too close. The rest of the lot remained unmoved beneath the haze. He stiffened on the bench, panning the black expanse.

Another flicker, winking nearby.

"What's wrong?" Lauren turned, frowning. "What is it?" Her eyes moved back and forth between her father and the window. "Dad?"

Rising to his knees, Glen palmed a porthole at the glass to cut the glare and leaned into the pane. He laid his forehead up against the window, felt the soothing transfer of its cold into his skull.

"Dad," she repeated. "What is it?" She rose behind him, her breathing doubled over, tripping through the panic branching out inside her chest. "What are you looking at? What do you see?"

Several booths away, Hank was gaining his bearings, still laid out across the floor and softly cursing with a palm pressed to the strip of bone between the socket of his eye and temple.

Out in front, water gently lapped the porch's edge. Then, it began to climb, stretching out across the deck planks. It lingered, pooling, hunting, coating Helen's last known location, sampling her mark, reading her body's signature.

"Seal the door."

Lauren pressed a hand against her his lower back. Her fingers laid themselves against her palm as she began to roll his shirt into a knot. "Dad, what?"

"Seal the door." Glen turned, eyes snapping like the severed ends of live wire. "I said seal the goddamned door." His voice was loud now. Laj and Jesse looked up from their task, turning toward him.

"What?" said Jesse. He kicked his eyes back to the door, returning them to Glen again.

Outside, the water started forward, resuming its trek across the planks.

"Seal the goddamned door!" Glen shouted, jumping from bench to table to floor, grabbing the remaining can of spray foam on his way back to the entry.

Laj reached down. "Hey, hey…what—"

"Check the porch. It's coming. It's moving. It knows we're here now." He threw a wild look back to Laj. "They drew it in. It knows. It knows we're in here!"

Glen shoved the straw into the seams, blasting the solution out along the floor gaps, then up the middle, the sides, hemming the ruined work to seal the fractures. It blew out from the openings as he moved along the gaps, expanding in consumption of the voids, slow to cure in the plunging cold and dampness of the mountain night.

Laj frowned, and through the glass he caught the lazy flow just several feet now from the threshold, inching nearer as Glen worked to patch the voids.

"Jesus Christ."

Laj now began to show the first marks of panic as he closed his eyes, pulling air into his lungs. The big man wagged his head, then began to pace, clapping his palms together. The tic had found his mouth again, twitching at the corner. He dropped to his knees and started repositioning bags behind the cured rework of the seams.

"Gimme a hand. Lauren, the bags," shouted Glen. He snapped his fingers, waved her over as he joined Laj to help him reinforce the space beneath the door. "Rice. See if we've got more of it. We'll need more. Much as we can get. And check the back doors, make sure they're still good."

Lauren nodded, backing along the open face of the counter before she turned and disappeared around the corner.

Tony joined her. He kicked into a jog, calling after Lauren. "Got some more in the pantry! Over here!"

Glen and Laj were in a frenzy, staggering bag-on-bag along the base of double doors in sandbag fashion as the liquid ran itself against them, pressing up along the outer edge. They jumped up to their feet and backed away, watching the water hunt the glass, running vertically and sprawling out across the window as it sought them out.

Jesse was on his hands and knees now, having come from sitting on the floor. It seemed he didn't trust his legs. His face was long and slack, unable to articulate his thoughts as he stared into the pulsing mass of liquid at the windows.

Hank's eyes were all that showed, peering just above the bag of frozen berries mashed against his damaged face. By those alone, terror had revealed itself.

"What the hell is it, man?" Glen panted, hands shaking. "The fuck *is* it?"

Laj shook his head, eyes pried wide in awe, disbelief. He watched the liquid climb the glass and then break left and right, branching widely like a liquid mapping of the human nervous system.

Glen switched from leg to leg, ready for the breach.

Laj stared at the water's upright configuration. The tic had doubled, nearly tugging one side of his mouth into a constant sneer.

"It'll hold, right?" asked Glen. "It can't get in, right? We sealed everything."

The water seemed to thrust itself along the bottom of the door, testing its integrity. Its climb continued up above, fanning out like sheets of coral. Every several seconds it would deconstruct and dribble down the glass again, rise and reassemble someplace else. It was utterly intentional, strategic, as if running searches out along the glass in systematic fashion, methodical in its attempts.

"No telling," said Laj. "It knows we're in here. If it can't see us, it can sure as hell sense us. Our heat, maybe. Maybe it can hear us." Still on his haunches, he leaned closer to the door. "Maybe even taste us, smell us." Laj reached out and held one hand against the glass. The water moved across the other side, panning the section of the window for a point of entry like a set of long and sprawling liquid fingers. It seemed to sense the heat that passed through the pane, where it pooled and lingered at the point of contact.

Glen shook his head. "Wouldn't do that."

Disconnected from his curiosity, Laj turned and looked at Glen. He quickly snatched his hand away and came up to his feet again, taking a step back from the door.

"It's searching," said Glen. "Sending feelers out. Almost like a proboscis."

"You've seen something like this before?" asked Laj, pulling a double take between Glen and the water crawling opposite the window.

"Not like this, but similar." said Glen. "Nemertea. Ribbon worms. They're aquatic, found in the North Sea." Glen leaned into the glass, observing how the liquid tendrils branched across the window, then retreated back into the larger arms of water. "It's how they hunt. They send out a proboscis as a means of seeking out and grabbing prey."

Laj dragged a palm across his mouth and turned back to the window.

Glen gestured toward the bottom of the door. "Seal's holding. Seems to be so far, at least. Look." The liquid spun and cut against the metal and glass, clearly aware of its proximity to them, working out a means to reach them.

"Yeah, but only a matter of time," said Laj. "Time's all it needs."

"Here. More bags." Lauren stepped between them, a plastic sack of rice in hand, larger than the others. Her face was red from crying, her words clipped tight by panic. "Five more bags like this in the back. Tony's bringing another." She stopped, for the first time introduced up close to what the water was doing. "Oh my God."

Glen took the sack and laid it at his feet, focused more on getting Lauren out of there. "Go get the other bags. Stack 'em near the back doors, and I'll meet you back there in a sec. We'll line them up the same back there."

"Dad, it..." She refused to pull her attention away, hypnotized by the impossible. She watched it hunt the glass. Beads of sweat broke out across her brow. "It wants in. It's trying..."

"Lauren," said Glen.

She twitched in his direction. Her mouth was moving without words.

"Lauren, the bags."

She stared at him.

"Lauren," he repeated, more firmly now. "Get the bags. Now."

Lauren slowly backed away. Finally, she turned and left, passing Tony. He stepped back and eyed the water coursing back and forth along the glass outside the doors. The image seemed to lock his legs in place. He stayed that way till Glen came to his feet and left to help his daughter with the service doors in back.

CHAPTER
TEN

"Fuckin' done it now," said Hank.

Between the swollen nose and bag of frozen blueberries mashed against his face, his voice was pinched into a nasal whine. His eyes burned on Laj. "You big, stupid cart mule dipshit. You happy now?" Hank pulled his knees up tight against his chest. He dropped his head, murmuring something down into the crook of his folded torso.

"Yeah," said Laj, nodding. He shoved the sweat across his forehead with his palm. "I am. I'm happy this lady's safe with us now, not out there like—" He dropped his head, closed his eyes. "Damn it, man. Left to you, she'd be gone now too."

"You damn straight," said Hank. "That's for damn sure. And you know what else? That watery shit wouldn't be up here lickin' on that fucking glass like a sheet of sugar, trying to get in at us now, would it? It'd be fat'n happy doing whatever the fuck it does out there, none the goddamn wiser." Hank let his head cock back against the wall, the bag of frozen fruit laid out across his eye and forehead. "But nah." He rocked his crown against the trim work of the counter. "Nah. Your stupid, junior firefighter ass had to go and drag her old bones back in here, put her up like bait in here with the rest of us." He blew a shot of air between his lips. "Well, it has her scent now. Ain't no comin' back from *that*. It knows she in here now. Knows we *all* in here."

Tony turned and held his palms upright. "Hank, why don't you—"

"Hey…HEY!" barked Hank. "Why don't you just shut the fuck up, Tony? Huh?" Hank pulled his head away from the wall and let the pack fall down into his lap. His nose and socket were deformed and swollen tight, like overripened plums. His face was caked in blood that gathered in his mustache, blotting out the features of his upper lip. "Biggest fuckin' pussy in here. Just shut the fuck up." Hank clapped those final syllables against the floor with his open palm, black hatred in his eyes. Wayward spittle rimmed his lips.

Tony stared into the corner of the room, shifting on his feet. His breaths came fiercely, shamefully. He gathered and released a clutch of denim in his fist.

"And you. Ohhh…" He pointed at the old woman, baring an overcrowded set of teeth. "What in the living, breathing hell was *you* tryin' to do, huh?"

The shell-shocked woman simply stared ahead, still tucked beneath the blanket.

"Where exactly was you two gonna go?" asked Hank. "Hm?

Y'all feelin' all slick, trying to just slip on through them doors. Thought you was just gonna…run away." Hank shuffled fingers through the air like running legs. He shook his head and hocked a pinkish wad of spit onto the floor. "Tell me, now. How'd that plan work out for you?"

No response.

"Hm?" He cocked his head. "Better yet," said Hank. "How'd that plan work out for your stubborn-ass husband?"

"Enough," said Laj.

Helen's eyelids fluttered in succession, the sound of Hank's voice seeming to register no more as words than would a pig's grunt.

"Oh, I'm sorry," said Hank, ignoring Laj's intervention. "You disturbed now? Huh?" He shoved himself up to his feet, the countertop across his back. "Have I made you uncomfortable?"

"It wanted me to touch him," mumbled Helen. Her eyes widened. "Told me to touch him."

"The fuck are you croaking about?" said Hank.

Helen only sat there, eyes wide and gone. The others watched her, waiting for something more that might make sense of what she'd said. Waiting for the words that wouldn't come.

Jesse came up straight, ironing out his slouch to add two inches to his already looming stature. He took a step toward Hank. "Jesus. C'mon, man. That's en—"

Hank spun to face his friend. "You can kiss my pasty white country ass, Jess! You supposed to be my boy! Have my goddamned back!"

Jesse turned his eyes away and stitched his lips into a surgical line.

"Got knocked the fuck out, then woke to you slinkin' round here with these clowns."

"Hank, the girl," said Jesse. "You ain't gotta talk—"

"Just shut the fuck up and keep your Judas ass away from me, Jess." Hank mashed the frozen fruit against his face again. "Talk however I damn well please. We done warned all them dumbfucks what was out there. Couldn't just take my word the goddamn stove was hot. Had to venture out and lay both hands on that shit to make sure."

"Hey!" spouted Laj. "That's enough! We're done with this!"

Hank didn't seem to hear. "Know what though, Jess? You right. I'll be damned." Hank grinned and slung an arm into the air with artificial realization. "Sure as shit, you right. The *girl*." Hank came up off the counter, stepping across the floor toward Jesse, looking into his eyes. "With her around, I ain't even got to talk to you. I ever want to talk to a little bitch, I'll just talk to her instead."

Hank turned away, head cocked back beneath the frozen bag. "How's that sound to—"

Two fists grabbed him by his flannel collar. Glen yanked him close, then swung the man around, cranking down into the knots, twin tourniquets against his throat. His face went red, then purple, the canyon of his still-good eye erupting with petechiae beneath the pressure. Glen threw Hank across the counter's edge, casting him across the line of stools. Hank plowed through them, falling to a standstill at the center of a tangled nest of seats and metal legs.

Hank cursed and kicked a chair from underneath his

outstretched legs, tried to stand, but the heap of stools beneath his torso caved and sent him to the ground a second time. With the rush of blood that filled his head, his nose broke wide again, spilling out across his mouth and shirt.

"Shit." Hank grunted, then moved to intercept the flow inside his open palms. Blood ran between his fingers, pooling on the floor. He let out a laugh and dropped his hands. "Well fuck me." He shook his head. "There they are."

Glen stood there in the moment's aftermath, chest heaving, furious.

"Knew you had a set of balls tucked up in there somewhere." Hank laughed. "Maybe you ain't such a puss after all."

"You think this is funny?" said Glen.

"This?" asked Hank, pointing to his face. "Nah, brother. This ain't a bit of funny." He shoved the toppled chairs away and rolled onto all fours. He stayed that way a moment, then came up to his feet and snatched a napkin from the counter, pressing it against his face.

"Then what the hell are you laughing at?" asked Glen.

"What's funny," said Hank, "is how, deep down, we all the same person, and you ain't even come to realize it." Hank let out another laugh, a nasal stutter. "Same instincts, same motivations, same anger, same person in the end, Glen. You ain't so special, after all. Same person, you and me."

"I'm nothing like you," said Glen.

"Don't be so sure, Glen," said Hank, suddenly serious, voice low. "We all have it in us. The need to survive, to protect our own."

Glen stared back at Hank.

"Them instincts don't come gently, Glen," said Hank. "Make a man angry, mean as hell, especially when things don't work out as planned."

"Dad," said Lauren.

"That a threat?" asked Glen.

"Ain't no threat," whispered Hank. "It's a fact."

Glen felt the insubstantial outline of two hands upon his lower back, thin and small.

"Dad?"

The word came through as no more than a distant sound, as if originated in his mind, buried in the drumbeat of the blood that packed his head, hot with rage.

"Dad."

He turned, finding Lauren standing at his side. She slipped her arms around him, held him tight.

Flames consumed Glen's face, his neck, no longer borne of fury but of shame at having lost his temper in front of Lauren. This wasn't what she needed. He felt the tremors pass between them as she pressed her body into his.

"Lauren…I…"

She squeezed him tighter. "Dad, sit down."

"Go on," Laj mouthed.

"Yeah," said Glen. He coughed, clearing the cobwebs strung across his throat. "Yeah, let's sit. We'll sit now."

Hank ticked his eyes from one face to another, black and quick like jumping spiders. He dragged a stool up from the floor and posted on its cushion. It was at that moment Hank appeared to realize the bag of frozen fruit had been destroyed, but clearly wouldn't bring himself to fetch another. Instead, he let his head fall back and clipped his nose beneath his index finger and his thumb, waiting out the clotting.

Mere feet away, the water swept the building's front, slightly higher now, more persistent than before.

The diner largely sat in silence now, and after a while, someone dimmed the lights again, more for visibility of the threat outside than for the benefit of sleep. Sleep was the last thing on their minds. As for the mess, they'd clean it up in the morning.

Helen huffed her broken prayers into the air. At her chest, a corner of the blanket folded over, toppling forward onto her lap. She didn't move to fix it. Her lifeless mind had clearly parked itself in some dark alcove of existence, a sensory limbo reserved for the few that saw too much, understood little, sucker punched and robbed blind, reality lifted from possession.

CHAPTER
ELEVEN

GLEN WOKE TO THE PASTE of morning on his tongue and teeth. His neck was all but sprained, contorted in the narrow confines of the booth. By some miracle, he'd found sleep, salvaging the last remaining hours of the night that burned down fast and hard, gone without remorse. The morning sun spilled through and bathed the inside of the restaurant in a blend of yellows, marigold and buttercup. And though the rays were cold, their quarters were somehow rendered warmer now beneath their hues, effectively deceiving.

The sunlight showcased something Glen had somehow missed. Beachfront photos, mostly black-and-white, different sizes, set in mismatched frames were hanging on the wall. Through the haze of lifting sleep his eyes began to drift across the images. Several featured strangers spanning different eras, differentiated by attire, hairstyles, sunglasses. Others were more plain, simply landscapes of the surf across a variety of regions. One caught his eye particularly. It was Ocracoke, North Carolina, he could readily tell. An image that was impossibly familiar. One specific location.

Glen sat upright. The weight of fear and panic slumbered in his gut, shifting irritably with his movement. Nightmares had infected him throughout the night, hellish visions going off like flash bombs on the hypnogogic edge of sleep. He detached from the photograph, suddenly convinced he'd not yet pulled away completely from that edge. Sweat beaded on his brow. He felt its coolness in the open air. It told him he was here, now, awake in full. He blinked hard and found the picture on the wall again. It was just a beach. Nothing more.

Glen pushed a sleeve across the perspiration on his forehead. He spotted Lauren seated at the counter alongside Jesse. The two of them exchanged a napkin in a game of tic-tac-toe. Lauren vacantly had placed her mark and pushed it back to Jesse. Her eyes were elsewhere, running through the windows of the diner, blank and sightless. Her actions seemed to be on autopilot, detached from whatever ruled her thoughts.

Jesse didn't seem to notice. He frowned, holding pen to paper, lips tucked beneath his teeth in thought. He struck his mark and pushed the square back to her.

"Your turn," said Jesse.

Lauren didn't seem to hear him.

Jesse rolled his head, neck cracking on its pivot. He exhaled through his nose, repeating himself. "You're up."

"Hm?" Lauren turned to him, oblivious. The BIC seesawed

in between her fingers, both ends making ticking sounds against the counter.

Jesse laid his chin inside his palm and nodded at the napkin.

"Oh." Lauren seemed to re-engage with her surroundings. "Yeah." She struck her mark.

Jesse slumped. "Well, damn."

The guy wasn't the brightest. Glen could see that plainly. He was certain Lauren could, as well. She was a kind girl, though, sympathetic to his condition, undoubtedly slipping him a couple victories along the way, even in her present state. In her younger years, when most kids would snap up any win they could without the slightest hesitation, she'd always managed to impress him with her grace and humility, virtues most adults had never even come to master. Things that came to her with natural ease, without a second thought. Age five or six, intentionally slowing stride to lose a race to slower friends. Maybe slipping peeks between her fingers in a game of Marco Polo, not so she could find the other players, but steer herself away to stretch the game, build their sense of pride in having them believe they'd been such skilled players as to keep her guessing, somehow always falling shy of finding them inside the borders of the ridiculously undersized, inflatable arenas. Pools far too small to play the game, but she was always sure to make it work, make it fun for all.

The recollection pulled a subtle smile. He'd almost forgotten those little, precious details of her nature. Not that he believed she'd lost them. No. He'd simply felt as if he'd hardly seen her in more recent years. Life had rushed up underfoot and knocked them down, time and time again. And so along the way those small reminders had been washed away, caught up in the churn that seemed to wipe out everything in its path. His smile fell at the thought, at what he'd missed along the way. What they'd both missed.

The smell of cooking bacon brought him from his seat on aching legs. He saw Tony at the grill, the left side of its surface laced with hefty strips of country pork, the other with a mound of hash browns and fried eggs. A pot of grits was cooking on a burner. He flipped the eggs and scattered cheddar over top. Lauren turned toward Glen.

"Dad, he's making them the way I like them. Same way you do." She smiled, only slightly, but it was the first real sign of life she'd shown since Glen had watched her from his seat. He wasn't entirely sure if it was real or forced. Still, it eased the knot inside him, if only a little.

"He asked how you want yours," continued Lauren, "but I didn't want to wake you. I told him just to do yours same as mine. Over medium, cheddar-topped."

"If there's any other way," said Glen, wincing as he straightened his back, "I don't care to know about it." He stretched the knots of muscle that were studded out across his frame like tumors, souvenirs of restless sleep. "What you two got going on over here?" He exhaled, blowing the question out into the air. Glen tried to muster up a smile and looked at Jesse. It wasn't too convincing.

"Your kid's been schoolin' me at some tic-tac-toe. Like it's some Olympic sport and she been training eight nights a week." He gave his head a wag and drew another breath.

"Take it easy on him. Let him come up for air from time to time, all right? It's only decent."

She let out a sound. "Yeah, not a chance."

"Y'know, I got a kid her age," said Jesse, the words lazy on his southern drawl as he prepped another game on the face of a fresh napkin. "Angela. Well, least that's what *I* call her. *Angie* now's what she wants to be called. *Ang* even. I think that one's the latest. Hell, I can't keep up." He paused in thought. "So *big* all a damn sudden."

Glen pulled up a seat and sat down at the counter beside them. "She live around here? With you?"

"Her mama," said Jesse. "Yeah, her mama got her full-time. Couple counties over, but she don't tend to let me come around much, y'know."

Glen nodded.

"Bring a little money, food sometimes. Kind of grease the skids, make it harder for her mama to say no. Guess it's kinda like a barter system, if you will." He doodled on a corner of the napkin, driving the tip of the pen around in tiny circles, its markings looking like a trail of bubbles. "Yeah. Her mama." Jesse paused, grunted, an entire history laid out in that single sound. "Ain't an easy woman to deal with, but she ain't never turned down money or food. Gets me in the door time to time, so whatever, y'know? It's worth it." Jesse laughed, a slight grin flickering into existence. He turned to Lauren. "Hey, y'all about the same age and all. Sometime...I mean, after all this shit..." Jesse caught himself, correcting course. "Sorry...*stuff*." He cleared his throat, bunching the napkin on the countertop. "Anyway, when it's all done and over with, this whole nightmare, you two should get together. You'd prolly get along, the two of you. She ain't got many her age to hang with. Least not to my knowledge." He struck an "X" in the first block and returned the square to Lauren. "Least the ones she do have around these parts ain't worth a wooden nickel in a slot machine, if you know what I'm saying."

Lauren smiled politely. Forced. This time, Glen could tell. She etched an "O" into the soft paper, tattering underneath the wet ink. Lauren pushed the square across the table, looking up at Jesse.

Jesse didn't move, didn't seem to notice. "I was supposed to see her last night." The statement came out like a confession, guiltily released. He turned to look outside, nothing now but water from the diner to the shadowed edge of forest. The road was swallowed up completely. His voice was soft, broken. "I should be there with her now. Not here. I should be protecting her."

"You try reaching out since all this started?" asked Glen. "Make sure she's okay?"

"No signal round here. Not a damn lick. Guessing y'all noticed that already," said Jesse. "Ain't stopped me from trying, though."

Glen and Lauren didn't answer. There was nothing they could say.

"I'm gonna get there," Jesse said. "Have to." His hands were on the napkin, but he didn't take it. Instead, they shook in place, stalled out on the counter. "Gonna find her, keep her safe. That's what dads are put on this earth to do. And if I gotta walk through watery hell to do it, so be it."

CHAPTER
TWELVE

Most of them ate together that morning, scattered out across the counter and booths. Hank, unsociable as expected, sat with his backside angled toward the others as he downed the eggs and bacon in silence several booths down from the farthest of them. Even Helen managed to get some bites down, though hunger by and large was clearly absent in that lonesome void that seemed to claim her mind and body. When she wasn't eating, which was the majority of the time, she stared into the melamine plate, head dancing on her neck with just the slightest nod of slipping thoughts.

Tony never bothered sitting down to eat. Instead, he'd rummaged in the back room till he'd come out with a wood-grained electronic unit coated in a sweater made of dust, which broke away and scattered in the air around it as he lowered the contraption to the counter.

Laj banged his mug of coffee to the counter like a gavel and began to speak.

"Need to figure out what this is, how we might manage to get ourselves out of here. This place ain't gonna hold out indefinitely, and nobody's coming." Laj cast a glance back to the caulked door. The nervous tic began to play the corner of his mouth again. "If I'm being completely honest with you, I can't believe our weatherproofing's held at all. Least as well as it has." Laj pulled his large open palm across his face and exhaled.

"No argument here," said Glen. "And you?"

"What about me?"

"Holding up," said Glen. "You good?"

"Tired is all. Brain refused to let me sleep last night," said Laj. "Had worse nights though. So, yeah, I'm good." He gulped another mouthful of coffee, set the mug down again. "Kind of night all sorts of memories seem like they come off the leash, run laps around my damn head."

"Know a little something about that," said Glen. Laj returned a nod and stared into his mug.

The seven mostly sat in silence, save the reluctant tick of utensils as they navigated plate and bowl.

Lauren kept her sanity by doodling in a composition notebook Tony kept beneath the register. She'd been deep in thought, the pencil in her fingers moving through the pages with a certain power all its own. Glen found a sense of peace by merely watching her at work, remembering better days.

Sitting at the kitchen table of their new home, the floor around them had been buried in the aftermath of Lauren's fifth birthday party. Friends and extended family had already left, and the air still rang of candle smoke and several different perfumes. Glen and Claire were beat, and the thought of cleanup was enough to make them want to light the place on fire and start over somewhere else. They'd exchanged the joke and laughed for several minutes through an exhausted, nearly drunken haze of delirium.

At the table, Lauren sat with her new art kit. She'd opened up the pack of drawing pencils and had waded deep into the thoughtful, meditative state they'd eventually come to refer to as "her pocket." That moment was the first time they had realized what a passion Lauren had for art. It became her sanctuary. A cathartic state through which she'd process life around her: thoughts, events, feelings. And she'd been good. More than good.

The memory stirred Glen without warning. He'd not even realized, not till now, that Lauren hadn't drawn again since Claire had passed. At least, not that he had seen. It had been such an integral part of her existence that he felt ashamed for not realizing this.

How could he have missed it?

At the counter, Tony toiled with the vintage Cobra CB radio. The unit whistled in and out of static as he turned the knobs, speaking quietly into the handheld microphone.

"Anything?" asked Laj, nodding toward the CB.

Tony shook his head. "Nothing."

Laj laid his mouth against his palm and turned his focus to the parking lot, watching, thinking.

Outside, the water stayed its course, increasing in its depth, devouring now the front porch and the lower portion of the diner's face. It was up at least another inch or two since he'd last checked. At the double doors, a bolt of current broke the stillness on occasion, sweeping past. It spun and roiled there against the glass and metal, though their makeshift weather seal had maintained its integrity, nary a drop of water seeping through the structural reinforcements. After each attempt, the water fell back on the glass again as if regrouping for another pass.

"Hell, if the water don't breach our reinforcements first," continued Laj, "the food will run out soon enough. Won't last long between us all."

"We're in a damn diner," said Jesse, throwing eyes around the room. "Should have plenty, right? Ask me, reckon food's gonna be the least of our worries at this point." He glanced over his shoulder, catching the carcass of an animal of some sort, large and brown, deformed. It thumped against the doors, turning over in the surging current. Shortly after, the water fell to stillness once again.

The horror in the room was palpable. The air grew thick with silence. Several laid their utensils down, what little appetite they'd salvaged now abandoned altogether. Lauren made a sound and turned into herself, resting the composition notebook on her elevated knees as she continued sketching. Glen reached an arm around her, making an attempt to bring her in. Lauren didn't yield, solidified where she sat.

"Actually, Laj is right," said Tony, tossing the mic onto the counter. He switched the CB off. "Last shipment came last Friday. Yesterday's never made it. We got food, but it ain't a whole lot. Not what you might think. Enough to hold us for a bit, but not indefinitely." He broke an end of bacon from a larger piece and laid it on his tongue, appearing to second-guess the absent-minded move. "Probably smart to start rationing what we got."

"Unless we figure our way out of here first," added Laj, lifting his mug.

Tony shrugged. "There's that."

Lauren looked up, broken from "her pocket." "Unless?" Her eyes staggered confusedly. "What do you mean, *unless?* We can't afford *not* to."

Laj turned to face the sky outside, suddenly uncomfortable. "We will," said Glen.

"We have to," Lauren said. "Wednesday, Dad," she whispered. "You know we have to make it back by then. We *have* to."

"We'll make it," Glen said. "Promise."

Lauren offered him a look that told of a conditioned distrust in that word.

"There's also the fact that we ain't even got a clue what the hell that shit is out there, where it even come from," said Hank. The group turned toward the sudden voice to find Hank stretched across his booth, eyes drawn up atop the purple swell of nose and socket. "Ain't that something we should prolly be fixin' to figure out instead of how long we can stretch out this group camping trip?"

Several nodded, no one spoke.

"So?" Hank sat up in his seat, not without discomfort. "What we got, then? Can't tell me ain't none of y'all been thinkin' this over."

Laj shook his head. "Plenty of thinking. All I been doing." He looked up at the group. "Only thing I figure is that it ain't just water."

"Well, no shit," murmured Hank.

"What I mean is that I think it has to be something *in* the water. Water doesn't move, doesn't hunt, doesn't attack on its own."

"Clearly," said Hank. "That ain't exactly no revelation, *Jee-Hod.*"

"You got better?" asked Laj, moving past the bigoted remark with no small degree of effort. "I don't hear you offering up."

Another moment passed in silence.

"Been thinking," said Glen finally, toying with the cooling eggs on his plate.

"Have you, now," said Hank. He fell back on his seat, letting the backrest thrust a breath through swollen sinuses.

"Last year, my class was studying—"

"You're a teacher," interrupted Jesse, more affirmation than question. There was a tinge of surprised amusement in his voice. "No shit."

"High school biology," said Glen. He released the fork onto the plate and pulled a napkin from the small black box, wiping off his hands, his mouth. "Anyway, studying climate change, global warming." He rolled his hands across the air in a flourish of generalization. "Effects of permafrost soils, glacial melting—"

"Here we go," spouted Hank, squeezing out a laugh. The group turned. He dosed his coffee with a splash of whiskey. "Oh, I'm sorry. I didn't mean to interrupt your pitch there, lefty." He raised his cup to Glen. "Global warmin', was it? Where was we?"

"Permafrost," Glen continued. "Bacteria, viruses, dormant for decades, centuries, maybe longer. So, let me back up here." He shifted in his seat, cleared his throat. "2016, Yamal Peninsula in the Arctic Circle, out there in the Siberian tundra, anthrax surfaced. Infections started cropping up here and there around that time, and the thought is that some infected reindeer died and iced over some seventy-five years back, trapping the bacteria there inside the permafrost until a heat wave thawed it out, released it back into the ecosystem."

"The hell is permafrost and where you even going with this?" Hank swigged his coffee, appearing to fight the taste of the concoction till he'd passed it from his mouth and down his throat.

Lauren cut her eyes to Hank, glaring through the narrows.

"Might find out if you shut up, let the man talk," said Laj, peering over his shoulder. "And you might wanna throttle back on the booze unless you dig time travel, wanna journey back to last night."

Hank sucked his teeth and took another sip of coffee, this time smaller than before.

"Frozen soil. Permafrost. Whatever. Point is, I don't think

it's the water itself that's moving. Not on its own, at least. It's whatever's in it. My guess, according to those anthrax findings, same thing could've happened here with some microorganism that's bled out from the Appalachian highlands somewhere. Something that's been trapped there, frozen till now. Preserved millions of years, even. Prehistoric." He tossed his palms into the air, sat back in his seat. "Or, maybe not. Just my theory. Something that's been running through my mind. Would at least explain why we've never seen anything like it before. Would also coincide with last week's heat wave and the heavy rains."

"Theory's better than nothing," said Laj.

Hank pushed his lip up flat against the undercarriage of his nose and drew a breath. "Appalachian highlands, you say."

Glen nodded. "Mhm."

"Your radar might be runnin' hot," said Hank. "We ain't that far north, pal."

"Wouldn't have to be," said Glen. "Permafrost's been discovered up in Maine and New Hampshire and—"

"And that ain't here," interrupted Hank.

"And you didn't let me finish," said Glen. He felt the pressure rising in his neck, his temples.

Hank's mouth shifted sideways, twisting with distaste.

"Who's to say some of that runoff didn't make its way into some stream or river, wash its way down south with all that rain?"

Hank rolled his eyes. "And who's to say it did?"

"What's wrong with you?" said Lauren, still glaring.

"My daddy didn't hug me enough." Hank winked.

Lauren turned away and screwed her fists another turn into her hoodie.

"Enough. Never said it did, never said it didn't," said Glen. "Just some educated guesswork. Like I said, a theory. Best I've got."

"All right, well, ain't here nor there," said Laj. "You can argue with a brick, but it ain't gonna get no softer for you." He stood and approached the window, back turned toward the others as he spoke. "Keep talking, Glen."

Hank clenched his jaw, muscles squirming at its edge.

"Right." Glen blinked hard, a cleansing action. "Not sure any of you have noticed, but that water out there ain't always moving. It comes in spells," said Glen. "And you can pretty much always tell where it is. Where it's heading."

Tony looked up from the bar top. "How you figure?"

"The way it ripples. Like the wind raking the surface."

"What makes you think it ain't?"

"Because last night, the way the fog laid out across the lot the way it did. The way the water shuddered underneath it, moved here, there, but the fog..." Glen paused, a smile almost emerging on his lips. "See, while that was going on, the fog stayed put, didn't move one bit. That's not wind."

Laj scratched his chin, then propped his arms up on his waist, pitching elbows outward from his torso in the image of some great transmission tower. "Huh."

"I mean, go on. Take a look out there right now," said Glen. "See for yourself." He lifted a finger, gesturing toward a section of the pond. "You can see it. Fog's gone now, but you can still see clear as day it isn't any wind causing that action. Check the leaves up in the trees around us, the grass. Nothing."

The others turned and watched the open stretch of water, the land surrounding. All around, the trees were still, holding their breath, foliage lifeless in the golden chill of morning. Sunlight dressed the leaves with subtle strokes of light that gleamed in place, not the slightest wink of movement. Oaks and pines both high and low stood still, resting from the constant whip of mountain air that normally drove them hard. But all had fallen calm now, patient, yet portions of the water trembled in the nothing, its sprawling surface shifting over irregular swaths of space that seemed to come and go at random to the oblivious eye.

"That's where it is. Two o'clock, along the grassy bank there by the signpost, moving west. See that?" Glen pointed, tracking its movement with his index finger. "That mass right there, rippled surface, even bigger now than it was before." He lowered his hand, shrugging. "Least it seems that way to me."

"You noticed all this and didn't tell me?" asked Lauren, her face crossed with a wounded look.

Glen shook his head. "Last thing you needed to know about. Got enough going on without adding to your worries."

"I can handle it," scoffed Lauren. She crossed her arms. "I'm not some little kid."

Glen pressed his eyes between his fingers.

"You're shittin' me," said Jesse. "That?" He squinted, shook his head. "I don't know, man. Still just looks like wind to me.

Just a breeze." But as he glanced from tree to water, back again, the checksum of his observation hit him. He keeled back in his seat, ballooning his cheeks with sudden revelation. "Well, shit." He frowned and shoved a thumbnail in between his teeth, began to trim the slender edge of skin away between his incisors.

"Again, I'm spitballing here. Just my theory," said Glen. "Believe what you will, but I don't see any wind out there. Just as still and easy as can be."

Jesse raked his scalp. "Well, believable as anything else, I guess," he said. "So, guess the good news, or about as close to any as we're bound to come right now, is that we can see it. Can at least tell where it is."

"Long as the wind's dead," Laj said. "Wind picks up though, reckon we'll lose it."

"I'd imagine so," Glen said. "Would rub its border right out. Blend it in."

"Still, it's something we can maybe work with, right?" asked Jesse. His voice was laced with a kind of fragile hope. "Something we can use?"

The question went unanswered. They all sat there for a moment in the neutralizing clutch of morning rays that doused the length of countertop. They brought some scant degree of actual warmth, this time without deception.

"Maybe if we had a higher view," mumbled Lauren, arms still folded in defiance. "Might be easier to spot it then."

Glen turned to face her. "Yeah. Hey, that's not a bad idea, actually." He looked at Tony, hopeful. "This place wouldn't happen to have some kind of roof access, would it? Some way to get up top from inside? Maintenance hatch, something along those lines?"

Tony swallowed the last of his coffee, then set the mug down with a thoughtful breath. "Actually, yeah. It does."

CHAPTER
THIRTEEN

"Ain't used it in a minute."

Tony balanced at the top of a ladder mounted to the floor and wall, patched with age-browned metal peeking through two layers of paint, tan and pea soup green. The portly man was forced to lean out from the narrow construct as he pushed against the antiquated hatch above his head with one arm stretched upright, the other anchored to the rod of steel along the ladder's left. He shoved against the latch, arms soft and shuddering as he grappled with the apparatus.

"Want me to give it a go?" called Laj.

Laj waited at the ladder's base. The rest of the group stood several feet away, gathered just outside the shelves of dried goods and canned vegetables and fruit within the confines of the open stockroom. Standing there amid those last supplies, Tony's mention of abbreviated stock rang true in every observation. Given their party's number, there was no doubt they'd exhaust the supply in little time if they didn't figure a way out of there.

Tony gave it another try. Beads of sweat now dribbled down his balding head as he folded forward, pushing up from the ladder rungs, shoving his upper back against the underbelly of the age-locked hatch. "Yeah," he panted. "Yeah, you give it a shot. Damn thing may as well be welded shut. Hell, far's I know, might actually *be* welded at the topside." He came down to the floor and swiped the perspiration from his head and face, moving aside as Laj stepped up the rungs. The fixture's reinforcements rattled in their concrete sockets as he climbed, exorcising ghosts of powdered rock that disappeared into the air.

"Careful, man. It ain't the most secure thing. Old as all hell." Tony struck a palm across his brow and watched the big man climb. "Ain't even never used it, far as I can recall. Maintenance folk usually put a ladder up against the side of building, get up top that way. Like I said, wouldn't surprise me none if the damn thing's sealed off up top."

Laj reached the ladder's peak and gripped the lever on the hatch. He pushed. It didn't budge. Laj frowned and hammered at its edge with an open palm. Four hard strikes in, the action knocked it loose and broke the grip of two support brackets, freeing them of their hold. One split in two, dropping free and hitting the floor in an explosion of rusty flakes. He shoved upward and, with a sucking breach, pushed the access panel up and over. The square of metal arched and slammed onto the rooftop, raining bits of dirt and rust, freeing a stash of seedpods that spun down into the open space like tiny helicopters. A trail of water dribbled from the panel's rim. It skated down his left arm, spattering on the concrete floor below. The others scuffled back, eyes moving from the man to floor and back again.

"It's okay," said Laj. "I think it's fine. Just water. Plain water. Look." He swabbed the moisture from his arm with the fingers of his right hand, holding them up to show the group. "See? No movement. Just water." There was something unconvincing in his mannerisms, fighting nerves thrown into motion by his own concerns, poorly hidden.

"Gonna head up top, take a look around. Gimme a sec." He scrambled up into the opening, hauling his massive torso through the hatch onto his knees, rising to his feet on the gritty surface of the roof. Laj turned and leaned across the opening, his head and shoulders no more than a silhouette against the sky beyond. "Anything happens, you shut that hatch and lock it, seal it best you can. Secure yourselves." He turned and trudged away, disappearing beyond the opening with a graveled crunch, a stop-go sequence of steps that faded out into the distance.

Several moments passed in silence. Glen called up from the ladder's base. "You good?" Stepping back, he listened for response.

Silence.

The group stood back by several feet around the ladder's base, waiting for the worst: a rush of water through the hatch, spilling down into the space below. They fixed their eyes upon the opening up above, surveying the square of light until their vision fuzzed along its borders, washing the edges out of sight.

"Laj, you good up there?"

There was a thump, a sound that seemed to shake the ceiling up above, something heavy hitting gravel. A lengthy gust of wind crossed the open hatch. It produced a long and mournful note, rising up to fill the room.

Another moment passed before they heard the gritty rise of footsteps in the distance, coming closer to the opening. Laj squatted, peering down across the opening's edge.

"We're good. Come on up."

———

The air up top was cold but still, a radiant chill that held them at its ready edge, threatening to cut at any moment. The lofty space was occupied with smells of architectural age. The scents of tar and mildew, mixed with subtle notes of organic decay, spilled in from the damp expanse of woodland slopes, their trees like color-coded walls that rose up high around them. Two birds called out from someplace hidden, shrieking high, low, high, alternating notes of steady conversation between two distant ends.

The group walked over to the building's rear and lined up at its edge, guarded by a brief and multilevel wall of cinder block that overlooked the water-coated asphalt reach of property. The land extended roughly 150 feet from the rear wall of the building to a rocky incline, transitioning to solid earth and closely held ascension of the thinning trees and brush. Left and right were level stretches that bled out into a dappled palette of the trees, lower in their elevation, dissolving into blackness out among the timber stalks that crowded out the higher rays of morning. The water was more scant on those opposing ends, but still there for a good eighty to a hundred feet or so before it halted at the slight ascent of wild terrain. To the right, a travel trailer rested parallel to the diner's immediate side, maybe fifteen, twenty feet away at its closest edge.

The group observed the water's surface, a pristine doppelgänger of the clouds above, its presence indiscernible from glass.

"Ain't seeing much," said Tony. "No movement."

"Yeah, well that don't mean much of nothin'," said Hank, running lengthy scraps of beard between his fingers as an exercise of thought. "It's out there. Best believe that."

Glen nodded in agreement. "He's right. No telling." He turned and started for the building's front, wrapping Lauren at his side beneath his arm. She stiffened and pried herself away, separating from him. A rush of anger crossed him. He felt his face and neck go red. This wasn't the place or time for her bullheaded defiance. It's the kind of thing that would get her killed. She thought she was big, independent. She was just a kid. A stubborn, clueless kid, no matter what she thought she was or who she thought she was fooling. And then a rush of something else crossed over Glen, a brand-new kind of hatred for this place, these circumstances, all of which were only driving him and Lauren further apart.

The others followed Glen and scattered out along the upward jut of cinder block that formed the building's crown, starting low at the edges to the left and right, ascending to a peak at its midpoint. It bore the architectural standardization of almost every small-town outfit of the 1940s, sporting some ancestral resemblance to the general stores in cinematic ghost towns, aesthetic knockoffs of the Alamo. The lot sprawled out beyond in full disclosure, their parked vehicles, the pumps, the roadway, all objects in between submerged to some degree amid a generous quantity of water.

"And there it is." Glen pointed toward a stippled patch of water some forty feet out, moving edge to edge across the middle of the submerged parking lot. It moved with patience, intentional as can be beneath its simple measures of conceal-ment. The wind had died off once again, leaving all surround-ings still and quiet save the lingering motion of the liquid mass that drifted out across the substrate.

"Be damned," said Laj, pacing back behind the others as he moved along the edge to gain a better point of view. "He's right. It's right there, clear as day."

Glen stooped and picked a stone up from the rooftop at his feet, turning it over in his hand, feeling its weight. He turned his eyes back to the water, watching the movement of the shivering patch of shifting boundaries and dimensions.

"Dad, what're you doing," whispered Lauren. He had her attention now. "You're not going to—"

He held a palm up to his daughter, halting her. By this point, several others had taken notice, curiosity in their eyes, tucked beneath an overlay of sour fear.

Glen reached back and chucked the stone across the lot, watching it strike the water opposite the mass. It met the water with a clap, throwing a rippled beacon out across the surface.

"You outta your goddamned mind?" yelled Hank. He flipped around and came toward Glen. "The hell're you tryi—"

"Shh!" Glen struck the man's words from the air, bringing him to a standstill. Beads of sweat had sprung to life across Hank's brow and cheeks, flushing red. "Watch," Glen pointed. "Look at it."

The wake collided with the patch of water, crosshatched as it spread across the shapeless form. It halted, then reversed, moving back across the lot at such a speed to generate a wake unto itself, plunging toward the origin of disruption. The liquid rolled, displaced in the manner of a large, imposing mass that glided just beneath the surface.

At once, perhaps in a primally instinctive move, the group receded by a single step.

"Motion," said Glen. "It hunts by picking up on motion in the water."

"Just what the hell is it?" Tony pointed at the turning mass. "How...tell me how the hell that's even possible."

Glen shook his head, at a loss for words. He frowned in thought, the threat more real somehow beneath the light of day. No tricks of eyes or other explanations thrown out as protective cover, justifications for the things they couldn't understand, didn't know, *refused* to know.

"Same shit me and Jesse seen," said Hank. "Same shit we all seen with the deer, the old man last night. Same shit's been nudgin' that glass up front, trying to get in at us."

Hank propped one foot up on the ledge, leaning on his knee. He pulled a mutilated Winston from his ear and clipped the filter in between his lips. He snicked a match across the strip inside his palm and sucked the flame, shaking it from the cardboard stick before he flicked it out across the building's edge. The nutty punch of first smoke marked the air, lingering in the stillness as he let the wisps flow from the corners of his mouth. He took another drag and held it, then set it free, twin jets expelled beneath his nose.

"Ain't a one of you believed us yesterday. Not a hollow-headed one of you. And damned if you ain't still struggling with it now." Hank took another drag and cinched his eyes up tight like drawstrings in the process. "Ain't sure how much more you need to see." He spoke in word-shaped huffs of smoke, waiting there for some response.

Tony simply stared at Hank.

"Well? You a believer now, little big man?" Hank took another drag and bumped a lump of ash onto the roof beneath his feet. "Tell me, who's drunk now, huh? Who's *high?*" He drew that final word out long, a gray-white cloud emerging from his open mouth in punctuation of the statement.

"You done now?" said Laj, eyes turned elsewhere.

Hank shrugged and turned his sights back to the parking lot. He licked his lips and pulled another drag from the cigarette, releasing it through his whistling nasal passages.

"We could outrun it, right? Now that we know where it is. Now that we can see it," said Lauren. The sour panic coursing through her suddenly had seemed to warp her tone into a sort of frantic hope. "We…we could lead it way out there, then make a run for it. We could be gone before it even comes, before it catches up."

"It's not safe, Lauren. Least not yet it isn't," said Glen. "There could be more at the outer edges, out of sight somewhere."

"More?" asked Lauren, her expression molded into something difficult to place. Some midpoint between a look of morbid amusement and fearful disbelief. The panic started bleeding to the surface once again. Suddenly, she looked cold. "What do you mean? Why would you say that?" Lauren folded her arms, working them against each other like two strips of kindling.

Glen let out a breath. "I don't know. Just talking. We don't know anything really. Not nearly enough." He instantly regretted having said it, nearly reaching for her, then decided against it.

Lauren swallowed, frowned, staring down across the edge, trying to peer into its filthy depths. The others seemed equally unsettled at the suggestion there could be more than one, but Glen was doubtful that he'd been the first to entertain the notion.

"Besides, it's fast. It can move," said Glen. "Saw that just now. And most importantly, we've nowhere to go. At least not till help comes. Someone with the means to get us out of here. Nothing but mountains out there." He exhaled, raked his chin. "Too dangerous. Too many unknowns right now. Someone's coming. They have to. I still believe that. Just a matter of time."

"Ain't no one coming and you know it," said Hank, staring out into the trees. "That deer aside, ain't seen no signs of life since me and Jesse showed."

Something racked the westward gulf of sky, a punch so sharp the group recoiled in unison, electric shards of sound unfurling out across the open range of cloud and timber. Glen reached up and touched his temple in response to hairs that lifted from his scalp, a static tingle passing underneath.

Hank's eyes twitched across the open air, his movements sharp despite the weight of alcohol within his system, nervous like a deer downwind of human scent. "The sweet hell was that?"

The sky broke wide again, a double crack that exorcised a murder of crows from the treetops, stippling skyward like a deconstructed shadow.

"Those gunshots?" This time Glen reached out and took Lauren by the arm, pulling her close. He didn't wait for her compliance.

The group listened, a fading thrum of frantic wings the only lingering sound. Then there was nothing.

"Others out there. Like us. Scared, defending themselves," said Laj. "Can't imagine that'll prove too helpful though."

"Yeah, well," said Hank. "Could be they ain't just shooting water. People lose all kinda sense in stressful times. Get unpredictable, make tough choices. Sometimes," he said, pulling another drag from his cigarette, "folks get desperate, take desperate measures, do things they might not normally do, find they *have* to do."

The others turned to look at him, letting the moment pass them by without remark.

Hank simply sat there on the rooftop's edge and watched

the trees, listening to the world around them. The air was flat, calm, devoid of sound and movement. From their vantage point, the mass was no longer visible, the parking lot a sheet of utter glass.

It was all too quiet, too still.

Far up on the distant mountainside, a flock of birds burst skyward through the forest's ceiling. Lower on the mountain came another, then another, drawing closer in a domino effect of wings and shrieks, thousands of birds released into the air like wisps of smoke unfurling from a burning fuse.

They all watched the forest. There was something in the distance, moving closer. Something fast, coming down the mountainside, straight ahead. They squinted in the sunlight, listening to the split and gasp of something pushing toward them. Closer now, they tracked subtle movement in the treetops, boughs of pines and maples stirring one by one, shaking free the needles, the leaves, the birds that fled in terror as whatever was approaching picked up speed, rushing toward the mountain's base. The distant gasp had now transitioned to a roar, a brutal sound of shattered trunks and limbs along its route.

It was the rush of water.

"God help us," said Laj.

Lauren's breath stopped in her chest. She backed away, tripping through the legs of the others that seemed rooted where they stood. Glen caught her by the arm, dropping into a defensive crouch.

A muddy torrent blasted through the forest's edge not

more than a hundred yards ahead, ripping shattered trunks and vegetation from the limestone-studded earth and hurling it across the road, across the parking lot. The rolling tangle plowed into the line of gas pumps. One pump ripped free and slammed across the asphalt, but the others held themselves against the impact, catching the majority of trees and undergrowth that lodged themselves against the metal bodies as the deadly current raged between, heading for the building's face.

"Back!" shouted Glen. "Get back!" The others, transfixed by the inbound horror, broke its hold and fell away, bracing for the impact. Hank jumped to his feet and pitched, staggering back onto the cinder blocks as his balance left him. His eyes went round and wide as momentum held him to his course, reeling back and over the building's edge.

CHAPTER FOURTEEN

HANK LET OUT A CRY as he went over. Jesse threw himself against the ledge and grabbed Hank's fast-retreating arm. Hank's lean body clapped the outside of the building with a gaseous yelp. He was wheezing, clawing at the topside of the building like a dangling rat when the water hit the diner's face. Jesse's face went red, springing veins along his forehead and his neck as he fought against the pull, sliding forward on the rooftop grit. Hank's forearm inched itself away from Jesse's grip, slithering through the fabric of the flannel sleeve. The water's impact sent a jolt throughout the building's cinder block construction as the water seized and thrust two cars side by side against the wooden porch, which was instantaneously decimated by the impact.

Hank's eyes bulged in terror as Jesse strained against the ledge, looking down into his old friend's panic-stricken face. The porch's overhang, several feet beneath Hank's kicking legs, let out a long, defeated groan. It had caught the upshot from the water's strike, shielding Hank, but now began to lurch and pull away, collapsing with the sudden absence of the pillars that had held its outward weight aloft.

As the overhang released its hold and crashed across the two cars wedged against the building's front, Glen appeared at Jesse's side and draped himself across the building's edge to grab Hank's other arm. Jesse cast his body's weight behind him, fighting the gravity that dragged Hank downward toward the water. Frozen, Glen stared down at Hank. Hank's eyes switched to Glen, a desperate, silent plea for help. Glen held tight, but didn't pull. A puzzled look had crossed his face, fast transitioning to a panicked mask of indecision.

Let him go. Drop him. Deliver him.

Hank slipped down another inch, closer to the churning water.

Jesse, wild-eyed, looked to Glen, back to Hank. "Glen, pull!"

Glen felt something shift inside him. It could be so easy. He could blame it on slippery hands. They were wet, of course. That part wouldn't be a lie. He was sweating like a shower door. Hank had been a threat to them. They'd be better off without him. *Safer.* More *efficient.* As for Hank himself, he was miserable. Maybe he'd prefer it this way. Maybe he would even ask for it if he could only make it past the moment's sudden shock and that stubborn instinct to survive, all other preferences aside. Yes. Maybe he would ask to simply be let go. He'd tell them they were better off without him. And Glen, he would readily agree.

Deliver him.

"Glen!"

Glen frowned and turned to Jesse, disengaged from what had stalled him.

"Pull, man! He's slipping!" shouted Jesse. "I can't hold him!"

With that, Glen came back to the moment and began to pull, fighting off the black, beguiling thoughts that clouded him.

What the hell was that? His heart was pounding.

Glen placed one foot against the ledge for leverage, pushing as the dangling man began to rise along the wall, the building's edge. Hank came flailing back across the ledge onto the roof with Jesse gripping one side of his body, Glen still locked onto the other. Hank stared at Glen, possessed by disbelief and utter terror.

Glen's stomach turned.

Breathless and depleted, Hank had hardly landed on the rooftop when they heard the scream.

Glen let him go. Hank and Jesse both had shifted at the sound, turning toward the source. They came back to Glen once more, questioning wordlessly before the recurrence of another long, eviscerating note.

From the inside the diner, down beneath their feet, the scream had come again.

And again.

CHAPTER
FIFTEEN

Laj and Tony were the first to turn and scramble through the hatch, down the ladder. They took two rungs at a time, then dropped the remainder of the way down to the floor. As the rest of the group spilled downward one by one through the opening, the two men had already made their way back to the front of the diner where Helen sat, pressed against her husband's bloated corpse, floating opposite the doors. It thrusted with the motion of the water, wet flesh playing glass in movement forward and back again, shrieking songs of overblown balloons.

The two stopped suddenly, thrown forward on their weight.

The devastation at the front of the building could now be seen in its entirety. The two cars were shoved practically bumper to bumper against the building's face, laid flush against the cinder blocks that framed the openings of the doors and windows. Two windows had been fractured. The cracks were large, striking upward from the corners of the glass like bolts of lightning.

Damaged, but not broken.

By some miracle, the insulation that had sealed the doors was still intact, as was their glass. The shelter of debris that heaped itself along the front had absorbed the brunt of the water's direct assault, capped off afterward by the porch's deconstructed overhang. The resulting creation was a sort of morbid terrarium. Only instead of rocks, there were cars. Instead of turtles floating in the water, having risen by at least another six or seven inches, a human body.

Helen moaned and leaned into the pane of glass, pressing her lips against her husband's waterlogged expression as he bobbed on the other side.

Tony was the first to step forward, just as the others had begun to wander in. On their faces was a look of threadbare fear, absolute disgust. Laj held a rearward palm up to the group that followed close behind, halting them beyond the farthest edge of the countertop.

"Ma'am?" Tony found himself within a foot of the woman now. He reached out to her, fingers trembling. "Helen?" He touched her, grazing a coat hanger of a shoulder underneath her blouse.

The woman spun and gripped him by his pant leg. He buckled at the knees and caught himself against an edge of the checkout counter, dashing a cup of pens across its surface, then the floor.

"He came back to me! Don't you think?"

Tony put his hands into his hair and looked into her grief-hewn face, feeling the look of horror on his own. Her wishful eyes awaited his response. Their tether to reality had been severed, perception of the world now reborn through the twisted lens of madness. She was gone completely, oblivious to the water's assault, to the state of her deceased husband, to reality collapsing all around her.

"Ma'am, I—" Tony threw a helpless glance to Laj. "Here, why don't you—"

"Just look!" Helen swung her hand behind her, slapping the glass. "Look at him!" The insulation creaked between the seams, and Tony swallowed down the brick of fear that came up in his throat. He watched the two doors shift against each other, chattering with the impact of her open palm.

Outside, the water shuddered, visibly excited, waves of chills pocked out across its surface. It thrust itself against the opposite side of the windowpane, then thrust again, this time applying long and constant pressure, eventually settling out to recompose itself in wait. The doors relaxed. The seams held tight.

"Satan took him from me, but he has no hold on my Fred." The woman's voice had suddenly calmed, almost explanatory in tone. "He's a man of *God*, you know." She nodded at Tony, smiling sweetly, appearing to search his face for signs of understanding.

Tony struggled just to breathe. It was all too much, too fast.

The water's assault.

The bloated body.

The woman's plunging madness.

He frowned and tried to move his lips into position for words that wouldn't come.

Helen's smile dissolved. She frowned back at Tony, frustration rising. "You do understand, don't you? You see? He's risen again in the name of Jesus!" She was back up on her feet now, ushering their attention to her husband's corpse, taut and gray, bobbing on the water like a satiated tick. Another squeal cried out as his cheek became acquainted with the glass again. The woman brought her hands up to her lips, giddy fingers twisted up as if engaged in some rheumatic quarrel. She closed her eyes, squeezing tears beneath her lids that fell across her face. She fed a dose of whispers to her palms and fingers, a makeshift instrument of prayer.

"Everyone…handles their stress differently," Glen whispered vacantly to Lauren. "That's all."

"Dad, stop," said Lauren.

Glen continued.

"Everybody's grief. All handled…in different…ways." He felt his sentences emerge in buffered fragments.

"Dad," she said.

He reached out and squeezed her shoulder. "This isn't… doing you any good. Why…don't you head to the booth, hon? I'll be over in a few."

"Dad, I think we're past that now." Lauren's tone was flat. "We're way past unseeing any of this."

Helen sucked a dose of air and stumbled backward from the door.

Outside, the collapsed overhang began to shift, sliding across the vehicles beneath it. The wood shrieked across the metal roofs as it fell away, slouching down into the water on the other side. The lot was visible again, and past the ruined overhang that floated like a broken dock, the surface of the water pulsed and shivered.

At the door, a pinkish broth escaped Fred's gaping mouth, the slightest trickle, moving to such a full expulsion that the buoyant carcass rocked in place beneath the force, a rhythmic surge of liquid spouting from the dead man's lips and gushing into the bed of water at his backside.

"No, no," groaned Helen. "Nononono. Oh God, noooo, Fred, noooo." Her face went flaccid, and she backed up into the fold of people standing just behind her, shaking free the newest course of horrors being served up to her already fractured mind.

Lauren couldn't pull her eyes away from the performance at the doors. "You don't need to worry about me, Dad."

For a moment, Glen forgot what Lauren was responding to. What he'd even said to her not several seconds prior.

"It's been long enough."

"What?" said Glen. He fought against the horror at the glass, drawing him in like quicksand. He couldn't pull his eyes away. The cool, dead tone of Lauren's voice offered an equally unsettling undercurrent to the horror of the moment.

"Since we lost Mom," said Lauren. She was staring at the corpse. "If that's what you're worried about," she said.

He pulled his eyes away, looked at Lauren. The context of her answer made its way to him. He gave his head a shake.

"Yeah…I—I know," said Glen, stealing glances left and right. "Still. It's not that. We don't need to bring that up. It's just—" His mind moved between his shell-shocked child, the water's attack, the potential of another, and what was happening at the glass right now. As for another attack, the debris had seemed to form a barrier along the front. Between the broken overhang and cars, it seemed to offer some protection against a direct hit, should it come again. At least for now.

"I feel sorry for her," said Lauren. Her eyes were shining now against the light. It wasn't the fearful look that he'd expected. The fearful look he felt she *should* have. A look to match the way he felt inside, perhaps the way he even looked. After the attack, after this, her face showed nothing more or less than utter empathy, understanding. Maybe even a comradery of sorts between the woman and herself. Her eyes weren't even on the corpse that slid across the entryway. Not on the damage dealt across the diner's front. They were on the woman, as if there were no realization of the other happenings at that moment, no other points of focus laid before her. "I know what she's feeling."

For a moment, Glen just looked at Lauren, unsure what to say, to think. He was having trouble forming basic thoughts. Did she understand they'd just been attacked? Did she even see Fred's body? Not just that. Did she see what was *happening* to it? Surely so. Of course she did. It was right in front of her. More so than the corpses that had come before, this was something on another level. Seeing it had thrown his own guts down in to a tailspin. Was this some kind of defense mechanism?

Despite her blunted response, Glen wanted to put his hand across her face, to cover Lauren's eager eyes, to remove the feed that played without consent. But there wasn't much that he could do. Seemingly, not much he *needed* to do.

"Yeah," he whispered. "So—so do I."

Laj now was standing at their left, Tony out in front. Laj leaned forward, laid a hand on Tony's shoulder. Tony jerked, nearly coming out of his own skin.

"Jesus," he panted. He swiped the backside of his hand across his mouth.

"You got something we can use to cover this up?" said Laj. He voice was low, artificially calm. The big man's chest was moving double rate, and the twitch had started tugging at the corner of his mouth again.

Tony licked his lips, nodding. "Uh," he said, pausing, seemingly disoriented. "Yeah. Maybe." His right hand worked his neck, kneading lumps of meat along its base. "I uh…" He gestured, looking like he'd had the wind knocked from his lungs, confused and turning slightly where he stood. "I got some…some tablecloths. In back."

Glen took Helen by the shoulders, turning her around, and led her farther back into the room. Head in hands, she closed her eyes and panted. Her breath was wet and hitching in her throat, quick and shallow. Having moved her to a nearby stool, Helen had begun to rock, her torso keeling forward and back again.

Glen turned to Lauren, standing at his side. "Keep an eye on her. Nowhere near that door, hear me? Especially not those broken windows. I need your help with her right now, okay? It's important."

Lauren nodded, the growing vacancy within his own child's eyes inspiring a greater sense of unease than anything else at that particular moment.

"Hon, you good?"

"Hm? Yeah." Lauren said, tried to shake it off. It didn't work. "Yeah. Dad, I'm fine. I'm good." She attempted an unconvincing smile. "Promise."

Glen paused, giving her another once-over. He laid his palm against the side of her head.

"Sure?"

"Mhm." Lauren said. She turned from him, placing her focus back on Helen.

Glen's hand fell away. "Right. All right. Okay."

Laj stood at the doorway, tablecloth unfurled from arm to floor. Glen walked over and joined him, taking one end in his hands and stretching its full length out between them.

Others gathered at the glass, watching.

They had to. They couldn't help it.

Expulsion of the liquid from the dead man's mouth had grown from trickle into a constant vomit, instigated by some hidden force to drag it from the clutch of human tissue. The siphon first ran light, then dark, a rosé evolution that in several moments went near-crimson as the corpse availed itself of all its moisture, impregnated with the remnants of blood and bile. They watched the body draw upon itself, a reduction not only of mass but of tonal quality, flesh embracing bone in such an act of rapid emaciation that puckered eyes and lips and ears until nothing had been left but deformed hints of features once intact, recognizably human only moments prior.

"Oh, God," whimpered Tony. He dropped down to the floor to bring a sense of balance to his sweeping vertigo. "Oh my God. I feel sick."

Glen reached down and laid a palm on Tony's back. "Just stay there. Take yourself a minute. Don't look at it."

The desiccated corpse bobbed higher on the water now, its mass reduced by half in its depleted state. Glen couldn't look away. It reminded him of classroom specimens he stored in jars of clouded formaldehyde: fetal pig, horse, frog, snake. The man's teeth cocked unnaturally right, shifted left of center, their misalignment bound beneath the insufficient catch of once-ample lips. The dislodged set of false teeth lifted easily in the final push of water coursing from his gullet, wriggling just behind the rigid cinch of lips, settling crookedly between his jaws when it had passed.

The men worked on in silence. They stretched the blue-checked cloth along the window and the door, blotting out the floating nightmare stalking just beyond the threshold. They moved opposite of one another, securing edge and corner via strips of duct tape, double layered against the cold that threatened to release it from the metal framework. The space was largely silent, most occupants that moved about infected by a common state of shock, notwithstanding Hank, atypically muted at his post behind the counter. His body canted sideways as he stared into a vacant corner, working the bottle and the glass in relative seclusion.

Lauren stepped down from her stool and over to the distraught woman's side. She was so calm, so collected. The fact that this was a point of strength of hers hadn't been lost on Glen. It was a point of strength just as much belonging to her mother. Claire had been no novice at concealing her emotions, ever-smiling, placating, dying inside all the while. This is something that concerned him, always had.

"You okay?"

"I think I'm going to need a little help, Dad," said Lauren, having fit her neck beneath the woman's arm. "She's not feeling so good, so I'm moving her over there instead. To the booth. Someplace she can maybe stretch out some."

Glen braced Helen's right side, helping her step down from her stool, easing her feet down to the floor. The integrity of Helen's legs was gone, rendered soft beneath her as Glen and Lauren led her to the set of benches closest to the doorway, nearly dragging her the distance. The doors and windows closest to the booth had now been shrouded by the tablecloth, blinding visibility of what lay beyond. They sat her down, helping her slide along the cushion's length and bringing her legs out flat across its surface.

Helen's face was waxen, sickly. She mumbled something unintelligibly, her breath rolling out beneath the lines of utter nonsense. She folded over, leaning into her arms. The movement seemed to squeeze a sound up from her throat, a low-slung ratchet like the warning of a pissed-off cat.

Opposite the covered doors, Fred's lifeless body nudged the glass. The rhythmic thump and squeal now filled the space, driving Helen well beyond the borders of her sanity.

CHAPTER SIXTEEN

Laj stood alone at the far end of the room. His upper half was painted in a blend of gold and shadow, knit into the ornate tapestry of morning light that fell across the corner wall and ceiling. Glen joined him, and the two men stood there in the momentary solitude of their respective thoughts. Glen's hands wrestled each other at his middle, fingers threading in and out, in and out. Feeling Laj's eyes on him, he moved them to his pockets, pinning them against his thighs.

They observed the vacant stretch of land that used to be a road along the farthest length of parking lot, its asphalt now concealed beneath the sunlit shimmer of a rising tide that now consumed the first two to three feet of sloping limestone at its distant edge. From the gaping hole that now existed in the tree line, rivulets of water trickled down between the stony crags to join the larger body at its base.

"Penny for your thoughts," said Glen, breaking the silence. "Quarter for a solid plan out of this."

Laj squinted through the glare. "Raise you a dollar if you got one of your own."

"Not a soul seen this whole time now. Nobody in, nobody out," said Glen. "We're being actively attacked now. This can't go on. We have to do something."

Laj raked his bearded face beneath his nails, moving slow and long across his cheek, his neck. "Best I figure, the hills, the mountains could be safer than here," he said. "Keep our asses out the low points, follow the highest out of here."

"That water just came down from high."

The sky split wide again, a sound like shattered rock that broke across the firmament, seeming to crack the void in several places. And then there was another, the sprawling aftershock of something great and hot trailing from behind. The treetops seemed to stir and settle in the wake, and Glen almost thought he felt those needled fingers dash across his brain again, the touch of some electric ghost. He reached up and rubbed his temples.

Both men simply eyed the sky and forest stretching out across the range of mountains. Neither said a word about it.

Glen turned to Laj. "But say we do that. Say we take the high ground. Then what?"

Laj shrugged, pausing in thought. "Then we keep on moving, try our odds out there, see where our legs will take us."

"There's still hope that someone comes for us," said Glen. "Still that possibility. Has to be someone out there."

Laj gave Glen a look. "Just you and me here, brother. Ain't no need to play it hopeful for your kid right now."

Glen didn't answer, but he really didn't need to either.

Laj gestured toward the undulating slopes of rock and tree that ran across their line of sight. "So, we can make a run for it, or we can sit it out right here, but me and you both know it's going to get in. Ain't a matter of *if*, so much as *when*. And when that happens, that's all she fuckin' wrote. And to be honest, I wouldn't rule it out none that the shit is somehow already in here with us right now."

Glen looked at him with an expression that betrayed his collected facade, throwing his thoughts into the open air without permission.

Laj's lips curled up like wisps of rising smoke, slow and thin. On a big man like Laj, a smile can be a threatening sight. It didn't quite belong, especially in that moment. Its seeming instability gave Glen a moment's pause.

"What? You thought you was the only banana in this bunch with a lick of common sense?" He snicked his teeth. "C'mon, man. You know you thought it too. I see it all over your face. You a terrible poker player, ain't you?"

Something let loose inside Glen, and a corner of his own mouth went up, no more than a flash before it disappeared again. He dipped his chin, acknowledging the fact.

"If it's true," said Laj. "What you been saying, that is. That this could be some kind of microorganism, something living in that water, shaping it, controlling it. If that's actually what this is, I think you know well as I do that it's probably already here with us. And if it ain't, it's bound to find its way in here sooner or later, and my money landing on the sooner side of that coin toss." He shook his head. "Won't take much, something that size. Could be anywhere. Could *fit* anywhere."

Glen nodded. "You and I are calling dibs on the same side of that coin then, my friend."

"So, tell me what you got," said Laj.

"Tell you what?"

"Your thoughts. Tell me what you thinking. Less I've been standing here clapping my jaws to no other than myself this whole time, talking to some figment of my damn imagination."

Glen let out a breath. "'Bout our only shot, taking the high ground out. Safer than low ground, for sure. Getting from here to any ground at all is our problem though. We're landlocked, water all around. Only way out is through it." He shook his head, then pawed a shaking hand across the grit of gray and black that marked his chin and jawline. "And I just don't see it happening, man. Least not yet. We'd have to be full out of options before taking to the water."

"We can *see* it though," stressed Laj. "You already showed us that. All we need's a spotter. Hit the water, spotter keeps an eye out for the mass, others make a beeline for dry ground."

"No way. Not yet at least," said Glen. "Damned sure not putting Lauren in that. We don't know enough about it yet."

"Ain't all of us even have to go though," said Laj. "Just a couple that can go find help, bring it back, hopefully before it makes its way inside. You say you don't want your girl out in that, and I don't blame you for it. Not a bit. But she don't have to even go, man." Laj turned back to the window again, watching the water spin in several places. This time the wind had picked back up, and he couldn't readily discern its influence from what was living in the water. "Just something to think about, man. That's all. I ain't trying to pressure nobody, but we need to face facts, make our smartest moves now, while we still can. Last thing we want's to be backed into a corner where shit gets hasty. Sloppy."

Glen shook his head in disagreement. "I hear what you're saying. I do. I just don't like it. Not right now, at least. We're miles from anything, anywhere. Send a couple folks out there, odds are we won't be seeing them or anyone else again before the water gets in anyway. It'll be too late."

"Said it yourself, right there," said Laj. "Water's gonna get in anyway. The hell are we waiting on then? What other options are we working with?"

He paused a moment, cracking his fingers one by one in thought.

"If we do it. If we go, then all of us go," said Glen. "No one left behind. But that time isn't now. We need to wait a little longer, make sure we weigh *all* our options first. Like I was saying, not out of the question, but if we do it, it's damn sure gonna be our Hail Mary. Just my personal feelings on it at the moment."

"I don't know, Glen. Seems to me you got a lot of *educated* thoughts on what's out there." The voice crawled up between the two men like a snake.

Hank had parked himself on the barstool behind Glen and Laj at some point in their talk. They'd no idea how long he'd been there. He swirled the liquor in his glass, meditating on its rise and fall along the translucent walls.

Glen kept his back to Hank, speaking into the windowpane instead. "I have theories, Hank. Like I told you before, just making some guesses as to what we're dealing with."

"Seem awfully specific, them theories." He took a sip. "Awfully *on the nose*, if you will."

Glen felt that if he turned around, looked Hank in the eye, he'd have a hard time staying put. Instead, he left his back to him, digging nails into his palm. "We still at this, Hank? Why don't you come on out with whatever it is you're getting at?"

"You might've hauled my narrow ass back over that edge, but that's that. And let's not act like you ain't had other designs out there." Hank drew another sip, baring his teeth against the burn and set the glass down on the countertop.

"What're you talking about?" asked Laj. He pivoted on a heel, facing Hank. Glen still faced the window.

"Your boy looked like he was weighing options when he had me by the arm out there," said Hank. "Like he was damn near ready to let me drop."

"That's some bullshit if I ever heard it," said Laj. "You should be on your damn knees right now, thanking Glen or God or whoever you feel needs thanking that you're not out there huffing water with them other bodies right now. You got some damn nerve."

"What do you want, Hank?" asked Glen, still staring out the window.

"Y'all want to mock my suspicions, make me out to be some

paranoid asshole with wild, unfounded government conspiracy theories and shit. But *you*…oh…" He chuckled. "You, Glen, lay out some real *specifics* and ain't nooobody got a thing to say about it." Hank swept his hand across the air to punctuate the statement. He brought it back across his glass and raised the drink. "Not a *damn* thing. But see, I ain't buyin' it. You wanna know what *I* think?"

Glen spun and took a step toward Hank. "Nah, man. Not really." He felt involuntary movement of his fingers in his palm, clenching like a primer bulb, again and again, his engine at the ready.

Laj read his face, the actions of his hand, and reached an arm across Glen's chest. "Take it easy. He's drunk." Laj leveled his eyes on Hank. "As usual."

Hank sucked his teeth and held his place, hanging his eyes on Glen. "I don't trust you. I don't think you are who you say you are. I think you got too many answers for someone who supposedly ain't got no part in none of this."

"You can't be serious," murmured Glen.

"*Whole* lot of answers. Scripting this whole thing out real easy, real clean. Just laying out them facts like you dealin' cards across the kitchen table on a Friday night." Hank held the glass up to the minor crescent of his lips and emptied its remains into his mouth, down his throat.

"Hank, I think we've been through enough this morning. Especially you." Jesse wandered over from the rest of the group, still tending to the moaning woman curled up in her seat, keeling to her side against the table's edge.

"Damn it, Jess. Can't you see the menfolk speaking over here?" Hank dropped the glass against the counter, sloshing a bit of whiskey over the edge. He did so with a small and crooked grin, head and eyes half angled toward the man. "You can go on, shuffle on back over there with the midwives. Looks like they fixin' to help that old broad birth a turd into the world." He wheezed a laugh into the air.

Jesse glowered, nodding at the bottle. "Startin' real early today, ain't you? Forget about what happened up top? Might want to hold on to your sense of balance."

"How about you just do you? I'll do what I gotta do, pal." Hank shrugged. "Deal how I gotta deal. Besides, ain't every day you got a human pool toy come knockin' at your front door. I mean, if that ain't a cause for celebration, I don't know what is." He spun the cap free of the neck and fed his glass another round. "But, Jess…long as you here, we having us a little come-to-Jesus time." He held the glass up to the light with one eye closed, spying Laj's distorted figure through the liquid. "Or Allah or whatever deity strikes yer particular fancy."

Laj clenched, a tectonic pulse of muscles rippling through his hardened jaw.

Hank winked and brought the glass up to his lips. He tossed the shot of liquor down his throat.

"Hank. Come on," said Jesse. He looked to Laj, shaking his head like an apologetic offering on his asshole friend's behalf.

Laj shook his head, dismissing the gesture with his hand. "Common sense done flown the coop, shit a trail across his brain on its way out." His eyes went narrow, sharp and white-hot like two glowing bits of shrapnel. "See, my man Hank here," said Laj, "is about to catch himself a bus on the corner of fuck around and find out. He just don't know when that joint coming. That bus run late time to time, give its patrons time to check themselves. Got a feeling it's comin' real soon though."

Hank set his eyes into a roll, ignoring the big man's words.

"See, what I'm 'splainin' to the fellas here is that, far as I'm concerned," said Hank, laying one hand on his chest, "Glen seems to know a little too much about our particular predicament."

"Oh, you ain't heard the half of it," said Glen. "You want to know what else I think, Hank? You'll love this."

At that point Hank's upturned lips came loose and dropped into a scowl beneath the blue-black swell of his defeated nose. Others approached, baited by the rising commotion.

"I don't claim to know where it came from or even if this is what it is. I'm a biology teacher, plain and simple. I study life, the science of it. That's it. No secret squirrel crap, no government testing. Okay?"

The group had gathered nearby now in full. All was quiet, all sound crushed beneath a nervous weight that filled the air. Hank sat unmoved, regarding Glen through blackened narrows.

"Like I already said, microorganisms. Rapid replicators, colonial." Glen could read the confusion on their faces, though no questions had been raised. "Basically, they're clustering, moving out in groups, packs, each cluster functioning as a single, multicellular organism." Several people nodded, whether out of pure placation or genuine understanding he couldn't tell.

"If I were to guess," he continued, "they're water harvesters, somehow drawn toward water sources, binding with the molecules, extracting it, collecting it. Reason I'm thinking this is because there are known species of water harvesters. Insects that collect it, y'know, small droplets and all, just not on this scale. They don't bind and extract on a micro-level like this. This right here is something different. I mean, if that's what's actually going on here."

"I ain't really got a reason to doubt you," said Tony. He was standing near the counter, more recovered than the last time Glen had seen him. "But could be anything, really. Why would you think that's what this is, of all things?"

"Because he's smart. That's why," said Lauren.

"I'll be the last to disagree with that, young lady," said Tony. "Don't misunderstand my question. Just wondering where he might've—"

"He has a master's in biology with a concentration in entomology," interrupted Lauren. Pride bloomed in her eyes, a look that caught Glen by surprise, something foreign he'd not seen in many, many years. A look that seemed to warm him, thaw him deep inside beneath the reach of self-awareness. Glen placed his hand on her head, smiled, and gently tousled her hair.

"The fuck is that?" said Hank.

"Means we got ourselves a bug-ologist," said Jesse.

Hank turned and scowled at Jesse. "The hell you talkin'

about, and since when did you know half of anything outside of classic TV trivia?"

"Me and my kid used to watch *Wild Kratts* sometimes," said Jesse. "Be surprised the shit you pick up from kid shows these days."

Hank rolled his eyes and turned back to his glass.

Glen grunted, pleasantly caught off-guard by the fact that Jesse actually knew what an entomologist was. Nine out of ten people didn't have a clue (ten out of ten in some groups), and if they thought they did, they quickly found they didn't, having assumed entomology had to do with infectious diseases, climate change, or some human condition they just couldn't quite put their finger on. People rarely ever knew it was the field of bugs. More specifically, the scientific study of insects.

"Just my hypothesis. A guess, honestly," admitted Glen. "There's something else."

"What's that?" asked Laj.

"Anyone else notice the trees around here?"

"What about the trees?" asked Jesse.

"They're changing awfully fast, awfully early this year. Thinning awfully fast too. They've already dropped half their foliage."

"What about it?" said Hank.

"It's a symptom of adaptation and stress signaling in trees to shed their foliage during times of drought," said Glen. "Had an awful lot of rain lately for that to be the case, which ties in with my hypothesis. If water's being harvested and pulled away from the trees and ground, that would explain the premature shedding even after such a rain-intensive period."

"Like I said," mumbled Hank, turning on his stool. "Got *all* them answers."

"Look, I have no idea if that's the case or not. No reason to speculate on one thing over another. I'm just basing it on other life I've studied out there in the world and going off what I've personally observed around us. Using the known to explain the unknown. All life's based on something. Nothing's truly new, wholly different. Not entirely. Just nature reconfigured."

An electric shot snapped off from somewhere out beyond, the percussive strike of splitting timber, a bolt that struck the air and crawled its way across the void. All turned toward the sound, yet again, no one said a word as if acknowledgment would curse them all, the presence of the sound somehow taboo, never really there. Opposite their inner circle, Helen breathed a woeful note into the surface of the table from the other end of the room.

"Bottom line, based on what we've seen, given large enough numbers, I think they're able to harvest and manipulate the water. I think that's what we're seeing. One seething colony, bound at the molecular level, collectively functioning as a singular predatorial entity."

Jesse scuffed his feet in place, chipping one toe at the floor. "Why us? If it's water they after, why people?"

"Human body's roughly sixty percent water," answered Glen. "I think it's intelligent enough to know this. To have learned this."

Jesse grimaced at the news. "Well, shit."

Hank smiled and came down from the stool. He stared at Glen a moment, eased his glance off slow and slick like melting ice, then left the group.

In the silence that followed, another sound caught their ears. One that hadn't been there prior.

It was the sound of dripping water.

CHAPTER SEVENTEEN

STANDING NEAR THE JAR POSITIONED on the countertop, they watched in helpless horror as it caught the slow, persistent drip beneath the leaking waterline.

"How long has this been going on?" asked Glen, whispering, as if, should it be infected by the microorganism, it might hear as well as it could feel, could hunt. Could maybe even pick up on the influence of their speech within the air, a butterfly effect of sorts. He couldn't totally dismiss the possibility. "Has it been the whole time?"

"No," answered Tony. "I'd fixed it. Storms last week had started it. Ain't leaked in days."

"That hit the building took must've knocked it loose again," said Laj.

"You think this was an accident?" Across the room, Hank was leaning forward, hands on knees. His eyes were on the jar. The fear was back again. The same fear that had filled him as he dangled from the rooftop. Glen could see it in his face, his eyes. Just more numb this time around, not frantic like before, tamed by the alcohol. "It knew," he said. "It wanted in, and it found a way."

Nobody answered. Then, with the realization that the water in the jar was moving, new horror flourished, filling them completely. This movement wasn't anything pronounced, overly exaggerated or overtly obvious, but those who looked for it could certainly see it. The water in the jar had begun to shift, more or less a sort of listing toward one end of the vessel than anything else. The waterline was canted, leaning, pressing on the glass wall of the jar, angling toward the ailing woman on the bench. Helen groaned and shuddered. Her head hung low and she appeared to be oblivious to anything beyond the fabric of her very lap.

Lauren sat across from her, blankly staring at the jar. The sense of shock still swam throughout her system, an overlay of calm atop whatever frantic storm was turning deep inside.

"You still have the lid to that jar?" asked Glen.

"I do," answered Tony.

"Gonna need that," said Glen. "We can trap it, maybe use it somehow. We'll need another container. And some bleach."

Plick.

Tony headed off into the back.

Glen stepped closer to the jar.

Plick.

The drops came only every thirty seconds or so. Nothing fast, nothing urgent. Still, all that was needed. Replication in the jar would take over from that point. Given time, assuming Glen's theory was a working one, it would eventually occupy every ounce of water in the container, growing stronger as it did.

After Tony reappeared with the requested supplies, Glen poured several inches of bleach into the yellow bucket Tony had retrieved, and then they waited. Twenty seconds later...

Plick.

Glen removed the jar and replaced it with the bucket. He capped the jar and twisted, sealing the liquid inside. Sweat beaded on his brow, and he exhaled, unintentionally having held his breath throughout the task. He set the jar down on the countertop. They all watched as the liquid leaned into the vessel's side. It branched, exploding up the wall into a network of translucent threads that held in place a moment, searching, feeling, then pulled away as the proboscis was retrieved.

"It's with us now," said Jesse. "It found a way in."

Beyond the water's reach, Helen groaned again, straightening in her seat. She opened her eyes, pained and eager.

"Close enough to touch."

Into the bucket, now serving as a disinfectant trap, another drip.

Plick.

CHAPTER EIGHTEEN

HANK SHOULDERED THE CORNER EDGE of the roof in silence, watching the trees, the distant mountain peaks changing color in the daylight's slow-drawn dissolution, their orange-yellow fire painting false warmth over the cold and unforgiving landscape. He hadn't eaten. None of them had since everything that happened earlier. Regardless, he'd not have felt his hunger had it not been ruined otherwise. The whiskey would've seen to that.

Most of the others shared the opposite end of the rooftop, also having relished the cool, outside air for quite some time, though beginning now to realize how they'd overstayed their welcome as the temperature began to dive as night crept in.

Finding him alone, Jesse made his way to Glen and stood beside him. "Tell me something," Jesse whispered.

Glen came to a stop, having walked the edges of the rooftop as he thought their situation over. Thought about the organism, how they might use the sample they had captured. Wondered if the bleach trap would effectively contain it, or whether it would crawl the pipe to some other point inside the building. Wondered if it already had, or maybe if there had been other leaks, still in action, somewhere out of sight. Pooling, waiting, hunting. Of course, he'd not mentioned any of this to the others.

"Hm?"

"What happened earlier?" asked Jesse. "Back when we was helping Hank."

Glen shook his head. "I don't follow."

"Come on," he said. "I seen the look on your face. You stopped pulling. You looked like you was weighing something."

Glen knew what he was talking about, but frowned as if he didn't.

"Options," Jesse hissed, frustrated. "Like you was weighing *options*."

Glen shook his head. He couldn't tell him the truth. The despicable, unfathomable truth. He couldn't tell him that he *had* considered dropping Hank. And not only had he considered it, but had gone so far as try and *justify* the action. Justify it through some imaginary yearning he'd convinced himself that Hank might actually have, pleading to be dispatched from his burden of a life.

Glen's stomach soured at the recollection. Shame bloomed hotly from his core.

He couldn't tell Jesse this. He couldn't tell him all about the voices. The ones that seemed to call to him from down below, glassy little words, but could've just as easily (and more likely) been inside his head.

Let him go. Drop him. Deliver him.

He couldn't tell him that because it would've thrown red flags. It would've raised alarm with Jesse, and he'd have raised alarm with others. Especially Lauren. And maybe rightfully so. Glen had left his medication in the truck, and hadn't had a dose since back before they'd stopped in at the diner. How long had that now been? A day? Two days? Lauren couldn't know this. His condition worried her enough already. The voices, the delusions that had followed Claire's death. Most of anyone, he couldn't let her know. Voices were the reason he was on them. And without them, well, the voices would return, as would the paranoia, the all-consuming angst. How long he had before they might return, he didn't know. What he'd heard while holding on to Hank had unsettled him, less because he thought the voices might be real, more because they likely weren't, because the medication might've started wearing off, because the PTSD might be at the door already, just waiting for a chance to be invited in.

"Don't worry about me," said Glen. "Guess I just froze up. Stress can hit me funny sometimes. That's all. Trust me. It's not what you think."

That wasn't entirely untrue. It was potentially worse.

Jesse held his gaze on Glen a moment, regarding him with cautious eyes. "Just making sure you was good. That's all."

"I'm fine," said Glen. "And I thank you for the concern." Glen picked up his stride. Jesse started walking with him, keeping to his side.

"You should know," said Jesse, "that even though Hank is a prick, and trust me, I know he is, it ain't exactly just because. He's been through some things."

Glen didn't know if Jesse was seeking his forgiveness, his understanding, but he wasn't feeling kindly toward the man who'd verbally attacked his daughter. He didn't issue a response. He and Jesse walked, rounding toward the building's rear.

"Some years back, he lost his little girl," said Jesse, slowing down while they were still out of Hank's earshot. "He and his wife didn't make it afterward. He's been on his own since, except for me, and he ain't never really processed it the way he should've. Just been an angry asshole ever since."

Glen stopped walking. Jesse had his attention now. Something sharp turned in his chest.

"But as a man, Hank ain't really bad," continued Jesse. He looked Glen in the eyes. "Don't doubt he ain't your favorite, but maybe that'll help explain why, well, he is the way he is."

Against Glen's will, he felt a wave of pity come across him. After everything they'd been through, everything Hank had said, had done, Glen strained for reasons to continue hating him. Despite his efforts, he was having difficulty holding on to any. The man had every reason to be bitter, angry, brokenhearted. Glen understood. He'd not fared much better under similar circumstances, albeit in his own, different ways. It occurred to him that he and Hank might very well have more of a connection than he ever would've realized. The realization was a sour one, something that he'd rather purge, spit out of his system like a toxin. But inconvenient, undesired as it was, it was the truth.

Again, shame burned in his gut as he reflected on the thoughts he'd come so close to acting on earlier.

"I appreciate you telling me, Jesse," said Glen. "I can only imagine. Been in a similar state of mind myself before, so his condition isn't wholly lost on me."

Jesse dipped his chin, then pushed his hands into his pockets. He looked like a weight had been removed somehow. The two continued walking.

For a while, they killed time toying with the waterborne entity, trying its responsiveness with pebbles, chunks of brick, nails, flinging them beyond the ledge and out into the soil-black expanse of water, regarding its behavior with renewed, gut-souring amazement each time it responded to the action with a fleeting measure of attention, abandoning the object, moving onward in short time.

But they weren't out there for the air or to screw around with the water. They had come up top to listen. Carefully. They'd listened for hours. And across the entire stretch of time they'd been up there, there'd been nothing. No sound of rubber tread on asphalt. Of engines. Of boats. Of aircraft. Nothing. Not even that horrific crack and hush of water cutting through the trees. Nothing but that same, sickening discharge that had come and gone, a seeming puncture to reality, ripping the sky in two. And for all they knew, that's exactly what had happened. Reality had ripped, and through the open wound the water dribbled in, slow and steady from some black, unknown dimension.

Jesse scuffled over rock and tar, eventually leaving Glen and wandering on his own, walking anxious laps around the roof's perimeter with his hands shoved deep against the inner seams of cotton pockets. In time, he rejoined the group, appearing at their edge with something small and soft in his hand.

Lauren made a sour face and looked away. "Aw, c'mon Jesse."

Jesse shrugged and cocked his head. "Found it dead, laying over by that vent. Ain't like *I'm* the one that killed it." He pushed the fingers of his left hand through its feathers, smoothed them out again. "Figured we'd try something. See how it reacts to this. Y'know, something real, living. Well, least close we're gonna get to it."

"Buddy, I think we all know how it responds to living things," said Laj.

Glen perked. "No, he's actually got a point. A good one." He walked over to Jesse, holding out his hand. "Mind?"

"Yeah, here, be my guest. It ain't a pet." Jesse laid the dead blackbird on Glen's palm, its plumage downy-soft, the bony underlayment calcified from rigor mortis.

"If we were to bait it, divert it. If we tossed something of flesh and bone out there, I wonder how much time it would buy us," said Glen, measuring the dead bird's weight inside his palm. "Surely more time than some inanimate object. We saw how fleeting its attention is."

"Only one way to find out, chief," murmured Hank, his words emerging from the creeping pitch at the opposite end of the rooftop. A shattered cataract of twilight haze obscured his exact location as they squinted back in his direction. "Give'r a toss. Find out if she floats." The words came out in singsong fashion, followed by a throaty click of laughter. Hank picked up the tune again, transitioning into actual song. *"If she floats, then all is fine. She'll sail till the end of time. If she goes down, that's all she wrote. Guess she shoulda bought a boat."* Hank let out another laugh. There was a glassy swish of whiskey as he took another hit and hacked across the mash of pebbles from a gag reflex.

"He's really losing it," whispered Lauren.

Glen hushed her.

Daylight had all but abandoned them entirely, but Glen could still decipher details of the parking lot in the waning haze of evening and gleam of rising moon. Rainbows glimmered on the surface of the water near the gas pumps where scant amounts of gasoline had emptied from the ruptured lines. He wound his right arm back and slung the lifeless bird into the graying void. The slight corpse caught a gust of wind and plummeted, dropping to the earth not more than fifteen to twenty feet out from the building's ledge. It met the water with a downy pat, not far out from the rear of Glen's partially digested truck, still resting between the lines of its parking spot.

Hank sat up and peered over the ledge. "Float or sink?"

The carcass bobbed, turning on the water's surface.

"Darn," said Hank, snapping his fingers. "Looks like ten more years of purgatory for us." He turned and flopped onto the roof again, keeling back against the wall behind him.

In the dying light, the liquid came to life as the colony assembled and moved in, a displaced plow of water heading its approach, arching underneath the last remaining threads of daylight wriggling across its oily surface.

This time the water took extended interest.

It roiled and frothed in greedy dedication to the task, harvesting the moisture stored within the scant amount of bone and tissue. In less than a minute, once its deed was finished, the aquatic mass moved out and disappeared into the gray-black settlement.

"It stalled it. Not long, but more than otherwise," said Glen. "More than using inanimate objects. It found something of interest, of value, in that bird."

"Not long enough though," said Laj. "We'd need more time. A *lot* more."

"No, I agree. But larger bait would give us that time. This was a bird. Imagine the time something larger would take," said Glen. "Might buy us a couple minutes, at *least*."

"In a perfect world, sure. Any normal day, we'd have options. Market's out of reach though. What kind of bait you got in mind?"

Glen shook his head. "Hell, I don't know. Doesn't even really need to be meat though. Could be anything. Anything of interest, water-bearing."

Laj released a pensive grunt. "Call it homework, I guess. Something to think on." He looked to the sky, then across the rooftop. The sun had dipped beneath horizon's edge completely, dragging down the final blush of sunset in its wake. With the disappearance of the blinding glare, they saw that Hank was gone now, moonlight swimming in the empty vessel he'd abandoned on the cinder ledge. In the falling darkness, the liquid boundary of the property revealed itself beneath the lunar bulb in rippling lines of neon white.

"Better get inside," Laj said. He clapped Glen on the arm, stepping around him on his way back toward the open hatch.

"Glad someone finally said it," said Lauren, burrowed deep inside her hoodie. "October shouldn't be this cold."

"Everthing's colder here," said Tony, turning one heel on the grit. "Twice as cold at night. That damp air pours off the mountains, comes through here with a vengeance. Come on. Let's get inside, warm up. Might have some pie or something we can heat up. Something to knock this chill off our bones."

Again, the sound came in from someplace distant, out across the range of mountains. A violent snap obliterated distant skies like thunder devoid of lightning. The aftershock growled toward them like a panther rushing through the blackness. Farther west, another strike cracked off, chasing the wake of the first across a crowded bed of stars.

The group dialed back their stride and turned to face the emptiness beyond the rooftop ledge.

"The hell is going on out there?" said Tony.

They waited. The hills exhaled through their prematurely thinning foliage, a reedy cry emerging from the shadows as an anxious wind swept through and flossed the sprawling bones of oak and maple. All else was quiet, any sounds preceding overwritten by the gusting wind, and those inevitably rubbed out by the next in turn.

The hairs across Glen's scalp rose up and tingled at their base. The air around them seemed to go to static, crackling with an energy he couldn't see, fading out to nothing in a span of seconds.

"Dad?"

He nodded toward the open hatch, taking Lauren's hand before she had a chance to voice her fear. "Believe I heard the man say something about some pie down there," said Glen. "Don't expect that'll stick around too long with this crowd."

Lauren fought to change the course of her expression, forming a brittle smile instead.

"Come on," said Glen. "See if we can't get ourselves a slice."

CHAPTER NINETEEN

"Tears in Heaven" played across the speakers overhead. It was the only station Tony had been able to bring in clearly. The only one that didn't sound like breaking surf. Some slight reminder of the world that still existed out there.

Glen scooped a bite of pie into his mouth. "Pie's good," he said. "No sense wasting it."

Lauren pushed the plate away, slice untouched. "I can't eat right now."

"I get it," said Glen. He laid his fork down. "We can talk. No pie required."

"This old people music," said Lauren. "It's so depressing."

Glen wagged his head both ways. "This one, yeah," he said. "Clapton wrote it about the death of his four-year-old son."

Lauren raised her brow. "Point validated."

"Indeed," smiled Glen.

"Why would someone want to write about something so

sad?" asked Lauren. "To just immerse themselves in their own grief like that?"

"Hard to say," said Glen. "Guess Clapton found it cathartic to face it head-on. To sing about it. Maybe bottling things up wasn't working for him, you know?" Glen released a breath and looked at Lauren. "Maybe there's a lesson in that."

Lauren shrugged. Her eyes stayed on her hands, wrestling one another in her lap.

"Now," said Glen, "What's really on your mind? Depressing as it is, it isn't the music."

"We're not going to make it," said Lauren, finally looking up at him. "Out of this place, I mean. And I don't want this to be it. This can't be it."

"Whoa," said Glen, leaning forward. "You kidding me?"

Lauren looked down at her lap again.

"Kid, look at me," he said. "Of course we are. What would make you even say that?"

"Because I have eyes. A brain," said Lauren. "A feeling."

"Listen to me," said Glen. "High school, prom, college, marriage. All that stuff's ahead of you. It's already written. Can't be unwritten. We're making it out of here, all right."

A moment of silence crossed them. Glen moved his fork around his plate. In the distance, the others talked, about what he couldn't hear, didn't particularly care. Through the speakers, Clapton broke into an acoustic guitar solo.

"That said," continued Glen, "gonna need to work on dancing when we do."

"What?" asked Lauren, looking up.

"Prom, wedding, all that stuff requires dancing," said Glen. "Maybe I can help you out with that. Just saying."

Lauren arched her brow, forming an incredulous expression. The corner of her mouth went up.

"What?" asked Glen.

"You don't dance," said Lauren.

"I dance," said Glen, feigning offense.

"Since when?" asked Lauren.

"I danced with Mom all the time," said Glen.

"I mean *real* dancing." Lauren laughed. "Not that slow stuff. *Old people* dancing."

"One day," said Glen, pointing at her, "you'll meet a boy, and I'll be there to remind you about this discussion we're having right now. I promise you that." He paused. "And at your wedding, daddy-daughter dances are never fast. Always slow. You know that."

"Don't make promises you can't keep," said Lauren, her smile fading.

"Never," said Glen, giving her a nudge. "Hold up."

"What?"

Glen looked around the diner.

"Dad, no." Lauren recoiled, smile restored. "Don't even."

Overhead, Clapton crooned.

"Come on." Glen smiled, rising to his feet. He motioned to her. "Stand up."

"No way," said Lauren, shaking her head. "I don't do the slow stuff. I told you."

"And I'm telling you that one day you will," said Glen. "And when you do, you're going to be prepared. So come on, stand up." He reached for Lauren. "We still have half the song left."

Lauren stood and groaned. "Dad, c'mon." She grinned. "This is so cringe."

"Embrace the cringe," said Glen. "Embrace it. Now come in close, arms out, like this. Here. Take my hands."

Lauren stiffly did as she was told, face reddened. The others in the room were silent now. They were clearly being watched. Neither bothered to confirm. As far as they were concerned, no one else existed in that moment but the two of them. Lauren relaxed, then leaned into her father's chest.

"There you go," said Glen. "Just like that. Back and forth. Easy, right? Just watch the kicks. Your mom was merciless."

She put her boot on Glen's toe, letting out a laugh.

"Funny girl," said Glen, smiling. He closed his eyes. Together, they swayed in rhythm to the music overhead.

"Getting out of here," said Lauren, suddenly serious. Tighter now, she gripped his hands in hers. "You really think we're going to?"

"I know we're going to," said Glen. He held his daughter closer as they finished out the song.

CHAPTER
TWENTY

SLEEP TOOK GLEN WITHOUT CONFLICT that night. Their adrenaline had been depleted, and the wave of lethargy that rose behind it was formidable. He and Lauren laid themselves across the stretch of vinyl floor that ran between the length of countertop and booths. The bench had cramped his back and neck the night before, hobbling him for half the day, and he couldn't bring himself to sleep another night cinched up like that again. The floor was hard, sure, but the trade was worth it. Rest was rest. His mind gave up the weight of their predicament and drifted deep and far, floating out amid the nothingness of utter exhaustion, landing somewhere in the recollection of a summer day, the soft and gritty burn of sand upon his back, the salty sting of sunbaked ocean drying at his front.

He knew this day, this dream, this past reality.

And it was never the same dream twice, though somehow never changing all the same.

Ocracoke, North Carolina. It had been their spot. That place they felt was theirs and theirs alone, at least inside the window of that single week each year, always one month out from end of school, right there in the dead of summer heat when all the ocean had transitioned to a warm and friendly bath with not a trace of cold remaining.

They'd finished an early lunch, peanut butter and honey sandwiches, rendered slightly stale beneath the graze of ocean air, yet somehow still the most delicious closure to their swim of a good hour or longer in the tireless surf. They'd laid there then, three beneath the sun. Claire was at his left, Lauren at his right. They stared into the crimson backlight of their eyelids as the sunlight wrapped them in its warmth.

When he awoke some indeterminate amount of time later, his wife and child were gone. He didn't even recall having fallen asleep to begin with. Glen sat up and squinted out across the water.

Claire bobbed amid the sun-flashed chop of ocean, too far out it seemed. When she raised a hand to him, hardly visible now among the undulating swells and valleys, rising, falling out of sight again, he raised a hand back in response, hesitant, uncertain.

The wind rushed up against his cheek, crusted by the salt. Lauren shoveled sand inside a nearby hole, having evidently been digging for some time now, her face intent upon completion of the task at hand. Her back was pink. The coat of sunscreen they'd applied was wearing off.

Claire's arm arced and fell, a broken windmill in the

sweeping tide. He got up from the blanket and approached the shore, still uncertain, his hand a visor at his brow against the sun. The wind picked up and drove a sheet of grit against his side. He braced himself against its bite as gulls took flight and screamed into the wind.

And then he saw that she was gone, sucked beneath the swells.

Glen broke for her, sprinting through the rolling foam that blustered toward him, rushed against his legs, snatched his calves and ankles. He leapt across the smaller crossing waves, hurtled past and toward the frothy channel slithering out and past his wife. The larger swells rose up and threw themselves against his legs, rupturing at his thighs, his torso as he plowed his way across the breakers out into the greater depths. He felt the savage pull that towed him outward, pulling his feet across the sand, carrying him beyond the ledge that dropped off down below and snatched his body out across the depths where nothing else remained but open space beneath his kicking legs.

Claire emerged again, her head no more than but a blackened freckle on the ocean's well-gnawed surface, drifting farther from the shore as Glen fought to overtake her, laid out and cutting sideways through the rip, the maneuver largely ineffective as the ocean gulped from underneath, a long and heavy pull that dragged his legs beneath him. The details of her face came into focus as he closed the distance, her eyes and mouth agape amid the swat of brine and froth that beat and sucked at her exhausted body, each counterstrike to every breach of surface twice as powerful as the one that came before. The ocean gulped from underneath, down and out, down and out. Another arm rose high, flopping over like a broken reed, exhaustion and futility upon her plunging face, a tail of bubbles bleeding from her open mouth. Overhead, the gulls converged to scream and tangle on the wind, their fevered cries competing with the battery of waves that overpowered all, reduced her body to the flaccid likeness of a cotton doll.

Glen lunged for her, fell beneath the surface, fought to grip the slickness of her wrist and arm to pull her back to him. She flailed against the current, her lower half ensnared within the unrelenting vacuum of the undertow that rushed beneath them. They breached the surface with a gasp and sputter of their limbs and in that moment, amid the choke and thrash and scream of feathers circling up above, he registered another sound.

The voice of a child. Their daughter, crying, advancing toward them in the ravenous current.

"Mommy…Daddy…Mommy…"

His heart stuttered at the sound and, as he turned to reach for Lauren, he missed her as they drifted farther from the shore in parallel. And as they did, the distance in between them grew.

"Get her," Claire choked. Her voice was wet, barking just above the surface. "Grab Lauren. Save her."

A burgeoning horror seized his heart, his face and, having seen it, Claire removed the choice from his possession, leaving him without an option. She shoved him free, releasing herself again into the current. It sucked her body out and down. Claire pushed her face up through the surface of the water, evicting the command again from deep inside. She shoved it through her desperate mouth into the air.

"Save our baby!"

Glen cut left across the flow, intercepting Lauren. He pulled her into him, choking, crying now at his shoulder. Left with only one free arm, Glen cut crossways to his right in a return to save her mother, his wife, now gone beneath the chopping waves and blackness running down beneath them.

Frantic, he spun left, right, the shore a far-off stretch of tan now, and for a moment the only visible element had become a narrow hedge of sea oats at the highest peak of dunes. And then the dunes had disappeared in full, those last reminders of the shoreline gone, and the ocean rose to touch the sky with nothing in between but hopeless space.

Glen's body numbed, panic gripping senses as he sucked against the clouds for air, catching salted spit of ocean at the backside of his throat, creeping down into his lungs. At his left, Lauren hacked, a liquid wheeze that sputtered, then held fast beneath the onslaught. More water found his lungs and, in the realization that his child had somehow slipped free of his arms, he spun to waves that boxed him in on all sides, rising up to meet him as the sky went black above, tucked beneath the filthy billows pressing low and urgent.

Claire's voice called to him from nowhere in particular, as much beneath him as above him, tackling senses from all angles at once.

Glen, our baby.

Glen gagged, the water spilling past his lips, down his throat, sinking him.

SAVE OUR BABY!

CHAPTER TWENTY-ONE

GLEN AWOKE IN DARKNESS.

He was cold, suddenly unable to breathe.

He was choking, a sensation tethered to the other side of consciousness from which he'd surfaced. His chest and throat were shackled tight, and he vaguely registered a wetness that had saturated legs and torso, in a ridiculous moment of half-witted confusion questioning his bladder before he shot upright, eyes wide, arms pawing at the liquid tendrils reaching down his seizing throat.

Beside him, Lauren's outstretched body jolted on the vinyl tiles. Inside a patch of moonlight coming through the window, her body glimmered as the water snaked its way into her mouth and nose, strands of hair locked in its flow across her face. It formed black threads across her cheeks and forehead, vanishing into the sinkholes on the greedy current.

Someone slapped a distant switch.

In the honest light that filled the room, all horrors were laid bare.

Helen's shrinking carcass folded forward on itself, water spilling from the openings of her face, slack with death. Her mouth, nose, eyes, ears relieved her body of all liquid, a mucal discharge plugging every orifice in its expulsion like some kind of hellish garden sculpture. Her lifeless body quivered under cinching flesh, stirring locks of gray and white atop the wincing scalp, gathered up along the ridges of her crown in rapid desiccation.

"Goddamn, *goddamn!*" shouted Hank. He was on his feet, standing near. He scrambled backward like a crab across the floor, stepping wide with arms out straight and broken at the elbows like two defensive claws. He turned and broke for the safety of the counter's height. Hank launched himself across its edge and slipped, fell back down again. He made another leap, this time catching the counter's other end inside his hands, hauling his body up across its surface. The writhing pool rushed out across the floor below, missing his feet by inches, thinner reaches running out ahead, scouting intersecting lines between the squares of tile like threadbare highways as the proboscises branched and hunted.

Laj stood before the others, stumbling backward from the scene in a reverse embrace of sprawling arms, eyes wide, breaths thin and insufficient as he pressed the others back to safety.

Glen's eyes plunged themselves against the borders of their sockets, vision melting down into a light-specked blur beneath the pressure. His chest bucked wildly as it filled with water, and every instinct of survival raged inside him, begging him to save himself. His body screamed in agony, a million tiny razors shearing muscle from his frame, gutting out his mind as the water penetrated deeper, deeper, harvesting the moisture from his body. His lungs wrenched beneath his sternum, feeling like their seams had come undone beneath the pressure, convulsing as they tried to process what had filled them. He forced his mind to deal with Lauren, placing her above himself despite his failing system.

Glen pulled Lauren from the floor, slipping on the slimy tile. He dropped her as his sight fell out into a tailspin. Voices came to him.

Release.

The water's fingers found his foot, his leg, rushing up the outstretched limb. He fell down to the floor and scooped her up again, raking water from her face, each time backfilled with another plunging course to rush upon her lungs.

Release her. Release yourself.

Vision half consumed by static black, Glen held Lauren to his chest and jerked a steak knife from the counter, shoving outward as he shambled forward. At this, the group moved farther back, falling back against the wall as far as legs could take them.

On the countertop, the water in the jar was wild, frenzied by the chaos of the moment. It leaned against the closest end to Glen and Lauren, seemed drawn to them. It thrust itself against the side, spattering and retreating, spinning in the confines of the vessel like a captive animal.

"Glen…Glen! Don't do it, man. Whatever you're thinking," pleaded Laj, backing Tony and Jesse toward the wall. "Please! Put it down, Glen. Put it down."

Hank cowered at the far end of the counter now, a gargoyle poised for flight along its edge. He shouted a string of warnings at Glen, passing through the filter of his panic as an ill-articulated thread of sounds.

The water crawled up Glen's chest, his face, another arm erupting up his leg to meet his genitalia, his rectum. It pried him open, transitioning inward.

He tried to cry out but his throat held tight, plugged by liquid ropes, the sound ascending through the passage as no more than bubbling fragments as he choked. Lauren purged her bowels in his arms, body rattling in the clash of hot and cold like death throes of an overheated engine.

So easy. So quick. Release her. Release yourself.

Glen stumbled off behind the counter, groping the wall beyond the sparking black that wrapped his vision, throttling out those last remains of light and life. He found his mark, fingers prodding borders of the plastic rectangle, the narrow slots beneath their tips. The water held them fast, a translucent snare that clung to face and leg and torso and trailed off somewhere on the other side of the counter, linking up to Helen's withered shell.

Glen found the fingers of his dying child. He wrapped her hand inside his left.

SAVE OUR BABY!

Glen blinked hard, a desperate gesture as the light of the

world around him went to pinpricks. His mind began to slip, reeling off into the plunging darkness.

He fumbled with the knife, gripping its handle in his palm.

And before his final dose of oxygen had burned away, Glen shoved the blade into the outlet.

CHAPTER
TWENTY-TWO

THE WORLD WAS STILL.

All five senses seemed to bind, folding into one another. The pulsing thumps within Glen's mind appeared as soft amoebas, shapeless throbs of light which spoke a blunted language, deep and foreign on the inside of his ears. He moved, or rather thought he did, a sensory trick, the deftly executed sleight of nerves. Behind the throbs ran one shrill note. It was an extended chime of emergency broadcast tests, a sound that filled his head like feedback from a microphone.

A strange smell rang about his nostrils: burnt hair and ozone.

His torso bucked and slammed his spine against the floor. The action jumped his lungs, and he heaved to purge the water held inside them, bursting from his mouth and spilling down his cheeks. His eyes sprung wide, catching the world in full, his pupils struck by spears of light that lodged themselves inside his optic nerves.

Glen recoiled against the pain that hit him from all angles. He rolled right, vomiting another mouthful of water. He heaved again, and this time it didn't stop. His esophagus unclenched and sent a putrid fountain to the floor. He panted there against the tiles as the world returned itself to order. Segregation of sound and shape returned, sensible again in voice and vision's reassembly, but the scene was more alive, more frantic than he'd realized as the chaos rushed his ears.

Something was wrong.

Something more than his immediate state.

Glen pressed his palm against the ground. He snatched it back at the agonizing touch of open flesh. His hand was raw, charred deep, cauterized and bloodless. He let out a wail and held it to his chest. Tears spilled from his burning eyes, falling out across his cheeks. He raised his head and looked around, thoughts and memories falling into place, a jigsaw-style assembly ushering Glen back to the moment, Lauren's peril like a shot of adrenaline to the enfeebled heart.

Glen kicked up to his knees, dizzy, vision laced with swarms of static flies. He fell onto his side, then rolled onto all fours again, crawling on his hands and knees to find Lauren. She lay sprawled out just several feet away, a veritable lake of pinkish water underneath, Jesse plunging her chest from overhead on rigid arms. He stopped and brought his mouth to Lauren's, lifting lungs beneath the half-zip of a throwback Nirvana hoodie draped across her chest.

"Lauren?" choked Glen, two intersecting lanes of sight disrupting equilibrium. He blinked again. "Lauren!" Glen grappled for her arm, her face, unmoving on the floor. He closed one eye to reign the double vision in, a trick of wasted drivers on a late-night journey home.

Jesse looked to Glen, then back to the girl. He drew his arm across his mouth, wiping clean the frantic rim of spit. "She ain't responding, ain't breathing. Shit, man." He fought to catch his breath and moved to plunge her chest again, rising overhead.

Lauren sputtered, choking.

Jesse jolted back and fell across the floor. He scrambled forward again and turned her on her side. At first the water trickled from her mouth, then ruptured like a broken pipe, bursting across the floor in pulsing intervals as the concoction fled her lungs and stomach. Lauren rolled onto her face against the ground. Another shot of water blitzed the tiles, and she wet herself again, an endless stream that shook her body, kicking her engine back to life again with yet another clash of dueling temperatures.

On the countertop, the water in the jar had settled, turning gently now.

Glen's mind fought to make some sense of what was happening, momentarily crippled by the massive dose of electricity that had taken his and Lauren's consciousness. They'd been spared, though nearly killed, and in the process the threat had been eliminated from their bodies. But he was frightened, still unsure. He frantically looked around the room. A copious amount of blood and water and God only knows whatever else adorned the floor, the seats, themselves. The air was saturated by a noxious blend of human waste and burning flesh.

But the liquid cast around them ceased to move. What puddles stretched themselves across the floor were nothing but.

Helen had transformed into a fetal curl upon her seat. What used to be a normal human body now was virtually mummified in full, fortified with the rigidity of some wooden totem.

Through the mental haze, a terrifying attribution came to Glen.

A Trojan Horse.

Laj hovered overhead and dressed the body in a coat of bleach from head to toe. He soaked the booth, the floor, any surface having crossed paths with the tainted water. What wasn't killed in the electric shock he aimed to wipe out chemically.

Glen reached over, pulling Lauren near, both of them impervious to the all-consuming stench of piss and feces marking them. Her body quaked within his arms, a hydrophobic shock which rooted her to father and floor, unable to move, to speak, sparing hardly a breath to cross her lips.

Glen hushed her, moving his hands across her shoulders, her cheeks, bringing his eyes to hers. "You're going to be okay. You're all right. Talk to me." He used his thumb to clear the detritus of something thick and yellow strung across the bridge of nose and brow. "Dammit, Lauren." He shook her, and the action sent her head into the lolling motion of a junkie trapped inside a dangerous high.

Lauren blinked a couple times, her gleam despondent.

For the second time, he shook her by the shoulders. "Lauren, give me something. I need to hear your voice. Tell me you're okay, hm? Talk to me! Say something!" He was frantic, running hands and fingers over head and face and arms and neck. "C'mon. Talk to me. Talk to me." Glen took the left side of her face inside his palm and worked it like a lump of clay. "Come on. Hey." He patted her cheek. "Hey. Right here. Talk to me!"

Her chin buckled, giving way beneath her bottom lip as the first real tears spilled from her eyes, now shuttered underneath their lids. No words, no sound escaped her open mouth, slack and dangling on its hinge. It was the calm before the storm. The kind of cry that infants give, sending mouths to war before the soldiers of their screams arrive for duty.

Glen regarded her awkwardly, as if somehow caught off guard, unsure of what to feel.

Happy she was responsive?

Fearful she'd been injured?

He'd never been much of an emotional man. His paternal tool kit was perennially half-empty on that account, yet the desire to calm her, return his child to peace, did not elude him. He wanted nothing more, yet all he managed to sputter out was "Honey, we're going to be okay. We're safe." He hoped it was what she needed to hear in that moment. To have her father tell her everything would be okay, as if the sentiment, those very words carried some magical property about them to work on levels only a parent's words could ever work.

His heart was raging in his chest. He wanted her to know he loved her. He wanted all the pain to go away, for her to be all right, to feel protected once again.

Glen felt a presence at his shoulder. He turned by half, finding Tony in his peripheral vision, at his ear.

"Hey," he whispered. He was panting, on the verge of hyperventilation. "Everything all right? She okay?"

Glen didn't speak. He turned back to Lauren. He didn't know. It wasn't a question he could truthfully answer in that moment.

Tony came down on his haunches at their side. He touched the floor to stabilize himself.

Finally, Glen breathed. "I think so." He felt the tears rise up inside, staying put as if the action to release them had been damaged somehow. Glen turned to Lauren. "C'mon, hon. Let's head to the back. Gonna clean up. Here, let's stand up." He pulled her close and lifted her from the floor on troubled legs, feeble under pressure. "Come on, I've got you."

Tony came to his feet beside them. He was shaking, still careful not to touch them. "Come on to the back, get you two washed up."

"I'm dizzy," Lauren croaked. Her voice had seemed to hitch itself down deep inside, dry and damaged like a wheel lodged tight and dragged across the supermarket floor. "My throat burns. Thirsty."

"There's water in the back," said Glen.

"No water," she whimpered. Her breath thinned out and seemed to slip between her words, losing traction in her voice, a viscous energy. "No. No water. No water."

"Or soda, milk. Anything you want. Okay?"

She nodded.

They shuffled through the open door into the back, over to the sinks. Tony followed close behind. Jesse loitered at the door with both hands lifted up behind his head, ceaseless movement of his fingers combing through his hair, the action played on loop and alternating one hand to the next. His face was red, swollen. It appeared that he'd been crying at some point.

Somewhere in the distance, Glen heard Laj call out to Hank for help. And then there was an argument, but he couldn't decipher what about, nor in that very moment did he even care.

CHAPTER
TWENTY-THREE

"ALL RIGHT, LOOK. WE'VE GOT a floor drain right there. Lock the door behind me when I leave. Slide latch right there. Keep folks out of here for a bit. Give you both a little privacy." The stocky man walked off into the pantry. He returned with several gallons of bottled water, placing them at their feet. "Use this. It's safe. They're sealed, never been opened." Tony took a step back, offering Glen a nod of nervous reassurance. Though his hands no longer shook, they roved in and out of pockets with a nervous energy. "This good? You two need anything else? If so, say the word, you got it."

"This'll be fine, Tony," said Glen. "But still, we can't be wasting our only good drinking water. We only have so much."

Tony scoffed. He pawed the air between them, striking Glen's words away. "We have enough. Whole damn rack of it over there. Drinking water's what we do have. Plenty of it. These'll get you started. Meantime, I'll try our luck with bleach and tap water, fill a couple pots, boil it to cook off anything might be in it."

"You sure that's a good idea? We know it was in the lines, likely still is."

"Should be fine," said Tony. "What the bleach doesn't disinfect, the temperature will."

Glen frowned, shaking his head in tandem with the danger playing through his mind, but he didn't care to argue with him. He was too damn tired, still too flustered from what they'd been through, concerned about his own kid.

Tony read him like an open page. "I'll be careful. Worry about yourselves right now. You two get yourselves cleaned up now with what we have here." The man moved to the sink and pulled two large stockpots from an adjacent rack, placing them on the burners, then brought another couple gallons to the counter. "We'll boil your clothes, get them cleaned and sanitized. After that, good as new, all right?"

"Appreciate it, Tony." Glen and Lauren slouched there in the middle of the floor as if two figurines with malformed bases, arms wrapped tight around their bodies. "You happen to have anything we can use to wrap ourselves? Something to cover up with once we're done?"

"Got some more tablecloths. I'll pull a couple for you both. Hand towels too. Small, but something you can use to wash, maybe dry off with."

For several moments after Tony left the room, Glen and Lauren lingered in an awkward silence. Glen crossed to the door and slid the latch in place, then turned to her and gestured to the open space. Lauren wasn't looking at him. Her chin was pressed against her chest, both arms wrapped around her torso. Her body shook. It was cold, sure, but Glen knew that wasn't why.

"So," started Glen, turning in a semicircle with a palm against the backside of his neck, "how you want to do this?"

Lauren made a sound like something poked a hole in her and let the air out in a sudden gush. She shook her head and turned away.

"Okay, well," said Glen. "Look, not many options. We got one drain here in the center. Trust me, not ideal on my end either. If I could take the pantry, take this someplace else, I would."

"It's fine," she said. "Is what it is, right?" Lauren drew the zipper down her front and slipped the hoodie from her shoulders, tossing it aside. "Quicker the better, right?"

"Right," said Glen. "But how—"

Lauren turned a finger in the air. "Turn around. We both will. Just don't turn around. For the love of God, I know I won't."

"Right. Yeah," said Glen, hesitating for a moment, then turning so his back was to her. "Solid enough plan, I guess."

"No turning," she said.

"Not a chance. Let's get this over with."

They tossed their clothes to the floor, forming a grotesque foothill from the soiled garments. From there, they cleaned themselves as thoroughly as they could with their backs to one another. They operated on verbal cues, so as not to violate each other's privacy. He could've left her to herself, then switched out. But, given the circumstances, Glen wasn't about to put Lauren to the task alone, risking another attack or, of equal importance, any unwelcome visitors.

They rinsed themselves in silence for the most part, listening to the slap of falling water as it hit the floor and found the drain. They could hear the others speaking from the front, voices baffled by the wall between, secured by a door of solid steel and single bolt that hitched the jamb inside a reinforcement sleeve. Glen looked around, taking in the fact the space was clearly something of a safe room in its reinforcements, evidently having once been one great walk-in freezer. Perhaps the building used to be a slaughterhouse, and they were standing in what once had been the meat locker, sides of beef lined up on hooks and steaming as they lost their souls against the frozen air. A chill passed through him at the thought, an imagined legacy of horror hosted in this cursed place where they stood. Where they nearly died tonight.

Glen hadn't passed too far beyond the boundaries of the moment before he realized what he'd thought was nothing more than heavy breathing had been Lauren sobbing behind him.

"Lauren?" said Glen, a soft, uncertain prompt.

No answer. Only breathing.

Glen paused, listening to her weep, uncertain what to say for several moments. "Hey, we're going to be all right, honey." Glen passed his words into the open air, his back still angled toward her.

Lauren continued washing, pouring, weeping, the breathy, painful notes embedded in the clap of falling water.

"I know you're scared. Look, I don't blame you. I am too. But we're going to be all right."

Another moment passed before she pulled her nerves together, just enough to speak again. "It got in here, Dad. First through the pipes, then through Helen. It was in her all this time, growing, and we didn't even know it. And then, it moved from her to *us*. It was actually inside of us." She kept her volume low, concealed beneath the water's movement, hidden from the others at the front. "I just—" she started, stopping short to catch her breath, to find her words. "There's no way. It could be anywhere. It could—it could *still* be inside of us." Her voice was shaky, chopped up by the panic cultivated through her racing thoughts, her words. "No way we're going to be okay. You can't even promise something like that and actually mean it. You just can't do that, Dad."

"I—" Glen began.

"Just stop, okay? Stop trying to make everything okay. To pretend like it is. It's okay for everything to not be okay. It's okay to admit that. That's normal, Dad."

Glen didn't speak.

"What's not normal is to keep acting like this is normal. Any of this. Like it's going to be okay. Like there's some kind of explanation for any of this. I didn't skin my knee. You can't just slap a Band-Aid on this and make it better. And not just this. Other things. You *always* do this. Why can't you just be real with me for once? Why can't you just be real with *yourself* for once?"

Glen still stood there with his back to her, feeling like she'd struck him with a brick.

Lauren had stopped pouring the water, standing just behind him with the last remains of liquid dripping from her limbs, her hair. It ticked against the tile below in growing intervals between each drop, the declination of its rhythm like the dying pulse of hope.

"I—I'm not trying to put a Band-Aid on this, Lauren."

Silence.

"I know this seems impossible. It's insane. It is."

Silence.

"But we survived, right? We beat it. And we can do that again if we have to. Whatever it takes to fight our way out of this. Hear me?"

Silence.

"Got it?" Glen's face swung sideways, left her standing just beyond the reach of visibility. "Hey. I need you to understand me. We're going to make it, okay? Trust me? I'm with you, and I'm not going to let anything happen to you."

A congested sniff. "Yeah." She clenched her hair, squeezing another spit of water to the floor. Lauren cleared her throat and swallowed down the last of her emotions in that moment. "Look, I'm done, Dad. Pass the towel?"

"Here," Glen reached an arm behind him, found her outstretched hand and passed the towel to her. "Me too. Wrapping up now. Let me know when you're good."

When all was done, they stuffed the two large pots with their clothes and left them there to boil. When enough time had passed, they pulled them from the water, letting the fabric cool a moment before wringing them out and hanging them to dry across the ladder's rungs.

Shortly after, Tony knocked. He came in with a bucket and a mop and set to sanitizing the entire floor beneath a heavy concentration of bleach and water, flushing all discarded waste into the drain.

"So, listen," started Tony as he capped the bleach and returned it to a low shelf. "Understand if you're not quite comfortable after all this, but we've cleaned up best we can out there." He pushed the mop and bucket up against the wall beside a rack of brooms and dustpans. Tony pulled a rag from his pocket, twisting both hands through its folds, scrubbing the slimy trace of bleach from palms and fingers.

Glen nodded his appreciation. "It is what it is. We'll keep close watch regardless. Don't think I'll be sleeping. Doubt any of us will at this point. Take shifts if we have to."

Glen paused, hesitating just a bit before he asked the question. "What about Helen?"

Tony frowned at Glen, unsure of the question. Lauren moved her eyes from Tony, to her father, back to Tony once again.

"Her body?" Glen leaned against a prep cart. "Can't just leave her there."

"Oh," said Tony with a sudden jolt of understanding, "Laj took care of her already. Whole space was soaked in bleach, her body included. Wrapped her up with some of the big black garbage bags I keep here. He's going to take her to the rooftop soon. Put her over the edge."

Lauren snapped her head upright and looked at Tony, face twisting in revulsion. "Put her over the *edge?*" She blinked. "You mean you're—you're just going to ditch her like a bag of trash or something?"

Tony moved his head in a sort of half shake, lost for words to soften his statement. He scratched at his neck, suddenly uncomfortable.

"Lauren, it's for our safety," said Glen. He reached out and set his hand against the backside of her head. "We don't really have a choice. Can't just leave her in here. Or even up there on the rooftop, for that matter. What happens if she's still infected? If something's left inside her still, gets out, comes back again?"

His words were incomprehensible, and she shook the nonsense from her ears. "What? Dad, I can't believe this. You of *all* people. You say what if she's still infected. Uh, Dad?" Her eyes sprang wide. "What if *we're* still infected? You gonna drop me off the edge of the building too? Just put me out like trash?"

"Lauren, you know that's not the same. Helen's dead. *Very* dead."

"I could be very dead too, Dad. Either one of us could be." She'd backed away from him, from Tony, arms thrust to the floor like two batons, fists like knots of knuckles at their ends.

"Use a little reason here, Lauren," said Glen, his patience dwindling with the entire thing, a creeping anxiety from near-death and sleep deprivation setting up shop within his nervous system. His head was buzzing now, a strange detachment taking over as he grappled with control of random thoughts that started running through his mind. Among those thoughts, the missing medication. The bottle sitting in the truck outside, two pills inside it.

"Dad, reason left town when water tried to kill us in our sleep!" Lauren swept her right arm toward the building's front, then tied it with her left across her chest. She was nearly yelling now. "I don't know if that's sunken in completely for anyone yet."

"What the hell would you recommend, Lauren?" Glen's face went red, blood pounding in his ears. "I think we're all just doing the best we can do right now, given the circumstances!"

The force of Lauren's breath picked up. She clamped her teeth down tight, locking her jaw in place. She stared into the corner of the room.

Glen turned to Tony, filled his chest with air, and held it there as if he were about to set an underwater record. Tony looked a little like a kid caught doing something wrong, waiting for his parents to devise a fitting punishment.

Glen closed his eyes, exhaled, and took another long and leveling breath of air. "Tony," said Glen, "the plan you and Laj came up with is solid. It works. Just fine. Thank you."

Lauren cinched the cloth up tight around her body, whitening the knuckles on her fists. She forced a growl up through her throat and left the room. An indecipherable mash of words spilled inward through the open door before she snapped it shut behind her, knocking them back down to no more than a subtle murmur.

"Hey, look," said Tony. "Ain't trying to upset the young lady, but not too sure how—"

"No," said Glen, lifting a hand. "No. You do whatever you have to do. She'll get over it. She's just being, well, Lauren, that's all." He plugged his eyes and squeezed, an effort to control the raging heartbeat in his head. Glen slouched against the cart. "Damn it." He dragged the open palm of his still-good hand across his features. "Am I the asshole, here? I can't catch a fucking break. Not once. Is it deliberate?"

"She's a good kid, man," said Tony. "She got a good heart. I get it. Can't fault her for that."

"It's all the damn time," said Glen, not bothering to acknowledge Tony's comment. He knew she had a good heart. He didn't need to be told that. She always had, same as Claire. She also had the same brick-hard stubbornness her mother had. And any time that side revealed itself, the weight of loss came crashing down again. That weight was constant lately, every day a different battle, a freshly opened wound for him to suffer. "I think we have enough to deal with already. Can't she give it a rest already? I don't need this shit right now. I don't." Glen held his hand across his mouth. It shook with dead-end anger, racing laps around his body without means of exit. "It's constant. Everything is pushback. Everything's a fight. I'm trying here. Trying my best."

Tony turned and killed the flames beneath the burners. He turned to Glen again and crossed his arms across his belly. "Most adults would've cracked after what she just come through, let alone somewhat her age. How old you say she is again?"

"Fourteen."

"It ain't you, man," said Tony. "Consider the circumstances."

Glen's shook his head, then let it flop both ways like a triple-beam scale. "Shit. Yeah, I know. I know."

"Hold up." Tony walked across the room and pulled a small bag from a drawer. He opened up the zippered tote and handed Glen a tube of first aid ointment and half a roll of gauze. "Here. Take care of them burns."

Glen took the offer in his hands, mumbling thanks. He unscrewed the cap and laid a bead of ointment out across the blackened ruts that crossed his palm and fingers. "Yeah, well." He winced and paused, waiting for the aching throb to level out. "Can't be strong all the time, but damned if she doesn't try. I worry about her. Life's dealt us a shit hand already. Can't imagine her *taking* much more. I know I sure as hell can't." Glen paused and kept his breath as he ran his finger through the viscous tracks of red and black that fought the treatment, sloughing off along the weeping surface of the open wounds. He dropped the tube and started with the roll, binding ribbons round the palm and thumb, between the fingers, wrapping it along the blackened imprint of the steel knife that had baked itself into his flesh. He winced and dealt a rocky breath into the room, swallowing the pain. The heartbeat in his head intensified.

"Look, I don't really know your girl, what y'all done been through already," said Tony. "Really don't know you too well neither, so don't get me wrong or nothing. But I'd be willing to bet she might be stronger than you realize." He took the medical supplies and zipped them back into their pouch, returning them to the drawer. "Let her talk to you. Know you don't have to talk her down from nothing. Don't have to hold all the answers, don't need to blame yourself when shit flies south. It's *this* she craves." He tapped at his ear. "Give her that. Let her know she's heard. Pure magic, the results. You'll see."

"You sound like a pro." Glen slipped a subtle smile between the pain.

Tony shaped his lips into a line, soft and reminiscent. "Yeah, well, I had a family once. A boy." Tony lashed the dampened rag across the edge of the stainless steel prep station, rubbing out dried bits of vegetables clinging to its surface. "Life sends some hairpin turns every once in a while. Handle with care's all I can say. Navigate with caution."

"Your son. What happened, if you don't mind?"

"He, uh…" Tony pawed at the nape of his neck. "Got tired of living. About ten years back."

Glen dropped his head regretfully. "I'm sorry."

Tony stirred the air with his right hand, a dismissive gesture. "Well, you get real good at lying to yourself after a while, Glen. Tell yourself all manner of nonsense. Sometimes blaming yourself. I know I did. Other times you'll make excuses, try to somehow justify the situation. Maybe distance yourself, find outlets for escape instead of facing problems head-on." He looked up at Glen, attempting a smile, then set to scrubbing at the dehydrated veggies again. At least where they used to be. He was doing no more than rubbing a square of naked steel now, hadn't seemed to notice.

"Nothing for you to feel guilty about, I'm sure," said Glen. "You did the best you could."

"Well…" Tony chuckled underneath his breath, holding the dirty square of cloth up high before he flipped it over. "Let's say some lessons are learnt the hard way. I wasn't always the wise old sage you see before you today." He stretched his arms out wide, reminding Glen of Christ the Redeemer looming high over Rio de Janeiro, on the bucket list collage he'd once made with Claire, still unfulfilled. A pang of longing and regret shot through his heart. Glen turned his eyes away. He shook his head and moved to speak but was cut off at the pass by Tony.

"No, no," the man scoffed, swatting the air. "I can see that damn apology coming a mile away. Keep it to yourself. Don't need it. Never did. You ain't done nothin' wrong, and I don't mind talking about it."

Glen closed his mouth.

"Look, this here is important, actually. Something I can pass along." He dropped the rag onto the table in a dirty lump. "Power of the ear, my friend. Strength in listening, understanding. Don't underestimate the power of the simplest things." Tony propped his hip against the table's edge. "He'd come to me. Just before it happened. He was upset about something. I was of course too busy to listen. Too damn busy working the diner, keeping it afloat, giving it *all* my time. Every ounce." He dabbed an itch at the corner of his nose, sneaking his finger into the corner of a watering eye. "You know, I honestly couldn't even tell you what he was so upset about now." He shook his head, lips soured. "Lived with a lot of regrets for a long time afterward, man. How I could've maybe done things different. I questioned everything. Every second spent, revisited, analyzed for flaws."

He took a moment to himself, listening to the muffled talk beyond the door and wall.

"Can I tell you how many nights I've dreamed about that moment? Dreams where I strain to remember what it was he was trying to tell me. What it was that I was too damn preoccupied to hear. In my dream, his words just disintegrate, never form. They were never really there. Not for me, at least."

"I'm sorry, Tony. I really am." It was all Glen could say. In his heart, he knew anything more would come off insincere, artificial.

"Like I said, ain't no apology required," said Tony. "Point is," he continued, "them kind of thoughts are a certain kind of cancer. The worst kind, eating you slow and easy until there's nothing left. You do the best you can, best you know how. Ain't nobody perfect, nobody getting it all right in this world, all the time. And the drive through life is gonna be damned hard if you always looking in the rearview."

The two men paused in thought. The noise beyond the wall had largely died off now. After a moment, the door swung open, and Laj edged through the opening with the body draped across his shoulder. The plastic crinkled, a thoughtless, utilitarian sound.

The door swung closed, and through the crack beneath it, Glen saw the dining room go dark, lights extinguished.

Glen stepped aside to let Laj pass. They exchanged a solemn

look, but said nothing. Laj continued toward the rear and made his way up the ladder. Glen took several steps toward the door, turning back to Tony. "Come morning, we all need to talk about how we're going to get out of this. We can't camp out forever. Going to have to make some hard decisions."

Tony grunted, throwing Glen a parting nod. He raised a hand. "Feeling it or not, you try and get some rest."

Glen drew the cloth up tight around his torso, reinforcing its wrap. Back up front, all was quiet, dark, nothing more than the occasional breath or stir existing now beneath the stygian haze. Bleach marked the air, a scent that pressed itself against his sinuses like the burning tips of matchsticks. Even still, a comforting odor.

A safe odor.

Glen worked himself into the booth where Lauren nested, tucked neatly up against the cushioned corner. He couldn't see her face, couldn't tell if she was still awake but couldn't imagine otherwise. He pushed his legs out straight beneath the table, heels wedged against the facing edge of seat across the booth.

Lauren's notebook lay open on the tabletop. In the fragile light, Glen could barely spy the outlines of her latest sketch. A building. Just the outline of it and the area surrounding. Above the entry on one side, a word:

EMERGENCY

A hospital. Familiar. Glen struggled to place it. By God, of course. The day her mother drowned. Where they'd taken him, taken her. Did Lauren remember this so vividly? Glen could barely conjure up the shape of the facility. He turned the page.

Another sketch. A room. A hospital suite. Standard fare. A bed, monitors, other basics. Also, there were racks. Several of them, housing what looked like computer equipment. Servers. There were people. Three of them, including the patient in the bed. Again, familiar. By God, the detail of her recollections. Had he suppressed these? Had he even been awake for this, or was he still unconscious, being treated at that time?

Glen's head throbbed.

Next page.

Himself, Claire, Lauren, together by the shoreline. Not *that* day. Another day. A good day. They'd traveled to Henderson Beach, North Carolina, to look for fossils. They'd woken up at 4:00 a.m. to catch low tide, starting out with flashlights till the day had broken just enough to see the shoreline unassisted. That day had yielded thirty-two fossilized sea biscuits, sixteen small shark teeth, and a fractured megalodon tooth that Claire had spotted sticking through the sand, only recently unraked by the waves. She'd reburied it for Lauren to excitedly discover on her own. Glen's eyes watered at the memory.

He closed the notebook and returned it to the table.

Beside him, Lauren shifted at the window. One deep breath, inhaled and released.

Glen thought about the water, the contaminant. It could be anywhere, inside anyone. They needed a plan. They'd been breached, and this space was no longer safe. And by now, it was clear nobody else was coming.

Up on the countertop, the water in the jar had calmed completely. As if it, no longer drawn to anything of interest around it, had simply settled down to rest. Glen watched the jar, two pieces of logic suddenly connecting in his head as he considered this.

It had *known* that Helen was infected.

It had *sensed* it, reacted to it.

It had leaned into the woman's presence back when she was merely ill. It had gone into a frenzy when she'd purged, when he and Lauren had been attacked. It had known. If they'd have somehow put these elements together sooner, they'd all have known, as well. Its reaction could have warned them all. Going forward, it could *still* be used to warn them.

Amid the weight of breath-studded silence, a glassy turn of another kind of liquid called from the other end of the dining room. In the shadows, paranoia flourished and Hank's gaze held Glen in its unforgiving embrace as he brought the bottle to his lips.

CHAPTER
TWENTY-FOUR

LAUREN HAD BEEN LYING AWAKE, staring at the ceiling, when the floodlight on the signpost at the corner of the lot had started throwing fits. For hours, she had alternated from her side onto her back. Her eyes had been swimming laps around the ceiling tiles, their dividing lines, old water stains that, as clouds can do, had begun to take on strange, albeit familiar shapes. Every fiber in her body ached. Her abs and chest and lungs were radiating knives and needles, a sensation that only worsened with the passing hours. The headache had been there from the moment of the attack, severe from the onset and never getting worse, never getting better. It felt like a maul had split the left and right hemispheres of her brain. It no doubt was reeling from dehydration.

The irony.

Outside, the floodlight flickered, snapping on and off. A rhythm settled in: two short, one long, two short, one long.

Rags of fog slowly moved across the lot. Lauren let it take her vision with it as she stared, having turned away now from the ceiling. The fog staggered left to right across the dark water, its movement diced up by the strobe-like sputter of the failing light.

Glen, stretched opposite of where she lay, had at some point fallen asleep. Despite all that had happened, his body still allowed it. He stiffened, shoving his feet against the section of the bench's cushion next to her. She knew he must be so exhausted. That his body must've desperately needed rest. Still, she felt resentment forming like a waxy residue inside her head. Senseless as she knew it was, it almost felt as if he was indulging in some limited reserve of sleep they both should be withheld from at this moment. Some luxury they both should ration.

Somewhere in the night, a loon shrieked. She looked up from the gray-white drifts and searched the blackened walls of forest rising up around them. But when they came back to the spurling sheets of fog, something else was there, standing in the water near the forest's edge. A form that Lauren was certain hadn't been there before. The spotlight flickered, keeping with its steady rhythm: two short, one long. The form, clearly now a human figure, moved toward the diner, crossing through the water. Lauren didn't trust her eyes. She wondered if sleep had finally slipped in through the back door undetected, letting in a nightmare with it.

Lauren stopped breathing; she was too petrified to even realize she had, squinting out into the night. Her left hand rested on her father's shin. Like a trap, her fingers closed around the muscle of his outstretched calf. She stared into the broken darkness, unable to speak, unable to parse reality from dream.

A person. A *woman*. Outside. In the water. But how?

The signpost's strobe lit up the woman's figure in a series of successive bursts, capturing the long, slow strides of her legs with the trademark jagged movement of a flipbook animation. She was soaked. Tendrils of her hair crisscrossed her face. Behind it, her eyes were almost shell-shocked, wide and frightful.

No. Not frightful. Closer yet, Lauren could more plainly see the woman's features. Her eyes. They were, more accurately, excitedly unhinged.

Lauren's grip intensified, driving nails into Glen's leg. Her breathing quickened. Glen opened his eyes, not yet seeing, not yet awake. Lauren didn't notice. She was staring at the woman, who now also seemed to have spotted her. The woman raised one desperate hand and shook it in the air.

"Lauren?" Glen pushed his body higher in the seat. His daughter didn't answer, and her fingers held his leg, nails hooked into the flesh like talons.

"Dad." It was all that she could manage.

The woman waded toward the diner through the splits of broken lumber that had gathered on the surface of the water. It scattered, colliding with a portion of the fallen rooftop with a muffled drumroll. The section floated just beyond the cars that still were angled parallel to the front of the diner, half drowned where they rested in the water's depths. The spotlight flashed.

Two short, one long.

Glen grimaced, more awake, more aware now with the pain that radiated from the set of nails embedded in his calf. "What's wrong? What—Jesus, my leg. Lauren, hey…that hurts." He tried to pull free of her grip and at the same time worked to spot what Lauren was staring at. "What's going on?"

"A lady. There's a lady out there."

"What?" Glen winced and yanked his leg free. "Lauren, are you asleep?" Glen sat up. He rubbed his palm across his still-adjusting eyes. "What's going on with the light?"

The woman stumbled through the island of debris and placed her weight upon the floating section of the porch's roof. She hoisted her body from the water's depths and began to crawl across the platform. It dipped beneath her weight, sinking several inches down into the water as she stood, securing her footing. The spotlight snapped its rhythm in the darkness, capturing the precarious teeter of her figure as she raised a pleading arm to Lauren once again. Black leaves clung to one side of her torso. The left side of her blouse was torn away, no doubt snared by branches on her journey through the forest. Fresh wounds marked her arms and cheek, threading red across pale skin where blood converged with water.

"Oh my God." Glen was awake now. He bolted upright in his seat.

Lauren looked at him, wildness in her eyes. "Dad?"

"Please!" the woman shouted. Her voice was blunted by the glass, yet still sharp among the nothingness of night around them. "I need help. Let me in, please!" The floating rooftop pitched and she spilled forward, bracing on both hands. She was sobbing uncontrollably. They could see this through the curtained fringe of hair that fell around her face.

Lauren had pulled away as if this woman were some kind of creature, sitting tightly at the farthest end of her seat now. The rest of their space had started coming into focus through the tunnel vision of her irrational fear (*was it so irrational, though?*), and she realized Jesse and Hank were standing in the aisle. Hank glared through the window with a blank and almost dubious expression. It was the expression of a man engaged in silent, desperate combat with the story that his eyes were telling him.

"You've got to be fucking kiddin' me," Hank whispered. Terror burrowed in his core, deep and sour. It wasn't one that stemmed from fear of this stranger. This woman seeking help. It was something else entirely. It was the fact that she was still alive amid the threat he knew was waiting out there. It was due to the fact this made no sense at all.

"Impossible," said Jesse. "It's impossible. Where'd she come from?" He eyed the stranger through the glass. "How the hell is she out there, man? How?"

Wide-eyed, silent, Tony shuffled down the aisle behind the booths, stalking this impossibility from one window to the next, looking for the source of this seeming illusion.

"From the trees, the forest up there" mumbled Tony. "She— she must've—hell, she had to've come down from somewhere up around Sawyer's Mill. One of them homes up there. The new ones. Them cookie-cutters all crammed in up there. Never seen her before."

"That's a good mile or so uphill," said Jesse. "I mean, at *least*. It's all the way up top near the cut-through for the power lines. That's impossible."

"Maybe that's where all that water dumped from yesterday." Tony looked from face to face. "Maybe it already made its way through there, could've missed her." He turned to face the woman through the glass again. "But how?" He laid a hand against his head. "She's—she's *in* it. Chrissake—she might as well be swimming out there for all the opportunity it's had to take her."

They all were frozen stupid with a million logic bombs exploding in their minds, momentarily locked out of the realization that this was a person needing help, just like them, trapped out there in the open. Trapped out there with the water as they sat there contemplating the how's and why's of her existence, here and now.

The stranger had moved closer to the windows, crawling toward them across the shingled platform. "Please!" she wailed, her choked-off voice now transitioning to a shout. Even from inside the diner, they could hear it ricochet across the far-flung regiment of trees. "God, let me in!"

"Dad! Oh my God. We have to help her. Before it gets her. Dad, we—"

Glen shushed her.

In the distance, the water shivered.

The woman made her way closer, climbing now onto the near-submerged trunk of a Toyota Camry that had wedged itself against the window. She laid her hands against the glass, clapping it beneath both palms. "Let me in!"

"Jesus Christ," choked Tony. His eyes were on the hairline fracture that extended from the window's corner. "Don't," he hissed.

"Just hold on!" shouted Glen, holding up a hand to suppress her panic. "Don't do that! Just hold on a second."

Close behind the woman, Glen watched the mass that stealthily had gathered. It simply waited, resting where it was. It seemed to ripple with anticipation, and Glen was unsure if it somehow hadn't come to knowledge of her presence.

"Dad? Dad, come on!" Lauren was staring at him. "We can't *not* help her!"

Glen paused. He stared at the woman. As if he needed just a moment to consider. As if actually entertaining the idea of exposure to *it* again, just to save her. Of finding some way to see it through at any cost. The very notion of it was insane. Slowly, the source of this bizarre compulsion dawned on Glen. One that went beyond the basic, human instinct most would have to help another in a time of peril. There was something... *familiar* somehow. Maybe something in the facial structure. The mouth, eyes, ears. He...saw *Claire* in her. Not that she bore much resemblance to her in any real manner. But the more he thought it through, the more actual it became. Hell, the woman's blouse even had begun to take on some small measure of familiarity, and the more he scraped the years of memories for that validation of this petty, insubstantial detail, the more he'd almost become *certain* Claire had worn one almost exactly like it. No, not almost. *Exactly* like it. He was sure of this. The smell of his ex-wife had even manifested in his sinuses, all the more connecting him to the insanity of this desperate urge to save the stranger. The resemblance, real or imagined, pulled him like a gravitational force. Begged his feet to move, his hands to busy themselves. His mind to work out some solution to the matter.

Despite it all, the situation was all wrong.

His temples pounded. First signs of a migraine whispered sharply in the darkness.

"We can't, Lauren," said Glen, shaking off the spell.

Lauren looked at him. A puff of air escaped her lips. "She's not like Helen. It's not too late. We can—"

"It's a decoy." He swallowed down the bitter hatred for himself. He knew they had no choice though. Pressure mounted just behind his eyes. A lump moved down his throat and lodged itself beneath his sternum. "It's using her."

Glen spoke softly. He didn't want to raise alarm with the woman on the other side of the glass. If he panicked her, she could and would break it in, no problem. She stabilized herself on the floating dock, glancing left and right, checking her surroundings. It rocked, setting out a wave that moved across the lot. At her immediate rear, the living water shivered, waiting. The woman was oblivious to the fact.

"What do you mean, a decoy? *Using* her? How could it—the water—it—it would have to be—"

"Intelligent," finished Glen. He was staring into the woman's widening eyes now, clearly having heard what Lauren said. Whether she had actually understood, he couldn't know.

She frowned, wiping free the threads of hair that striped

her face. She shook her head, then rapped on the glass with the knuckles of her right hand. "Open up." Her voice came firmer now. Authoritatively. She looked to the front doors, still barricaded by the cars. "You have to let me in. There has to be a way in. Please!"

Lauren started sobbing. Heaving gulps of air that at first came dry until the tears were mined from deep inside, wherever any moisture might've still existed, then began to pour across her face. "Don't do this, Dad. We have to. We have—"

The woman knocked again, this time harder.

Hank and Jesse came forward a step, as if they wanted to restrain her, grab her wrists, protect the sanctity of their enclosure had she not been on the other side, out of reach.

She formed a small fist, then started thumping dully at the glass.

"No," said Tony. "Don't do that. Don't."

Glen made another calming gesture to the woman, this time without effect. He turned, whispering to the others just beyond the woman's visibility of his lips.

"This…sounds batshit. I know," he said, sliding the backside of his hand across his mouth. "But I think it's baiting us. She should be dead by now. Should've never even made it three steps from the edge of those woods out there."

Behind her, the water had begun to shift, moving softly now across the platform, licking at the edges of the Camry's trunk, pacing clearly several inches from her folded legs.

It waited.

"Look at it," hissed Glen. "At her feet. You can see it. Just waiting."

The others followed his direction.

"Waiting," repeated Hank, the realization of Glen's observation hitting him. All the while, he'd assumed the worst, at least as he perceived it at the time, that she was probably infected, same as Helen. That she likely made it past the larger body of the ancient germ somehow without it taking her at once, but had still become infected through exposure. Letting her in was not an option. No. He'd die first seeing to it. But that it might be using her, that it *knew* she was out there and had intentionally spared her for the moment, this struck him like a rock. This was not something he'd anticipated. Not even close. Chills dropped through his body at the gravity of the notion.

Glen nodded.

"Please." The woman was now choking on her tears. "There's nowhere else. Please."

Tony gestured toward the front doors, blocked by the cars, weather sealed against the water. He shook his head, signaling the futility of her demands. Even if they *wanted* to, they simply couldn't. She had to understand that. She had to see the truth of the matter. There was no way.

She slapped the glass again. Hard.

The others winced, biting down against a silent prayer.

It felt as if they were being watched, observed to study their reaction to this cruel inevitability. That they'd been cast into some hateful social experiment, pitting every natural instinct of their preservation over that which urged them toward an act of selfless mercy. Glen felt sick.

The woman let her arms fall to her side, then looked

confusedly across the scattered vehicles, as if considering whether one of them might offer some safe harbor from the water. It only took a fraction of a moment to realize it was a foolish, childlike hope.

She slumped, resulting in a hollow, thunking sound against the Camry's steel. The water knew. Through whatever prehistoric sense it used to read its prey, it registered its loss of opportunity. The ruse was up. It moved on her. Before the woman could release a scream, she was gone, ripped beyond their line of sight into the black tide opposite the floating fence line of debris.

Then, a gunshot.

Everybody jolted, thrown from one point of horrific confusion to another. That was when they realized Laj had disappeared.

Another gunshot.

The spotlights blinked: two short, one long. All was quiet, save the lingering broadcast of the gunshot dancing off into the night between the mountain walls.

CHAPTER
TWENTY-FIVE

Laj was standing at the edge of the roof when the others found him. The handgun dangled from his right hand, and his gaze was lost along the broad expanse of misty water covering the parking lot and roadway. The stutter of the signpost lights lit up the parking lot like flashbulbs at a crime scene.

"Did that lady a solid, this one," said Hank in a deadpan tone, looking over the edge. "I respect that." Floating in the water, the woman's partially headed body drifted through the mist beneath the lamplight. Tony and Jesse stood beside him, staring. Lauren's vision was obscured by the wall the three men formed. For that, she was grateful.

"Laj?" said Glen. He crunched one step closer on the graveled roof. "You okay?"

Laj didn't answer right away. For a moment, he just stood there. Far away, another loon's cry pealed out of the blackness.

"When I first went overseas, my mind was clean," said Laj.

"As a young man, I was brand-new in that stupid, carefree sort of way. A good way."

The others didn't speak. All around, the night was heavy.

"When I came back, that part of me had been stripped down, broken in. My mind, it was stained by then, all scribbled up. Seen a lot of shit. Things no human should ever see. Kind of shit that never leaves you. It changes you, because once you see it, then you know. You know what evil's out there in the world. How deep the darkness really goes. I learned firsthand in that deployment that the devil come in many forms. Of all them forms, I ain't never seen one like this."

Glen wanted to say something, but he wasn't sure what. Empty statements had no business here. They were well beyond those.

"Reason why I never had a wife, never had no kids. A family. Seeing what I seen, I couldn't justify bringing a family up in a world that dark. A world that evil. Not once I knew." Laj shifted on his feet. His breathing moved in pointed bursts, too small, too fast, like the panting of a tiny dog.

Glen noticed Laj was still holding the gun. His hand was throttling the revolver to the point of tremors.

"Times I wondered if I'd messed up. That I'd maybe made the wrong choice. Maybe, you know, things would've actually been okay. Maybe things weren't as bad, as dark as I'd imagined them." He shook his head. Against the flicker of the spotlight, the others watched its slow and thoughtful wag, back and forth. "But, I'd been right." He laughed softly to himself, a downy breath of validation. "This right here, this tells me I'd been right the whole damn time. Ain't nothing to regret, after all."

"Laj," said Glen, "why don't you go on and put that away."

Laj turned and looked at Glen confusedly, almost like he'd forgotten where he was, what he was holding. He seemed to hesitate, then reached back and slipped the gun beneath his waistline.

The spotlight flashed: two short, one long.

Again, from the darkness, the loon screamed.

CHAPTER
TWENTY-SIX

"WE CAN'T STAY HERE." GLEN wrapped the mug of coffee in his palms. It steamed white, a tattered flag that thrashed against the morning air. From the rooftop ledge, he studied the water. It seemed to celebrate the touch of day, shaking off the night and reaching out in formless sprawls of roving death that flared against the light. Remnants of gasoline still loitered where it trickled from the broken pump, Technicolor patches slipping in and out of the debris. The bodies were no longer present, swept away before the dawn had come.

Tony stared into the water. His eyes, same as the others, were bruised and sleepless. "So it's been said. Question is, do we really have a choice?"

"Always a choice," answered Glen. "Always." He paused and moved his eyes around the water, deep in thought. "Decisions of necessity, not necessarily matters of desire but outright need." He turned to Tony. "And we *need* to move, *have* to move.

Nobody's coming for us, Tony. Last night was just a preview of what's to come if we stay camped out here much longer. It got in. Through Helen, like a Trojan Horse, it got to us. And when it failed, it tried to lure us outside, using another survivor like bait. Just look out there. Look at it."

They turned their eyes back to the lot, searching the vast expanse of water like two castaways marooned. A segment of the liquid plane was sliding right to left, its borders hardly there in ways which knit into the substrate of surrounding water, trailing from all edges as it moved. Glen sensed they were in the presence of a creature that had been here since Earth's dawn. Incalculably ancient, locked away inside the ice before it had an opportunity to claim the world.

"We're being hunted," said Glen. "Stalked." He pointed toward the roving flat of liquid. "Ask me, it's getting smarter. Evolving. I've been sitting up here, just watching them for hours."

"Them?" asked Tony.

"Like I mentioned before, it's not just water. Can't be. Water doesn't move on its own. There's something in it, shaping it, controlling it." Glen paused and held a knuckle to his cheek, pressing it against his molars, gnawing at its inside as an exercise of thought. "Like we talked about before, I think this is some kind of colonial microorganism."

"Look, I'll be honest with you," said Tony. "You gonna have to break it down a little more than that, throw a little English my way."

"By colonial, I mean the microorganisms colonize. They

cluster, moving by water as a single mass, a single entity. The water itself is basically used like a body, used for transport. Maybe more, maybe even nourishment. No telling."

Across the rooftop, the static whistle of the CB could be heard as Lauren sat and worked the dials and switches. Two small windows glowed a sallow orange on the unit's face, illuminating needled gauges that lay dead. Though Tony had abandoned the device a long time prior, Lauren had picked up where he'd left off, toying with it throughout the remainder of the night. She couldn't sleep. Neither could Glen. He had helped her take it to the rooftop out of earshot of the others as they got some rest, or at least did their best to. Having teetered on a fragile, lucid edge of sleep, Jesse joined them shortly after, moving to escape the waking nightmares playing at the backside of his eyelids. Still below, somehow, Laj and Hank slept on. Laj had clearly slept through plenty other horrors in his days. He was no stranger to the wicked. Hank had simply drunk himself unconscious. Twice he'd woken up in tears, immediately passing out again.

Not having picked up any hint of signal since the radio had been unearthed, they didn't know if the '70s-era behemoth was even functioning as it should, or if there was simply nothing out there in the endless ether for it to latch on to. Lauren sat before it on the gravel, scrolling up and down the frequencies, not out of hope so much as something to preoccupy her spastic mind, her hands.

Tony simply sat and stared into the haze beyond the rooftop ledge. "So, what you're telling me is this is basically a no-shit, literal body of water."

"Mhm." Glen took a sip of coffee. "Body of water."

"Be damned," mumbled Tony. He worked his grip against the mug of coffee. "Ain't that some shit."

"There's something else," said Glen.

Tony's brow went up as he drew a sip of coffee.

"Noticed it last night, first with Helen when she was sick, then with me and Lauren."

"Noticed what?"

"The water," said Glen. "In the jar. It knew."

"What're you talking about, *it knew?*"

"Something extrasensory. Has to be," said Glen. "It reacted to its own. In Helen, in us. It…*excited* it. It really came to life inside that jar, tried to reach out, connect with its own."

"You sure?"

"Positive," said Glen. "And that's something I think we might be able to use. Something we can use to pick up on infection in our group."

"Can we trust that?" asked Tony. "I mean do we know for sure that's what stirred it up? Last thing we want to do is stoke the paranoia, falsely speculating on who is and isn't infected. Folks are already coming undone as it is, some more than others, if you know what I'm saying. They don't need no encouragement."

"I agree, and it's why I've debated whether or not to say anything about it."

The two fell silent, considering their dilemma.

The CB shrieked, and Lauren spoke into the handheld mic. "Hello?"

The airwave razzed and squealed, wildly swinging high and low. Jesse reached across and slapped its wood-grained top. It went to static once again. She dropped the mic into her lap and turned the knob. Jesse leaned back on the rooftop's ledge and dumped a breath.

Glen and Tony watched the shape glide across the lot, tossing light across its rippling surface. "She ain't gonna pick up nothing," said Tony. "Far's I know, it never worked at all to begin with. Noisy-ass paperweight. That's about it."

"Let her try," said Glen. "Least it's something more than sitting around, doing nothing. Screwing with that thing is probably about the only thing keeping her mind glued together at this point. Cell phone's dead from signal hunting this whole time. Just let her do her thing."

Tony shrugged.

The CB chittered, winding back into another squeal. "Hello?" said Lauren. "Someone, hello? Anyone out there? We're at the Ocean Diner. We're trapped. Hello?"

"Anyway, maybe something we can sleep on, but I'm leaning toward cluing the others in on this. We don't exactly have time on our side right now, and Lord knows we can use any intel or tools we can get our hands on. Could be a pretty major asset, the way I see it."

Tony nodded, considering Glen's point. "You concerned at all about having it in here with us?"

"It's contained," said Glen. "And I feel like we've had bigger concerns at this point. It doesn't set too well with me, no, but if we can use it, if it can help us strategize, stay aware, then I'm all for it."

"If you're confident about this," said Tony, "let's go for it. Let the others in on what you've found."

Glen dipped his head in agreement. They sat another moment listening to the squabble of the CB radio before he spoke again.

"Anyway, these microorganisms, if that's what they are, I think they break off, replicate, form new clusters, repeat," continued Glen. He pointed to another area of the lot where the water roiled at the edges of the gas pumps, jutting from the liquid like a grove of trees, metal trunks, rubber limbs. "Each one's intelligent. We know that much for sure. We've seen it search for us, crawling the glass, hunting for us, gaining access. And last night, seeing what it did—with Helen, me and Lauren, the stranger at the window. How it tried to bait us. It's damned smart."

The CB let out a flanging drone that cinched into a high-pitched hiss, needle-thin.

"Each mass essentially functions as would any other multi-cellular organism." Glen turned to Tony. "Like you or me. Any other creature. They think. Even if on a primitive level, they strategize."

"How many we talking?" asked Tony.

Glen shrugged. "No idea. I'd be guessing. Maybe a few, maybe a dozen or more. Longer we stay here, the more they replicate, spawn new clusters. And the more that happens, the more water they're going to harvest, tow this way, raise the levels on the diner, flood us out."

"Jesus."

"Exactly," Glen said. "So, now that you and I are playing from the same sheet of music, you can see the not-so-long-term issue here."

Tony set his coffee down and turned on the cinder block ledge. He pressed his face into his open palms and breathed, an effort to scrub away the angst that crawled across his nerves.

"How the hell are we supposed to manage getting out of here though, Glen? We're blocked in."

"Going to have to wade through it."

"Come again?" Tony shook his head and waited for the punch line.

"It's the only way."

"Yeah?" said Tony. "And where we gonna go? Ain't a damn thing out there."

Glen shook his head. "Don't know. Anywhere but here."

"Nah. Sorry. That ain't a way, Glen." Tony's words came up an octave, fast and shrill, and his torso took a rigid form that stuck out like a hitcher's thumb from where he sat. "Tell me how exactly that's supposed to happen. You saw what it did. You know firsthand what it's capable of."

The CB hummed and fell into a line of static. Jesse smacked its top again, driving it to silence. "Come on. You trying to kill it?" came Lauren's voice. She brushed Jesse's arm away and set to spinning dials again. The unit sputtered.

"Yeah, and I've been thinking about that," said Glen. "We also know its weakness now. Last night gave me an idea." He prodded the bandage at his palm and tried to make a fist, wincing as the scabs broke free, the swollen flesh packed tight and fighting action.

Tony frowned into his coffee, watching the oily shapes divide and touch the edges, variegated through their centers. He grunted, waiting for the rest.

"The electricity. The shock," said Glen.

Tony turned to face him. "You damn lucky you and your kid ain't dead," he said. He glanced at Lauren, back to Glen again. "Risky as hell. Can't blame you in the least for what you done. Smart as hell there in the moment, but if people came equipped with nine lives, y'all done cooked off seven or eight with that shit. You can't afford to chance another go like that."

The CB fizzed, then wound into another manic squeal.

"No," said Glen. He shook his head, "My point is that it killed it. The electricity. It stopped it. Whatever the hell it is, it wiped it out. The whole connected mass of it."

"Yeah?" Tony arched his brow. "And like I just said, almost killed you too. Both of you."

"But we don't need all that voltage," argued Glen. "Something just enough to kill it. Or even at a minimum, maybe just disrupt it, force it back."

"What exactly you got in mind?"

"Car battery," said Glen, now turned and leaning on his knees toward Tony. "Rig some jumpers to it, keep it on us when we move. Should pack enough of a punch to get us out of trouble on our way out, God forbid we have to actually use it." He held his palms against the mug, feeling the heat pass through the bandage, soothing the open wound beneath. "Would hurt like hell, sure, but wouldn't be enough to kill us."

Tony's body seemed to let out some degree of slack, and he

looked across the lot where daylight pooled and flickered on the water's surface. "You have been thinking, huh?" He raked his cheek, eyes calmer now in contemplation.

"That I have," said Glen. He took another sip of coffee, cooling fast beneath the morning cold. The caffeine hardly touched the fog that filled his mind. Last night clung to every fiber like a sticky resin.

"Might have a set of jumpers in the supply closet inside, but I'll tell you right now we ain't got no battery." He looked down at the line of cars below, at least what ones remained, their noses nearly touching brick the way they all filed in like suckling pigs. "And I got a ladder we could use to make our way down to the cars, but can't say I know how we'd manage to pop the hood and lift one from an engine. Even if we ran the ladder straight down to the bumper, might be enough room to pop that hood but that don't do nothin' for the problem we'll have getting to the release hatch inside the cabin. Water's now up past the bottom of the doors, so you know it done made its way inside already."

They fell into a pool of silence, save the squabble of the CB in the distance. They mulled the issue over for a moment as they sipped their coffee.

The radio barked and launched into a droning sound like angry hornets. And then, a voice, barely audible above the static hiss.

"...42. Do you read? Come in."

Jesse grabbed the mic, lifting it with Lauren's hand still attached.

"Yeah, hello?" said Jesse. "You there?"

"We're here. Do you copy?"

"We copy!" yelled Lauren. "We copy!"

"This is Center 42. What's your location?"

The voice was fading in and out of static, nearly washed out by the noise entirely.

Glen reached down and took the mic from Lauren.

"We're at a place called Ocean. Ocean Diner. We're trapped. The water, it's everywhere. We need help."

The static roared, surging up and down, suffocating any speech attempted on the other end.

"Do you copy? Send help. Ocean Diner."

Static.

"Tell me your location," said Glen.

"...42. Can't...water."

Glen frowned and reached out to strike the unit, stopping short. The signal cleared, and words poured through again.

"...you leave? We can't come to you, but...safe here, for now. Not sure how much longer. We have care...doctor...shelter. If...make...in time...can help you."

"We're trying. Where are you?"

Static.

"Where are you? How do we find you?"

"Follow the noise," came the voice, barely audible. Static rushed against the words.

"Hello? Hey. Are you there?"

"...the noise..."

There was a snap, followed by a puff of gray that rose into the air. Everything went silent.

Glen dropped the mic, and they all stood speechless for a moment.

"There are others out there," said Jesse.

"But where?" said Glen, staring off into the hills. "We have no idea where they are."

Lauren looked up at her father. "The noise. She said to follow it."

Glen frowned, somehow equally and irrationally preoccupied with the familiarity of the voice on the other end of the speaker. He knew that voice. Or, it *seemed* he knew that voice. Behind his temples, the river in his head began to pick up speed, the dogged ache returning to its post.

At that moment, the sky broke open yet again, and a splintered crack rolled out across the woodlands like a fleet of sonic shrapnel. And then another, and another, hard like splits of oak.

"The noise. Only noise we've heard," said Lauren. "All we have to do is follow it. Follow it and find the others. She said it's safe there."

"For now," said Glen, working both sides of his head between his fingers. "Meaning we might not have much time if we want to join them. Otherwise, they might be gone before we get there."

Lauren watched him carefully, visibly concerned. Glen brought his hands down from his temples, pretending not to notice.

"Getting there is the problem. That still ain't been solved," said Tony.

Glen walked to the edge of the rooftop, scoping out the scene below. He paced the edge, then stopped and called to Tony.

"Hey, tell me something."

"Yeah?" Tony joined him at the adjacent end.

"That camper," said Glen, pointing at the nearby unit running parallel to the wall. "It has a battery, right?"

"Yeah," said Tony. "It does."

"Works?"

"Works just fine. Replaced it last year. That right there's where I lay my head at night." Tony made his way along the edge, toward the camper's front. He pointed to the tongue. "Battery's right there, fastened to the tongue behind them propane tanks."

"Looks reachable to me," said Glen.

Tony stared, placing one foot on the ledge. He leaned into his knee, giving it some thought. "Yeah," said Tony after a moment, his tone reluctant. "Suppose it is." He pushed his fingers up across his neck, working the muscles. He squinted back at Glen as if the notion were a tack that lodged itself inside his brain. He took a breath, swallowing down whatever pleading apprehension simmered at his core.

Glen looked at Tony, waiting for the unspoken suggestion to settle out inside his head.

"Ehh." Tony sighed. He closed his eyes and nodded, letting his hand slip from his neck and drop down to his side. "Shit. Yeah. All right. I'll pull the ladder, see if we can't give this a go."

All around, a bed of clouds went up in flames on mountain

treetops, heaped like shadow-ash against the orange and red of rising dawn. There were no more sounds. The world around them held its breath.

Glen clapped Tony's shoulder, giving him a nod. "Well, all right then. Let's wake the others, give this a shot. Maybe have that talk about the jar while we're at it."

CHAPTER
TWENTY-SEVEN

LAJ HAULED THE FAR END of the extension ladder's frame up through the rooftop access at an angle, hoisting it across the roof as Glen ascended through the access panel with the bottom portion gripped above his head. They laid it out and waited as the others followed close behind, spilling through the hatch.

Laj shoved a palm across his sloping brow and squinted through the reeds of sunlight jabbing through the treetops, whisker-thin and crosshatched like a wall of hasty basketwork.

"All right," said Laj. He swiped a hand across his nose. "You ready to do this?"

"Battery ain't held in place with nothin' but a nylon strap," said Tony, eyes pinched up against the early light. He pressed the moisture from his palms along the denim downslope of his thighs. He tugged his shirt free of his pants and let it fall across his belly. "Buckled on top. Simple setup. Should be pretty easy, in and out no problem."

Laj bowed his head. He sucked a breath of morning air, cold and moist. It was a plunging, cleansing act that filled his chest and drove it out against the inside of the buttoned shirt beneath his folded arms. He took a moment to himself before responding, as if finding his resolve to follow through as an accomplice to the idiocy of the act to follow, nodding all the while at nothing in particular.

"All right, yeah," said Laj, breaking from the stronghold of his thoughts. "Then tell me how we gonna do this." The big man gripped his nose and scrubbed an itch across both nostrils.

"Can't run it straight down to the tongue. Ain't got the room. Risk slipping free, falling down into the water that way." Tony stepped close to the edge and pointed to the unit's rooftop. "Bridge it ledge to roof instead." He gave a minor flourish of his finger like an artist's brush. "Wedge it up against that AC unit at the top right there. Shouldn't be no slippage that way. Roof's rubberized, anti-slip."

They picked the ladder up and walked it to the building's ledge. The two men slid both rails opposite each another, nearly maxing out its length before the sections came to rest and locked themselves in place. The metal construct made an awful racket as they pushed it out and over, grinding forward across the cinder ledge before they dropped it down onto the camper's waiting rooftop. It clapped the camper's surface with a metallic chatter, sharp and much louder than intended as the weight took over on the farthest end's descent. The two men worked the ladder's base up tight against the AC unit's side, then jerked the apparatus left and right to set the rubber feet in place.

"Show's all yours, buddy," said Laj. "Following your lead now." He dropped his hand against the metal frame and clapped it twice, then turned his eyes to Tony. "Should be right secure where she sits." He reached out, packing Tony's shoulder with an open palm, and Tony fought to keep from stumbling from the impact. "You sure you game for this, man?"

Tony nodded. "I'm most familiar with the rig. Only makes sense." He swallowed, squinting back at Laj. "I'll be all right."

Laj dipped his chin.

"Tony," said Glen.

Tony turned. "Yeah?"

"Listen." Glen walked over to the man, making sure he had his ear. "I know I don't even need to say it, but I'm gonna say it anyway. When you get over there, keep it moving. Don't hang around any longer than you have to. Get the battery, get back across that ladder."

Lauren stood against her father's side, fists tucked deep inside her sleeves like knots of cotton as she listened to the two men speak.

"You see anything funny," said Glen, "anything strange at all, you get your ass back across that bridge and do it fast. We don't need the damn thing bad enough to lose a life over it."

"And if we don't get our hands on it, could mean loss of life all the same," said Tony. "All in how you look at it. Way I see it, only real option's to just make sure we get the thing. We need it."

"Within reason, Tony," affirmed Glen. "We need to, we'll figure something else out."

"I hear you. I'm rather fond of staying alive anyway," said Tony, speaking through a nervous grin. "You know, given the option and all."

Glen returned a smile, grunting out a note of humor. "Can't say I blame you, buddy. Good to know."

Tony walked up to the border wall and kicked the cinder blocks that lined its base. He looked down across the ladder's length, blew his cheeks out like a globe, and stepped up across the ledge. With one leg lifted up and over, he laid his weight against the ladder's outstretched neck, measuring its behavior. The metal framework chattered, flexing slightly under strain before he brought his other leg around, dropping his other foot down to the next, and then the next rung after that, angled forty-five degrees and heading down and out onto the spongy membrane of the camper's rooftop sprawl.

Hank watched him from above, standing with his hands plunged deep and squirming at his thighs like two bagged rabbits. He squeezed his eyelids shut, an overt blink of someone fighting sleep, perhaps confirming their reality. He leaned out from the edge, looking down, and for a moment seemed to prime his mouth for words, then stopped, stepped back, and settled into silence once again.

Glen turned a fleeting glance to Hank and for a moment caught his eyes, an odd and rolling calmness in their wells. It somehow made him think of how the ocean dips and turns out past the blackened breakers in the predawn hours where the threat is at its greatest, past the false bravado of the pounding surf. The menace of the plunging deep, living just beneath the gliding surface out beyond where things seem safe and still, sucking like a hungry mouth from underneath.

Hank stared back, his expression blank. The look produced a sudden urge in Glen to move himself and Lauren to the farthest point of the rooftop, padding the void between them and the man whose sanity appeared to slough away and flit like ash into the crossing breeze.

CHAPTER
TWENTY-EIGHT

Tony dropped his head and tracked the course of his descent beneath his outstretched body. Through the rungs and down below, the water stirred to life and flowed beneath the makeshift bridge as if a dam had come undone at some upstream location.

"Shit," hissed Tony, freezing at the ladder's midpoint, staring down into the eager churn. "Shit…shit," he repeated.

"Just keep moving," called Laj. "You got it, brother. Keep on moving. You well out of reach. It's way the hell down there, you way the hell up here. You got this."

Tony squeezed his eyelids shut and leaned into the ladder. He pulled his torso tight against its length and pressed the softer portions of his body in between the rungs, feeling cold aluminum against his cheek.

Glen watched from the roof, and from the side, the man's position brought to mind a pasta press with nubs of dough emerging from the holes.

Tony drew a sideways breath across the metal surface. "It knows I'm coming. It can hear me."

"It's the vibrations," called Glen. "It can sense them through the ladder, through the trailer's frame. C'mon, buddy. Look at me."

Tony's breaths were coming tight and fast now. "Ah, shit, man. I don't know about this." He cranked the ladder's rail beneath both palms to reaffirm his grip. "Shit, shit, shit. Ah, hell. I don't usually curse this much. I'm sorry. I'm so sorry."

"Hey, right here," said Glen, crossing at the rooftop ledge to where the ladder rested. He took hold with both hands and fit his head between the goalposts of its peak. "Look at me."

Tony opened his eyes, then turned them upward.

The water down below licked past and roiled at the points between the wall and trailer frame, the sound almost a foreign language rising up to meet Glen's ears, its words a measured dance of reed and glass. Glen fought the urge to listen closer. A sense of madness deep inside that told him there was something speaking to him. Something floating upward from the water, just for him. Something he'd be better off not hearing.

"There you go," said Glen, speaking over what might try and work its way into his ears, his unmedicated mind. Glen held the ladder's peak, hands white-knuckled. "Right here with you, buddy. Step at a time. Take it slow. It can't get you up here, okay? It can't reach you."

Tony nodded, looking down.

"Nope. Don't do that. Hey." Glen slapped the ladder's edge. "Back up here, Tony."

Tony tensed and gripped the ladder tighter.

"Eyes up here. Right here. Don't look down there."

"All right, I got this," whispered Tony. "I got this. I'm—I'm going."

"I can go instead," said Glen. "Say the word, man. Ain't a bit of shame in that."

Lauren looked up at her dad, her expression telling of a silent hope those words were nothing but.

"Nope. No." Tony turned his volume higher, shook his head. "I can do this. I can." He slipped down to the next in line, and then the next to follow. The ladder jounced beneath his weight, and he started wondering how he even planned to haul the battery back to the building's roof. As it stood, it was all he could do to hold his own unburdened weight in place. He should've thought to bring a bag or other means to strap the battery to himself. He gave himself a mental slap at the realization. Too late now.

Tony's outstretched foot eventually found the spongy surface of the camper's top, and he stepped out to its center. He paused there in the crossing breeze to press his sweaty palms against his jeans. Twelve feet out before him was a sloping ridge of glossy fiberglass that spilled down to the unit's tongue. He pulled a coil of nylon rope from his neck and dropped down to his haunches. Tony drew the end around the air-conditioning unit jutting from the middle of the rooftop. He tied it in a figure eight and pulled it tight, leaning back and jerking hard to measure its integrity. Tony looked up to the party watching from the rooftop ledge. He held his thumb up high, nodding once.

He gathered up the rope and brought it to the camper's front, where he knelt and let it fall. Tony jerked once more against the tether, a final test before he laid his full weight on the rope and let his body slide over the edge.

The trailer's tongue jutted out beneath him in an inverse V. Tony dangled from the rope and carefully found his footing on the topside of two propane tanks. Carefully, he brought a foot down to the camper's metal frame. Behind the propane tanks, the plastic housing of the battery could now be seen.

The water resting not a foot beneath him was a flat of onyx, still and quiet as volcanic glass. Tony felt a small degree of tension slacken in his muscles. Some degree of ease began to find him, and he breathed a normal breath for what had seemed an endless hour.

The lid of the battery box was cinched down by the nylon strap. The buckle wedged itself against an edge of plastic trim, tight and unforgiving. Tony balanced now with both feet planted on the V-shaped framework of the camper's tongue. He doubled over, working at the buckle and the folded strap with anxious fingers. The strap snapped free and Tony cried out like a frightened child. He threw his arms out wide to brace himself, and when he did, the lid fell from the box and landed upside-down, floating on the water as it disappeared into the shadows of the camper's undercarriage.

"Shit, Tony! You good?" Jesse's voice reverberated off the water and the walls with the hollow chatter of an empty hallway. "Aye, Tony! Talk to us, man!"

Tony stood there for a moment with his hand outstretched

on the corner of the battery box. Despite the coolness of the morning air around him, his forehead went to liquid heat. He stared between his feet and watched the water underneath. It buckled, stirring to life from nothing. The water's surface rolled as if drifting across the back of something large and powerful that passed beneath. Tony downed the brick that wedged itself inside his throat and sucked a breath.

"Shhhhhhh…" He hushed Jesse with an upturned hand, then pointed to the water underneath his feet before he brought the finger to his lips.

He could hear the soft exchange of words, and then the group was quiet once again.

Tony braced himself against the propane tanks, then reached behind and slipped a multitool from the leather sheath suspended from his belt. He slid the pliers free and knelt to place their teeth around the nut securing the black line to the negative terminal. Snowbanks of corrosion wrapped it. The nut came loose, as did the powder laced around the threads. It disappeared in the gentle breeze. Tony finger-spun the nut to liberate the cable's hold entirely.

Now, the red.

The other nut complied with little effort, and Tony was able to slip the contact free and clear, just as with the black. This one came off cleanly. Tony pocketed the tool. Using the carry strap attached to the battery's topside, he hauled it from its case with ease. He wasn't quite so sure at first just how he planned to move the battery, a unit weighing every bit of forty pounds, but then he slipped his hand beneath the carry strap and found that he could hang it from his wrist, albeit painfully and not for long.

He knew he'd have to move with speed before the clamor drew the thing in close. The water was a web and he was like a fly ensnared, any sound he made reverberating through like tiny beacons. He'd made it down the first time without incident, but now the awkward weight of cargo slowed him, testing balance, making him clumsy.

Tony wrapped his other arm around the rope and placed a foot against the fiberglass. He pulled to lift himself, both legs splayed outright. The hardened rubber of his soles attacked the flimsy shell, and the sound was like a drum with every step, the surface buckling underfoot. Eventually, he rounded the topside edge and fell out on his knees, panting with exhaustion. Tony looked up toward the roof and flashed a smile of triumph at the waiting throng of people. At their end, Hank stared blankly, his face a mask without emotion.

Tony came up to his feet again and walked the battery to where the line was tethered. He laid it at the ladder's base and moved to disengage the knot of rope. And as he reeled its final feet into a coil dangling from his open palm, he felt the dampness at its end, and then the water as it dribbled from the fibers that had held his scent, wicking up the liquid where the rope had fallen unnoticed, having dangled like a strip of bait beneath the water's surface underneath the camper's tongue.

CHAPTER
TWENTY-NINE

The group was slow in their response.

It all happened so fast.

They'd hardly time to register the moment, take it all in.

Tony's hesitation at the touch of water.

Confirmation in the union of this thumb and forefinger.

The liquid strike that ruptured from the fibers of the rope and found his forearm, bicep, neck, mouth, nose, eyes. It all happened in a blink. He flung the rope away and clawed the water from his face, slapping it from his body. Lower, the water found his foot, and when it did, another hungry arm rushed up to reinforce the grip, seizing his leg in full.

Lauren blinked two times and looked up at her father in a dubious stupor.

"Tony!" shouted Glen. He scrabbled off along the ledge, his frantic thoughts now breaking loose and fleeing through his lips. "Shit. No. Nonono. Think...*think*, goddammit!"

Glen leaned across the building's edge and shouted out to Tony. "Grab the battery! Grab the goddamned terminals!"

The man was gagging now, rendered blind and deaf and thoughtless in his desperation, choking on the liquid fingers spilling from the length of rope, a massive wick that drew the liquid to the rooftop, to his body, to his seizing lungs. Tony heaved against the flow, its current doubling over now, flowing faster, stronger with the passing seconds.

Glen watched the water take his friend there on the camper's roof, out of reach, completely helpless. Spinning panic reeled him forward, bringing his right foot to the diner's ledge.

Laj grabbed Glen before he made it to the ladder, holding him by the arms. He rushed his face in close to meet Glen's eyes head on.

"Don't be stupid!"

Glen tried to jerk himself away. Laj snatched him by the collar, shaking him to a stop. "Don't," barked Laj, jerking Glen another time to reinforce the word. "Think *real* hard about this. Think about what you doing right now."

Glen jerked his face away, spying Tony's thrashing body in his peripheral vision.

"Hey!" yelled Laj. He laid his hand against Glen's face, forcing it back in his direction. Glen fired off a round of rapid blinks, staring back at Laj. "Go out there, you good as gone. Gone! Let it go, man. Can't you, can't *nobody* do a damn thing for him now. Let. It. Go."

Tony stood there drowning in the open air, face cocked toward the sky, arms seized tight and thrusting downward.

His eyes reversed themselves, rolling blind and white like lumps of ice.

Where the wet rope's track lay streaked across the trailer's rooftop, another arm of water followed, emerging at the sloping end and guided by the scent of Tony's body where he'd crossed the fiberglass just moments prior. Beneath the reach of water coursing from the bridge of nylon rope, the liquid bound him layer by layer, swaddling tight and gripping arms and legs beneath the mounting pressure. It held him like a sheath of liquid muscle, spiderwebbed into a grid of crossing jets that fused and spread and knit themselves into an all-consuming cloak, arresting breath and movement save the flutter of his eyelids over thrusting whites. And then it swept him from his feet and dropped him flat against the camper's roof. His head collided with the AC unit in a single strike that knocked his mind into a winking lull.

Lauren's stood there at the building's ledge, calcified with shock, choking back the emotions that were clawing for escape.

Glen stood not far away from her, watching Tony without recourse. He hushed her as she fought for breath, the five of them deprived of any action short of standing there in wait of the inevitable.

Tony's body lay in place beneath the shroud of water, rippling over every peak and valley of his anatomy, its sound of movement but the same sweet trickle of the streams and brooks that carved their way throughout the hills around them. And it was that sound that was so integral to the creature's camouflage of normalcy: disarming notes of nature's lullaby, a song whose roots plunged deep into association with the calming essence of the great outdoors.

Of the five that had been essentially immobilized by what they saw, Jesse was the first to break the vision's hold. He stepped back once, twice, then turned and started pacing, faster as he seconds passed.

Then, the body moved, only slightly, gliding forward across the camper's rooftop several inches, then a foot, momentum building as the tendrils towed him onward, sliding not so much as floating on the liquid plane. A tail of crimson striped his route, dispensed across the camper's surface in a water-blur of brilliance spilling from the open wound on his head like abstract art.

Jesse chucked his fists across his scalp, both hands moving to a single cradle on his head. He was racing now. He forced his eyes toward the gravel passing underfoot, evading truth of sight. He mumbled to himself, a hybrid groan of word and sound that leaked across his tongue just out of earshot of the others, some kind of private incantation for his ears alone.

"OhGodJesusGodpleasenoGodJesuspleasenononoGod nomakeitstopohJesusJesus..."

The body drifted to a stop and seemed to buckle where it lay, vibrating with the shorted twitch of failing nerve and muscle. Tony's jaw swung wide, pried into an exaggerated yawn. His body picked up movement, shuddering into action on the open deck, the sound a muffled drumroll starting low and mounting to abusive heights. His body slammed against the camper, and his chest became a rising swell as if engaged in breath, long and deep. Then, it dropped, collapsing flat, then went concave, impossible compression of the breastbone pumping one suspended shot of rose-pink liquid from his throat into the air. The fountain came in violent bursts with bubbling spills between. His flesh and muscles drew up tight against his frame in rapid dehydration as the water fled his body, spilling from the trailer's edge into the waiting pool below.

Lauren creaked a sound and gripped her father's shirt, rolling it into her fist. He turned and wrapped his arms around her, binding her against his chest as if to take her in and lock her safe inside.

"Trust me," whispered Glen into her hairline. "Can you do that for me? I need you to be brave, to trust me."

He held her out before him on extended arms and swept a mat of hair across her face, guiding it behind her ear across his middle finger.

"What are you going to do?" The question rushed from her mouth, a filthy thing tied to an answer that she didn't really want to know. Her face was turned away from him, afraid to bring her eyes to his, to see the truth behind them. Lauren pulled away and brought her arms up tight against her chest. "Tell me what it is. What are you about to do?"

He turned from her and brought a foot up to the ledge.

Laj stepped forward and slung an arm across Glen's chest.

"What do you think you're doing, Glen?"

Jesse had stopped pacing, frozen with his hands compacted in a lump of fingers at his front. He gawped at Laj and Glen, rendered mute with terror. Hank hadn't moved from where he'd been, seemingly unplugged from all the world around him.

Glen turned and looked into the big man's eyes. He took his foot down from the ledge and whispered loud enough for Laj's understanding only.

"Take your hands off me and put them on my daughter."

Laj flinched, blindsided by the order. He glanced at Lauren, and Lauren caught the look. A look that would have been too brief to notice had she not already had her eyes on them.

"What? What's going on?" Lauren took a forward step. "What did you say?"

Laj was back on Glen again. He didn't answer.

"We need that battery, and right now's when I need to get it. While the water's preoccupied with Tony's body," murmured Glen. "The battery's free and clear, but might not be for long. I'm going to get it, and when I do, I need you to keep Lauren away, keep her safe so I can cross that ladder and get the damn thing while we still have time."

Laj shook his head.

"Hey, man. Forg—"

The clap of metal broke them from their whispers. Both men turned to face the sudden clamor. She'd been quick, and in the two men's preoccupation, Lauren had already crossed the ledge onto the ladder, several steps into her descent, heading toward the camper's roof.

Glen knocked Laj's arm aside and launched himself onto the ledge. His screams unfurled across the open hills.

"Lauren!"

Laj tore at Glen's shoulders, his back, pulling him with all his strength as Glen clawed toward the ladder jutting up across the cinder blocks. The action wrenched Glen back a couple feet and brought his torso down onto the cinder blocks with a futile thud.

"No!" screamed Glen, clawing at the bricks. He reached out and latched onto the ladder's peak, shaking the entire frame. Lauren screamed, clinging to the ladder as it jounced above the void between the building and the camper.

"Let go!" shouted Laj. "Glen! Let her go! You're going to knock her off the goddamn ladder!"

"Get the fuck off me!" screamed Glen, kicking Laj above the groin. The giant man let out a huff. Glen's left hand was still upon the ladder with the right en route to join it. The apparatus lurched from side to side, rasping on the edge of cinder blocks as Glen fought to seize it.

"Lauren!"

Laj drove a fist into Glen's kidney, instantaneously doubling him into a wad that dropped away and hit the gravel rooftop of the diner. He let out a wail, sudden loss and agony rolled into one eviscerating note.

Beyond the ledge, Lauren kept on moving, halfway now down the ladder and descending toward the camper roof.

CHAPTER THIRTY

LAUREN DEFTLY MOVED ACROSS THE ladder, careful with the sound she made. For now, the water had preoccupations of its own. Preoccupations that should offer her sufficient time to grab the battery and bring it back across the ladder well before it turned its focus elsewhere.

At least this was her hope.

She hadn't any actual plan. Her only plan had been to stop her dad from going after it. She was lighter. She was faster. She could beat it.

Its assault on Tony hadn't ended. It was voracious, efficient, and when the entity had finished harvesting the moisture from his body, it hauled the empty husk away in its retreat along the path from which it'd come, gliding toward the camper's sloping nose.

Above her on the rooftop, Glen lay sprawled out on the ledge, gripping both rails of the ladder. Lauren looked up only fast enough to catch a glimpse of him, the look of devastation on his face. Betrayal. Utterly psychotic worry. Laj was still behind him, out of kicking range, ready for the grab. Glen said something. He was yelling at her again, the only choice he had. Lauren couldn't hear him, wouldn't hear him.

Instead, Lauren heard the body when it slipped across the front, colliding with the camper's metal chassis. She heard the splash to follow just a few feet out from stepping to the camper. The sound hit her senses like a boxing bell, signaling the closure of her window well before expected.

Her time was up.

She didn't turn at once to scope the situation, didn't care to see that withered body turning on the water's surface. In the corner of her eye, she saw Tony rush beneath her on the current and she fought the urge to look, to see the man-shaped husk that had only recently become her friend. And all in all, the manic upturn of her father's shouting up above betrayed what sights she spared her eyes, and better judgment told her that she'd best keep moving, stay on task, keep her mind and limbs upon the ladder.

The battery still rested at the ladder's base where Tony had left it. Lauren stepped down onto the still-dry surface, double-checking it before she knelt and eyed the unit's housing, the arch of plastic strap sprung high across its top. It was dry as well, at least as far as she could tell.

The box was heavy, and when she moved to lift it, she instantly realized her error. Her thin arms shook, and the strap was merciless in how it carved into her palm beneath the weight of the battery. Lauren grimaced, looking up the ladder, all the steps that lay ahead. She saw her father, standing now, beckoning for her return.

"Come on, Lauren," he hissed. "Just move. Moooove."

Lauren started climbing upward. The battery jumped one rung to the next, lifted and dropped, lifted and dropped, threatening to tip and plummet to the water down below as Lauren inched her way back to the roof. She tried to be as quiet as she could, but it was pointless. She might as well have been setting off cherry bombs.

Laj was standing at Glen's left now. The nervous tic was back again, tugging at the corner of his mouth. Jesse chewed his thumbnail as he chucked his feet in place, eyes unmoving from some point along the camper's surface. Several feet downwind along the ledge, Hank stood placid, cold, still as ever. He looked like a marionette in storage, slouched without the will or means to move.

As she climbed, Lauren moved her eyes between the ladder and the others lined up at its peak. That's when he saw the look on Jesse's face, a sudden change that brought him to a stop, feet stilled on the tar and gravel. She tried to see what he was looking at, but the fear of toppling over held her out of range. It was all that she could do to hang on to the battery and keep from falling as it was. Jesse's gaze had gone from vacant to concerned, and then had moved to utter terror as he wound his hand in circles, reeling her across the ladder with his mind.

"Move," mouthed Jesse.

Laj and Glen had turned to look, then tracked his line of

sight down to the camper, just beyond the ladder's base. Where the battery had been, an arm of water coiled like a serpent, originating somewhere past the distant edge of roof. It pooled in place, sensing Lauren, sampling hints of where she'd stood, where she'd gone.

"Jesus, move!" Jesse cut along the ledge, shouting out to Lauren. "It's coming! Move!"

In the cacophony of Jesse's words and Glen's launch into hysterics at the ladder's peak, Lauren finally brought herself to turn and look, hardly long enough to glimpse the eager stretch of water that now wrapped itself about the lower rungs, snaking upward.

"Oh my God."

Lauren kicked up toward the rooftop, hammering the rungs beneath her feet, fast and hard. Her legs burned, and her core was aching from relentless tension that had stiffened her against an accidental fall. She was only at the ladder's midpoint now, grappling with the battery that teetered on each rung, no longer mindful of the noise in her attempts to scramble farther away from the upward streak of liquid. The ladder flexed and chattered as she flung herself across the rungs, sometimes leaping two at a time, unearthing strength she never knew she'd had. The action liberated swaths of water into the pool beneath her, shaken free in sections, knocked from its upward trek in dashes littered out across the pond below.

Her right foot missed a rung, and her leg plunged in between and disappeared up to the thigh. Her stomach dropped and all nerves came to life at once. She reeled, fighting to stabilize herself, the forty pounds of cargo nearly towing her across the ladder's edge entirely before she somehow found herself upright again, thrusting from the trap and grappling closer to the building's ledge. She could actually hear the water now, somehow louder than the chaos sounding off above, a metallic lick that chased the frame and found her ears, closing in not far behind.

Glen was at the ladder's peak, arms outstretched and grasping for her.

"Almost there! Come on!" He slapped the metal. "Come on, Lauren!"

Lauren grabbed his hand, giving one last hoist to throw the battery across the ledge. She felt Laj wrap his hand around her now-free arm. Her body left the ladder as the two men wrenched her up and over. She tumbled from the ladder's peak, across the ledge onto the rooftop's rocky teeth. Laj turned and threw the ladder from the ledge, the liquid tendrils peaking then and leaping from its end, dissolved into a tail of mist that formed a rainbow on the morning light.

Hank remained unbudged, a catatonic figure save the slightest movement of his head and eyes that tracked the water's misty exodus. And then he brought his left hand to his cheek and crossed it with his fingers, moist and cool.

CHAPTER
THIRTY-ONE

"Want to tell me what the hell you were thinking?" said Glen. He pulled an arm across his face, slicked with perspiration.

Lauren lifted the battery and turned her back to him, started walking toward the open hatch.

"Hey!" Glen turned her by the shoulder. "Don't walk away from me. What you did is—"

"What, Dad?" said Lauren. "What was it?"

"Give it a rest already!" Glen yelled.

Lauren blinked and took a step back with the battery. "I did it for you," she said.

Glen face collapsed in anger. "No. Bullshit. Not this. Not the guilting. I need a *real* answer, Lauren. What the hell were you thinking? You could've—"

"Lost the battery?" Lauren said.

"Damn the battery!" shouted Glen. "To hell with the battery! I could've lost *you!*"

Lauren stared at him. Tears gathered on the surface of her eyes.

"Do you see me now?" asked Lauren.

"What?" Glen fell back a step and sent both arms into the air. "Of course I see you. What does—"

"You haven't seen me in a long time, Dad," said Lauren. "It's been a long, long time."

"I've *always* seen you, Lauren."

"Maybe it just feels that way to you, Dad." She laid the battery at her feet and shoved her arm across her eyes, swiping free the tears that dropped across her cheeks.

"*That's* what this was all about? You kidding me here?" said Glen, turning his head. "Not feeling *seen? Loved?*"

"It's what it's *always* been about. Ever since Mom died."

Glen stepped toward Lauren. "Jesus." He wrapped his arms around her, holding tight. "I see you, Lauren. I see you. Always have. Always. That's *never* changed."

"Maybe *now* you do. Now that you've been *forced* to deal with me. You don't have a choice in this place. Now that we're stuck in here and you don't have anywhere to run and hide and bury yourself."

"Lauren, that's not true," said Glen, dumbfounded. "Do you have any idea how much I love you?"

"You say that," said Lauren, sobbing hard. "You say that, but I think you made the wrong decision. You *broke* when Mom died. You *needed* her. More than you needed me. Why didn't you just let me go? Why'd you have to save me instead of her? You actually *needed* her!"

Glen squeezed harder, binding her against his chest. "Jesus, Lauren. How could you even say that? I need *you*. I loved you both. It was impossible. So impossible. There was no right or wrong. It was all so fast. All so fast, kiddo."

"That's another thing," said Lauren, her sobbing voice muffled up against Glen's shirt. "I stopped being a kid a long time ago."

"Yeah," said Glen, still holding on to Lauren. "I guess you did. Maybe I did miss that part."

He locked her body into his, just holding her. He didn't want to move.

"I love you, Lauren," said Glen. He shook his head. "I don't regret a thing. Do you understand me? Not a thing."

Against his chest, Lauren nodded, silent.

"Being your dad is *everything* to me," whispered Glen. "And I'm so proud that you're my daughter."

They stayed that way a moment. Lauren clung to him until the tears had stopped.

Glen let up on his hold as Laj and Jesse wandered past them on their way back to the hatch. Lauren stepped away and pushed her palms across her eyes.

"Heading back inside," said Laj, pausing. Jesse kept on walking, no longer really in the moment, functioning on autopilot.

"Y'all straight? Need help with that?" Laj gestured toward the battery.

Lauren cleared her throat and stooped to pick it up.

"Think I'll take it from here, thanks," said Glen, putting

out a hand to stop her. He touched her arm. "Not that I think you *can't.*"

Lauren tossed her hands into the air. "Stupid thing already almost broke my arm off." She sniffed, tried to laugh, failing miserably. She turned from Glen, holding back the rising wall of concrete in her chest as Tony's final image shuttled through her mind. The fact that he was gone had only just begun to settle in. "You take it," she whispered, afraid to test her vocal cords again, lest the fear and pain and grief come pouring out behind her words.

Glen picked the battery up. He leaned in and kissed his daughter's forehead. "Come on." Glen started walking toward the hatch. Lauren held her spot, finally calling after him in a congested, broken voice.

"What now?"

Glen turned. "Now, we figure out how we're getting out of here."

CHAPTER THIRTY-TWO

THEY'D ALL WIPED DOWN WITH a heavy dilution of bleach and pre-boiled water, a precautionary measure to ensure all regions of uncovered skin were treated. But the paranoia had already taken root, spreading through the group. Despite the measures taken, all were ill at ease with knowing any one of them could already be infected. It could already be inside them, maybe all of them, embedded like some logic bomb awaiting just the right conditions, the perfect time to strike.

The whiskey had already spent its final drops there somewhere in the darker hours of the morning, and as the day wore down, Hank had taken to the quiet corners of the diner in a search for time alone. The tremors had begun to show, and though they all had noticed, none had said a word. Now that the alcohol was gone, withdrawals would only hasten his descent into mental instability. Still, the crew was hopeful that he'd take a turn for better sooner or later. And should he not, the man was better on his own regardless, removed from conflict in his solitude.

Since they'd come down from the rooftop, Lauren hadn't ceased to move about the diner, searching and sorting and gathering food and any other acts that helped stave off recollection of what happened earlier. Anything to draw attention from the threat that lay in wait not just beyond, but for all she knew, within the walls around them. Anything to keep emotions locked up safe inside her core, out of sight, out of mind. And in her ceaseless state of animation, she'd found the set of jumper cables stashed between a broken wall clock and a partially used extinguisher inside the storage closet, just as Tony recollected.

"Dad," she called, untangling the knot of wires in her hands. "These it?"

"Looks like it," said Glen. He'd been watching her. Despite her manic state, he found watching her was strangely calming, despite the reason why and what they'd all just been through. The way she moved from space to space, hair pulled up into a messy bun exactly like her mother's, moving as her mother had, speaking as her mother had, comments zipper-quick, almost synchronized with every flash of movement. She had no idea how much she resembled Claire, almost such that both were right there with him, two in one, two planes of existence overlaid in seamless integration.

She passed them to her father, frowning at the strangely delicate smile he hadn't even realized he was wearing. Glen shook it off and took the bundle from her, and when he clamped them to the battery's terminals and touched opposing ends, a spark cracked off and told of solid charge, enough to exorcise the devil from a human body.

The battery was strong, sufficient to protect.

"How exactly is this going to work again?"

"Well," said Glen as he unclamped the cables, binding them around the battery, "we already know it can't handle an electric shock. Think we're going to have to get out of this place. Soon. When we do, can't hurt to bring a little power with us."

Lauren paused, digesting the concept. "How do you know?"

"Know what?"

"It'll work."

"I don't."

Lauren's face dropped, and she went silent.

"Just leveling with you here. You're not a kid. You were right about that, and so I'm not going to treat you like one. Thought that's what you wanted."

"It is," said Lauren. "Thanks."

Glen offered her a pensive nod, then placed the battery and cables on the prep cart's bottom shelf. "But, battery or no battery, we're getting out of here. That's a promise."

Laj stood against the open windows of the dining room, tending to the fractures in the glass. Using a bottle of super-glue he'd found behind the front desk, he carefully guided the applicator along each line, pumping it into the fractures. As he'd done so, he'd also watched the water levels heighten by the hour. It seemed Glen's theory had been right. With every passing moment, the tide was rising in proportion to the replication of the microorganism and its harvesting of water from the surrounding landscape and its inhabitants. A substantial wall of water had risen up to press the building's broad exterior, seeking points of entry among the cinder block and glass and steel that formed the sweep of doors and windows. As he worked and watched, the water pressed the double doors, their sealant groaning under strain, and Laj could tell it wouldn't hold for long before the seams broke free and let the tide roll in.

He'd marked a visual point of reference on a light post in the early morning, somewhere around six or seven o'clock, and now the clock read 4:15 in the evening. From what he could tell, the water was a good five or six inches higher than before, and so he estimated half an inch of water growth with every hour, meaning that, by this time next morning, they'd find themselves another six inches submerged, and twenty-four hours from now a good foot or more, at least. And this was making the assumption that their shoddy weather-stitch and crack repair would hold till then, with odds that it would hold out any length of time beyond that landing close to zero.

Glen joined Laj's side just as he was finishing up. Laj gestured toward the glass and shrugged. "Poor man's windshield repair. Always worked for that, don't see why it wouldn't work for this." He capped the bottle and pocketed it, turning his eyes back to the water, the forest all around them.

Glen matched his gaze. Along the lower half of the mountainside, three-quarters of the foliage had already dropped. The upper half was denser, though not by much. Roughly half the foliage had released along the higher regions, though within the next day or two, Glen surmised, it would've caught up with the state of the lower half, and the lower half would likely be reduced to nothing more than sticks from total dehydration. By then, the water surrounding them would be twice as vast, twice as deep, twice as occupied, twice as strong.

"Guess this is where we either go ahead and shit or get off the pot," said Laj.

The two men took their seats inside the booth. For several long and heavy minutes, they sat and felt the circumstantial gravity bear down on them. Glen's hands wrestled with each other, wadded up around his chin and mouth. Laj reached an arm across the backrest of the seat and turned his face into the twilight glow that spilled down through the window. It cast shadows from the condiments and shakers, three black pillars laid out long and flat across the table.

"Guess it's past time we start talking about how this is actually going to go down." Glen reached out and took the greasy set of shakers in his hands, fiddling with them as he broke the silence. "We're not even really talking options anymore. We're in the realm of inevitability here, only one way out of this. Hoped for other options, but I think we know by now that's just not happening."

Laj set his head into an understanding nod, his expression percipient, solemn. "I've been watching the levels."

Glen pushed the shakers back in place. "Pretty clear it's trending in the wrong direction."

"Eyes don't lie, do they?"

Laj brought his chin up just a little. "I'll be real with you. If you'd been up for setting out back when we talked this over last, I won't ready to go all in on that notion just yet." He turned to Glen. "Thought maybe somehow God might step in at some point, just reach down and pull a plug out there somewhere, let that shit just run on down to hell where it belong."

Glen looked up at Laj. "God?"

Laj raised his brow. "You take issue with that?"

"No issue here," said Glen. "Just thought you told Hank you were Muslim. And with what Helen said to you…"

"Name's Muslim," said Laj. "Never said I was one thing or another."

"Fair point," said Glen.

"I let folks think whatever the hell they care to think, make whatever assumptions they care to make," said Laj. "End of the day, they're gonna find a way to do it anyway, and I'm gonna keep on living my life just the same."

"Truer words," said Glen.

He turned sideways on the cushion, squinting out across the lake that shimmered sharp and slick like distant blacktop in the desert sun. The broken overhang still floated opposite the cars, teetering with the motion of the water just enough to chafe their metal sides with sharp, grating monotony. Glen found the shakers in his hands again, unable to sit still. His nerves were lit at both ends now, and underneath the table both legs jumped like pistons. He strummed the ribbed circumference of the shakers, turning them against his fingers like the spinning innards of a music box. "The hell is going on here, man? How big is this thing? Just here, or is it everywhere?"

Laj shook his head, transfixed by the distant stream that flowed beneath the thinning light. "No telling." He pressed a finger up against his nose, one side at a time, blowing irritation from each passage. "Maybe the man upstairs decided on a pop quiz. Said it's time to put the world to task, find out what we made of. Time to separate the strong from weak, only this time we ain't got no ark to sail us out of here."

Several bodies floated into view, out along the stretch of road, now a jet of swiftly moving water shearing past the distant tree line straight ahead. Soon after, something large emerged, a clumsy shape that toppled through the current, jolting end over end beneath the water. A wheel and tire breached the surface, disappearing as a set of handlebars, then a fractured headlight broke through, turning over, spinning down beneath the current as the motorcycle tumbled over rock and asphalt underneath.

The ruins of the medic building jutted from the water, splitting the current down the middle so it rushed along the edge of either side. The vines that dressed its angles, once lush and healthy, now dangled loose and dry like weathered nets of rope. A solitary stream spilled from a broken window, coughed into the bed of water gathered at the sinking base. The evening light reflected off the cross, illuminated in a shade of bloody orange, enhanced tenfold at that very angle, that very time of day, lit up like a taunting beacon for their eyes alone.

There would be no rescue here.

Lauren's constant patter sounded from the back room where she fed her nerves with actions largely devoid of purpose or necessity.

Just movement. Endless movement.

Every so often, she'd call out to Glen to announce some tool or gadget that she'd come across, and he'd return some word of praise to keep her spirits lifted. But truth be told, he knew the way she must be crumbling from the inside out by now, and he was without means to bring her any sense of peace.

"That girl keep herself busier than a moth in a mitten," said Laj.

"Funny you should say that. Her mama used to use that same exact phrase," said Glen. He smiled softly to himself. "Never heard it elsewhere."

"Y'all lost her some time back, did you?"

Glen dropped his head. "Yes. Yes, we did." He pulled a breath, squinting through the window. "Drowned some years back. Six now. Got caught in a riptide on vacation. Took her right out." Glen felt the wasp inside his chest.

"I'm sorry."

"Thanks." Glen dipped his chin. "Been a rough stretch, man. Just can't seem to get it right ever since. Neither one of us, I don't guess." He swallowed, unraveling the knot that gathered in his throat. "I feel like we'll never get it back. That maybe I've screwed up too much, let her down too much at this point. I don't know."

"You believe that?"

"Mhm." Glen nodded. He raked a nail across the underside

of knuckles, letting it hitch on each callus, jumping one patch to the next.

"Things were different before. *Claire* was different, so different from me."

"We're *all* different, man. All got our different ways."

"I know," said Glen, "but she was always so adventurous, so outgoing. Always up for anything. Given the opportunity, I'd more often choose a day at home. More of a homebody, I guess you might say. But Claire…" Glen laughed.

"What?" asked Laj. A smile crept into view. "Tell me about her."

"Okay, an example for you," said Glen. "There was this hot-air balloon festival. In Lexington, Virginia. Balloons Over Rockbridge, I think it was called. Lauren was six or so. Maybe five. Somewhere around there. Anyway, forecast spelled rain. Claire booked the trip anyway. She was damned determined to make that festival, to go up in a balloon."

Laj sat there listening, smiling quietly.

"Well, we went. And, right on schedule, as we were standing in this god-awful muddy line waiting to buy tickets for the balloon ride, the damn sky unzipped and let us have it. We were soaked. The balloons were deflated all over the fairgrounds as they waited out the storm, which, mind you, was striking out all around us, thunder and lightning, the whole show. Half the line had more sense than we did and left, but nothing of the sort for us. We stood out there and took that weather beating, and Claire and Lauren just laughed and laughed the entire time, despite the misery of it all."

"Sounds like you had some good times, man," said Laj, still smiling.

"We did, yeah," said Glen. "Yeah. I think we had more fun in the rain than in the balloon we eventually did get to ride in together." He turned the shakers in his fingers, slowly rolling them back and forth, back and forth. "But that was what Claire did for us. She was *life*. There was never a dull moment. Never." Glen looked up at Laj. "But me? What do I bring to the table? How could I possibly fill those shoes? She was everything I'm not. Everything that girl should have. Everything she deserves."

"Come on, Glen," said Laj.

"It's true," said Glen. "I mean, I'm trying now. Maybe too late, I don't know, but I'm trying. This whole trip, you know. It was supposed to be like the old days. Something fun. Something spontaneous. I couldn't even get us to the damn rental."

"Don't be so hard on yourself, man. Ain't no way you could've known."

Glen shrugged.

"And let me tell you another thing. Something maybe you're a little too close to the situation to see on your own. That girl right there?" Laj swung his head across the room. "She loves her daddy. Thinks a hell of a lot of him. Believe that."

Glen turned to face the counter. Lauren shuffled back and forth behind the counter, moving items underneath the shelves.

"And that wife of yours? Her mama? She ain't gone, brother. Believe that too. She still out there, and she love you just the same. You ain't let nobody down." Laj caught Glen's eyes and held them for a moment, making sure the message reached him unobstructed. "Feel what I'm telling you? Start talking that junk, start believing it, the only person you finna let down is yourself."

"I appreciate you. What you're trying to do here," said Glen, straightening in his seat, "but I've never been much on spirituality, matters of faith. Just never really been my thing."

Laj grinned. "Well, luckily for you, that don't really matter none. Universe ain't much dependent on what you do or don't believe." He winked and raised a finger, pointing it at Glen. "Universe is a big, confusing-ass place, man. Lot bigger than we are, than any personal beliefs we might hold. Lot older than we are. Lot we don't understand, damn sure never will."

"Mhm," said Glen. Through the window, he watched the water, ravenous and turning underneath the setting sun. "Can't argue that."

"Twenty-four years active duty in the air force," said Laj. He let out a short laugh. "Twenty-four damn years I served my country. Retired six months ago, pulled a hundred percent disability for my PTSD, got me a place up in these hills to fix up all on my own, just me and all that retirement dough. Time to settle down, enjoy life. The golden years, as they say, right? Thought I might even get me a cat or two."

"A cat, huh?" Glen smiled.

"Don't let the rough exterior fool you," said Laj. "Team cat right here and not a bit of shame in that. Dogs get on my damn nerves."

Glen laughed.

"Yeah, well, so much for all that now anyway," said Laj. "Here we are. Out of my hands, out of yours. To my point earlier: the universe and all that shit we don't understand, we just have no choice in the matter. No say at all. Go where life sends us, trust in the journey. Control is an illusion, my friend. Surety of life, existence, of here, now, tomorrow. You, me, all this." Laj gestured to the diner, the glass, the water outside. "Nothing is for sure. Nothing's certain. Never was, never will be."

"Yeah, well," said Glen. "I'd be lying if I said that brought me any peace."

Laj leaned forward, laying both arms on the table. "So, tell me this," he said. "All this talk on beliefs, of faith, you got much faith in this battery rig?"

Glen shrugged. "Can't say I have a lot of faith in much of anything right now, but yeah, far as faith goes, guess I do." He turned his eyes to Laj. "And after what went down this morning, I can't exactly afford not to." Glen fumbled with the shaker, turning it over in his fingers. "We kind of have an obligation to make it work now. For Tony."

Laj nodded.

"And for Lauren," continued Glen. "Promised her I'd make it back to catch the doc on Wednesday. Finally take care of some things. Going to do my best to make good on that."

"Today's Tuesday," said Laj.

Glen nodded his concession. "Ain't looking too good, is it?"

Laj shrugged. "Nothing wrong with dogged perseverance." He leaned into the table, laid his arms across the surface. "How 'bout you?" asked Laj. "Anything serious?"

"Serious is a relative term," said Glen. "To me, to her, yeah.

Serious enough. Time to take a solid crack at treatment. For both our sakes."

Laj decided not to press the subject any further. He looked up and gestured past Glen with his chin, across the dining room. "Thoughts on him?"

Glen looked back at Hank, knees drawn up against his chest and belted tight beneath his arms. He leaned back on the window with his eyes pinched shut, perspiration threading channels down his brow and cheeks. His body shivered like an engine with a cracked head gasket, and his crown juddered against the glass in such a way that formed a single, hollow note in aggregation.

Glen shook his head. "You really don't want my thoughts on him." He palmed an itch from his nose. "Never trusted him a bit. Sure as hell don't now."

"Could get pretty bad, pretty fast," said Laj. "Need to keep an eye on him, close as possible."

Glen stole a glance at Hank across his shoulder. "Wouldn't put it past him to toss the battery from the goddamned rooftop, screw us all."

"So, we gonna talk about this now or wait till that watery shit comes and tries to pick us off in our sleep again?" Jesse dropped into the seat alongside Glen and tossed an arm across the backrest.

"Question of the hour, my man," said Laj.

"Come on, let's take this topside," said Glen. "Can't plot much without full visual. And besides, not trying to clue your buddy in on every bleeding detail of this plan. I'm sure you can appreciate the root of that concern."

Jesse pushed his tongue against a wall of cheek and bobbed his head. "Unfortunately, I can."

The three men left the booth and headed through the backroom door.

Hank stayed put beneath a claw of sunlight groping downward through the window at his back, folded tight and glazed by sweat and festering in the moment like a splinter jutting from the flesh of sanity.

CHAPTER
THIRTY-THREE

THE TEMPERATURES HAD FALLEN HARD, sinking roughly ten or more degrees since they'd last sampled outside air, and a fine and silvered mist embraced the water like a wisp of spider's silk. A subtle breeze, a crisp delivery from the inbound night, broke portions into rags that spackled the expanse with all the pallid spontaneity of arctic camouflage.

The men lined up along the building's rear and looked across the back end of the lot where, several hundred feet out, the earth launched upward into scales of stone before it met the line of forest roughly fifteen feet uphill. The scene was placid, somber, largely devoid of sound or movement, as if something scrawled across an artist's canvas, depiction falling short of all those natural accents of the real. The sky was gray, dirty, its billows sagging low like water-swollen insulation in a burning house, stretched across the gulf of sky as far as human eyes could see. It groaned, the sound unfurling through the gray like granite slabs colliding somewhere out beyond the boundaries of our world.

Laj leaned against the ledge on outstretched arms, looking down along the disappearance of the diner's wall beneath the blackened water at its base. Several feet in depth, it rose to just above the bumpered edge of a concrete loading dock, merely inches now beneath the service door that led out from the back room of the diner.

"You hear that thunder, see them clouds? That's a storm coming, and when it does, we're done for if we stick around this place. It's almost at the door down there as it is, and we're pretty much out of sealant now. Tape won't hold it alone."

"How we plan on getting down there now?" asked Jesse. "Sank the ladder this morning."

"Rope?" asked Glen.

"Only rope we had was what Tony used," said Laj. "That's gone too."

Glen slowly made his way along the ledge, stopping just above the left side of the loading dock.

"Right here," he said. "Drainpipe. Old-school steel. Heavy-duty. It'll hold." He bumped it with the side of his fist, gesturing down its length. "Rope's not hard to fashion. Tear some strips of tablecloth, link them up, we'll be fine. Good enough for that short drop, at least."

Laj met him where he stood and reached out to the pipe, a paint-caked contraption roughly five inches in diameter, segmented down its length at three-foot intervals by brackets bolted to the wall of brick beneath it. The length of pipe ended several inches up above the surface of the water, so what sound they made in their descent would fail to be relayed to anything other than the open air and whatever shared it. He wrenched it with both hands. It didn't move. He stood upright and propped his hands on his hips. He ran his tongue across his lower lip, eyeing the pipe in silence.

"So, we all feel pretty good about this then?" he finally asked. "We gonna do this?"

"Good might be a bit strong of a word," said Glen. "But considering the lack of options, let's just say I feel okay."

Jesse snuffed and raked his nails across his scalp. "Heard that."

"Settled, then. Sounds like we'll be taking the pipe down." Laj pushed his hands into his pockets, laid a foot up on the ledge. "Glen, you on rope duty?"

Glen dipped his chin in agreement.

"Aight," said Laj. "There we have it, then." He scratched his chin. "Question now's how we plan on crossing that pond alive."

"And what then?" said Jesse. He turned and took in the desolation that surrounded them. "Say we get across the lot. What then? Follow the sounds? We even know what the hell they are, what direction they're coming from?"

"Best plan we've got," said Glen. "It's that or stay here. You know how that turns out."

"Shit," said Jesse, shuffling his feet.

Twenty to thirty feet out, a patch of water shivered across the center of the open plane. It moved with certain grace, and as it did, it was preceded by a minor swell that rippled out across its path like one great wrinkle smoothed across a cotton bedsheet. And every so often as it changed its course and followed its senses to potential prey, tiny whirlpools formed along its edges, spinning off behind it, where they died out in the wake.

The three men watched it cross in silence as they thought their situation over, weighing options. And as that single body crossed the center, they watched three more hunt the edges, two off to the left and one ahead, licking crevices of stone and brush the way a dog would navigate the bottom of an empty bowl at dinner's end.

"It's going to take a strong distraction," said Glen. "Something more than pebbles and dead birds. Something sizable."

"We're fresh out of bodies, pal," mumbled Jesse as he ran a thumbnail in between his two front teeth, a look of welling nausea on his face. He came down to his haunches, hanging his head. "Ain't no way this'll work. Ain't no got-damned way. Bullet to the head holds better odds than this. This is plumb insane." Jesse swung his head from side to side. "In-*sane*."

"Hey," said Laj, laying a hand on Jesse's shoulder. "There ain't no other way. It has to work, man. This is where we are now. It's the only chance we got."

Laj crossed his arms and shook his head. "Besides, we made it this far, right?"

Jesse nodded, a faithless action.

"Made it by putting all our heads together, working together, like we doing right now. We'll get out of this. One team, one fight."

Glen looked around the landscape, the fading sky above the

trees, citrus twilight starting its diffusion up across the blue-white dome.

"We need to go now, brief Lauren and Hank, get ourselves situated. Got to do it all before we lose the daylight. Place won't hold till morning." Glen clapped Jesse's shoulder, giving it a reassuring squeeze. "Besides, sounded like them folks on the radio might not be hanging around forever. We want a shot at finding them, joining up with them, this has to happen now. Come on. We got this."

CHAPTER THIRTY-FOUR

"Death march. That's all this is. Led to slaughter." Hank's words rustled up against the pane of glass, his voice a garbled whisper. "And we'll just follow right along. Pied Piper and his gang of merry fuckin' idiots, right? No questions asked. Yessir, ya big asshole. Whatever you say." He turned and threw an overblown salute toward Laj. "Shit." Hank turned back to the window.

"The decision is a team one, Hank," replied Laj. "Ain't no one person calling shots here."

"Then how's about we take a vote," said Hank, his eyes still boring through the glass. "Have ourselves a family meeting like we the goddamn Brady Bunch, see what them numbers look like firsthand?"

"Majority's already voted," said Glen. "We got two choices here. Either we leave or we stay here and die. It'll be inside this place in a matter of hours, maybe sooner. Our time is up here, Hank. Longer we stay, the worse our odds become."

"What if it's already in here, already inside one of us?"

Lauren's voice emerged like a mouse in hiding, and her statement was the elephant it had chased into the center of the room. The notion lingered like a stain, hopelessly apparent. Hank turned from the window, glaring across the room to where she sat.

"Come on out and say it, girl."

"Enough, Hank," said Glen. He shifted in his seat, not yet standing. "You need to calm yourself down."

Lauren turned her eyes away, working her fingers in her lap.

"Say it," Hank insisted. "Go on."

"She wasn't saying—" started Laj.

Hank unwrapped himself and spun his body toward the others, bolting to his feet and tilting under sudden vertigo. He blinked hard.

"Don't," snarled Hank, "tell me what she wasn't saying, *Jee-Hod*." He took one step forward, legs feeble, insecure beneath the single stride.

On the countertop, the water in the jar began to stir.

"I ain't stupid. I know how to read between the goddamn lines. I know you all done counted me out of your little escape plan, already got me pegged as sick, infected. Already made your plans to bait that shit with me while you fuckheads make off for the Promised Land." Hank swayed on his legs. "Well piss on that, you assholes. You ain't settin' *me* up. I'll keep my happy ass right here, where I'm safe and fed and sooner or later gonna be saved." His breaths were heavy and he looked to be on the verge of tears. "This ain't the first slice of shit I been dealt in life. Got myself through that, and I'll get myself through this. I'm a fuckin' survivor. I don't need shit from no one."

Laj came up to his feet, filing in between Hank and the others. "You sick all right, but we ain't leavin' nobody. We all stay together. I don't give a damn who it is. Ain't no one getting left behind."

The water thrusted, slung against the glass. Enough to bump the vessel forward on the counter. Hank's eyes landed on it, taking silent notice. Glen turned to find it leaning heavily in Hank's general direction.

"Fuck you," spat Hank, taking another step toward Laj. "You're a goddamned liar. It ain't even like it's something you can help. It's in your filthy blood."

Laj caught Hank's collar in a single fist and walked him back against the edge of the booth from which he'd come. The two men stood there in that seething moment, eye to eye, buried in the blackness of each other's hatred. All the air around them seemed to go to soup, falling thick and heavy, nearly muting out the world surrounding.

Nobody moved, nobody spoke.

Glen shifted on his feet. The heartbeat in his head was back, intense and banging in his ears. The action of the water in the jar unsettled him. His eyes stayed with it, transfixed by the action of its sprawling, wet proboscis. He opened up his mouth to speak.

Then, they heard the spatter.

They saw the liquid dribble down, hit the floor and pool there on the tiles beneath the two men's legs. Glen frowned

and looked to Jesse, back to the floor, at first uncertain whether
Hank had wet himself from fear. And then they saw Hank's
face recede in horror as his arms began to thrust, to fight the
big man's grip upon his shirt, wrenching now to free himself.
He worked to pry the fingers free, to peel away the hand that
held him like a trap. A shiver ran through Laj's body. His
torso buckled as the muscles tightened through his back, his
abdomen. Another dose of liquid fell. It smacked the floor
beneath them in a sudden rush, exploding in a single strike
across the tile.

The others shot up to their feet and backed away, stumbling
backward over stools and table corners.

"No," mumbled Lauren as she swung her head from side to
side. "No, no...not again. God, not again."

A sound emerged from Hank's clenched mouth, pushed
against the inside of his teeth, and, when he couldn't free the
snare, he opened up and screamed, thrashing for his freedom.
Laj turned sideways now, locked into a rigid post, a superim-
position on the graying light beyond the window. Daylight
glimmered through the water gushing from the sockets of his
eyes, down his face and crawling, falling to the floor, snaking
upward over boot and leg and climbing high to find Hank's
every point of entry.

"Oh, shit," groaned Jesse. "Naw, naw, naw, man. Uh uhhh."
He wrenched into reverse, slipping, stumbling to the floor.
He scuffled to his feet and blindly groped his way along the
countertop with arms outstretched behind him.

Glen grabbed Lauren, pulling her from where she stood. He

bumped her backward as she caught up to the moment, legs and arms delayed and finally finding life again, overcompensating in a series of frantic kicks and thrusts that nearly knocked them to the floor in their retreat.

Laj's body jerked and spun to face them. His limbs and torso jolted wildly, like a hand inside a glove searching for the finger holes. Hank scraped and pushed, fighting for his freedom as the liquid tendrils groped his body, found his mouth, his nose. A jet of water snapped from Laj's open lips and seized Hank's face, binding it into a liquid knot that caught the light of fading day in its refraction.

Glen faltered in his movement. He took one step back, stepping forward again as if in doubt, as if there might be something he could do to help. Lauren stood there with her mouth slung wide and weeping with a violent force. She laid her weight across her father's arm and fought to press him farther back across the room.

Hank's arms battered Laj's torso, shoving, raking at his chest and face. He gagged against the all-consuming flow that filled his airway. His limbs began to hitch, seizing as the organism occupied his every fiber, drawing muscles taut and utterly defiant as the microscopic lifeform looted every ounce of moisture from his aching, useless body.

Hank reached deep within himself, tapping into any final fumes of strength he harbored, using it to turn his face toward Glen. Bubbling to the surface, running counter to the tide extending down his throat, his final exclamation spat itself into the open, cutting through the shield of water.

"Save…her!"

Hank gagged, then opened on a sucking reflex as his throat expanded. The arm of liquid pushed its way into him double rate, bridged from Laj's face to his, twisting down into his body. Hank's right hand, slapping blindly, happened on the friendly wooden handle of the gun protruding from the back of Laj's belt.

Burning off his last reserve of strength and cognitive intent, Hank jerked the weapon free. He fought to raise the deadweight of his arm, stiffly numb and aimless like a windblown tree branch. Hank pressed the barrel to the big man's eye and squeezed the trigger.

The blast suspended time in such a way that seemed to throw those seconds into minutes. The entire right of Laj's head had disappeared beneath the path of the magnum round. The gun's delivery left a thousand steely needles screaming in the diner's air with nothing heard beyond their ceaseless pitch, even deconstruction of the window as the glass rained down in utter silence, opening wide their inner sanctum to the horrors just beyond the low point of the sill.

"Oh, God!" screamed Glen. They staggered backward, numbly slipping and stumbling toward the back room of the diner.

Hank's hands sprung wide and dropped the gun. It clattered to the floor as ropes of water drowned him where he stood, rushing through his body and back out again. The puddle at his feet began to branch out like an urchin spines, sprawling wide in search of others in a liquid grid. Hank's muscles stiffened, cinching him into a plank. He dropped and hit the floor. Laid out like a board, his flesh began to gather on his bonework like a cowhide drying in the sun.

Glen and Lauren fought the floor for traction, scrabbling on the greasy tile as Jesse helped them cross the threshold to the back room, slinging shut the slab of steel to close the route. He bumped the latch into its catch and scrambled backward, falling out across the floor. Glen eyed the half-inch crack beneath the door. He caught the scent of ice and pine and dirt that rushed the building, filled their quarters, bringing with it screams of birds that cried out like instinctual sirens, reacting to the liquid thing that moved upon its prey. The three of them fell silent, now listening to the sound of water coursing through the ruptured window, filling up their quarters like a cold bath drawn for their demise.

CHAPTER
THIRTY-FIVE

ALL THREE MOVED BACKWARD, MINDS struggling in the current of the moment, sweeping past them at a pace they weren't equipped to handle, weren't ready to accept.

They heard the steady gush of water coming through the diner's open face, the desperate groan of chairs that clawed for traction as the water swept them up and herded them across the floor. Something large and heavy hit the ground, the crash of shattered glass erupting just behind.

The jar.

They heard the water rush the shards across the floor with fragile notes of broken wind chimes. They didn't move, couldn't move, eyes locked upon the crack beneath the door.

It was with them now. Inside. It was coming, and there was nothing they could do but wait for it to seek them out. That, or try their odds against the elements outside.

"Lauren, the battery," said Glen.

She was staring at the gap, deaf with terror.

"Lauren!"

She jumped and looked at her father, head shaking in denial.

"The battery." Glen leaned forward, leveling his eyes with hers. He took her face inside his palms. "Listen to me. The battery," he repeated. "The battery, Lauren. Where did you put it?"

Tears dribbled from the corners of her eyes, pooling where Glen's hands met her cheeks. She blinked and held an arm straight out and pointed to the closet. And then she frowned and touched her face, felt its wetness, as if the brine were such a foreign thing. Hysterics claimed her as she wrenched free of his hands and clawed the salty liquid from her body with her shirt, again and again until Glen grabbed her arms and forced them to a standstill, bringing her to understand her tears were only tears and nothing more.

"Dad." She panted. "Dad?" Her eyes were wild, pleading. Glen could feel her heartbeat through her arms, jumping like a hunted rabbit.

"We're getting out of here. Now." He hushed her, trying to keep his tone on an even keel, although he felt it flinging wildly like a car without a driver. "Go get the battery."

She stared at him as if the order were too tall to fill, as if she'd been tasked with the impossibility of counting every grain of sand upon a stretch of beach. But, as her father nodded, touched her face, her hair, she calmed, coming back into the moment. She heard the rush of water in the distance. She saw

Jesse pacing at her father's rear, hands inside his hair. Lauren turned to execute the task at hand.

Glen turned around and spoke to Jesse now.

"Get up that ladder to the rooftop, scope the scene before the daylight leaves us. It won't be long. Find out where they are, see how many you can spot. Do what you have to do to move them as far away from where we're headed as you can."

Jesse gripped his head between his hands, clapping at his temples, closing on them like a vise.

"Whatever you can do," urged Glen. "We'll be up behind you. It's almost dark and we're going to be screwed if we're not out of here by then."

Jesse struck the ladder with an open hand and cursed. He struck it again and leaned his cheek against the icy metal.

"Hey," said Glen. "Come on, man. You with me?"

Jesse bobbed his head, dumping a breath, then began his climb up through the access hatch.

Glen heard the trickle at the far side of the room, closer now, clearer.

Find you.

He turned to look, seeing the water's sprawling fingers groping tile beneath the door and bleeding inward. Glen ignored the water, the words he may or may not have heard. His head was pounding. The driving pain was like a railroad spike that ventured further with each pulsing strike.

Find you.

He gathered up the length of shredded tablecloths he'd linked into a rope, triple-knotted at the points of intersection to ensure they'd not unravel halfway down the building's side. He looped them overhead and slung them low beneath his left arm like a giant sash.

Glen shifted on the floor, turning several times in manic contemplation of what came next. "All right. All right. Think. Think." He nodded, catching his breath. "Lauren, I need the battery."

She hoisted it onto the table, throwing the cables up beside it. Lauren backed herself against the farthest wall and waited, arms crossed and squirming on her chest. Glen removed a strip of tablecloth from the end of the makeshift rope and tethered both ends to the battery to form a sling. He pulled it over his head and across his chest and let the unit hang down his back. Both ends of the jumpers dangled up and over both sides of his chest from their origination at the terminals.

Lauren watched him work, staring at her father and the rig and rope that fell across his torso like some kind of insane cosplay, and in her distrust of the plan, with an unexpected wave of focused calm, she shook her head and muttered, "No, Dad. Maybe we can…maybe we can just…the rice…maybe block—"

"Lauren, it's already in here."

"But, just—"

"Lauren," he said, guiding her over to the ladder. "We're leaving. Right now."

And then the strange and inappropriate calmness passed as suddenly as it had come. She stared back at him. The realization seemed to finally land, and she saw that he was right.

The water had already joined them, its tendrils mapped across the floor and smothering every object in its path, climbing, snaking, hunting in its blindness, reaching out in hopes of finding something real, something living.

And if they didn't move, it would succeed.

Lauren took the ladder by the rails and started upward. Glen started after, trailing at her heels. The water down beneath them streaked across the floor and toward the ladder's base. Across the room, it choked the bottom of the door, pulsing through the crack with rhythmic chugs that racked the lock against its catch with every violent surge.

The water rushed the ladder's base. It whirled around the brackets, then began to climb.

"C'mon, Lauren. Go. Need to move. Fast as you can."

Lauren glanced behind her. She made a choking sound as fear rushed up to meet her throat.

"Don't do that," said Glen. "Don't look back. Keep moving. Just go. Go."

Her legs and arms moved faster, flinging wildly two rungs at a time.

Lauren shoved her body through the hatch and scrabbled out onto the rooftop, the backpack filled with dry goods dragging at her side. Glen came up just behind, hoisting up the forty pounds of battery and cables at his back, careful when he stepped out on the looser composition of the graveled rooftop. He took hold of the hatch and, before he threw it down, could hear the wet and soulless chatter of the water, echoing inside the open chamber just before the panel dropped. He stepped down on it, jamming it into the rusted frame, sealing it beneath its weight. He laid the rig down at his feet, followed by the rope, then he turned and came down to one knee, checking the laces on his boots, followed by his daughter's.

"What's our situation, Jesse?" asked Glen, wrenching down the double knots and moving to the next. "Tell me what we're working with."

Jesse paced around the borders of an imaginary space.

The temperature was falling. The darkness of the surrounding forest seemed to leach the last remains of daylight from the air, strained between the woody net of branch and brush, a murky film of twilight left behind. The lampposts flickered to life across the lot, two units mounted high on smoothed-out trunks of pines that barely cast their feeble glow across a stretch of twenty feet beneath. The details of the world beyond the jurisdiction of their yellow cones was fast dissolving by the minute.

"Hard to say." Jesse squinted, breathless in his panic. He shook his head defeatedly. "I—can't tell, man. I don't know. I ain't even gonna lie. Can't see shit out there."

"Damn it," hissed Glen. "Well give us *something*, Jesse." He stood and slung the rig around his neck and shoulder again. "Need you right now, buddy. Tell me what we've got. C'mon. This ain't the time to be flying blind," said Glen. "Need to know what we're heading into."

"Can't hardly see nothin, man," whimpered Jesse. "Honest truth. It's too damn dim, too dark. And besides, my eyesight ain't so good, 'specially at night."

Glen shoved a hand across his head. "Okay. All right." He turned on a heel, taking several steps, then turned again. "It's fine. It's gonna be fine."

"I'm sorry. But look, I don't think it's even out there, man."

"What're you talking about, it's not out there?" said Lauren. "Of course it is. It's everywhere!"

"I—I think it's all still gathered at the front right now, coming through the diner."

Glen stopped and looked up at Jesse.

Jesse spun toward Glen, the realization of his observation having struck. "I'll be damned," he said. "It thinks we're still in there. It's busy searching the diner right now. It don't even know we left. It's still inside!"

"We—we have a chance, then," said Lauren, her eyes darting from Glen to Jesse and back again. "We might actually get out of here, right? We have a chance?"

"Best chance we're going to get. We don't have much time. This is it," he said. Glen came down to a knee again and fumbled with the rope, unbinding the length with nervous hands, dropping it onto the rooftop. "This is our diversion. Only one we're bound to get." He stood and wiped his sweaty palms across his jeans, turning to look across the lot himself. "I'll head down first. When I get to the bottom, I'll wait for you, Lauren. You come on down and step off to me once you're close enough. Got it?"

Glen awaited her response. He watched her break into a set of fragile nods, then realized that she wasn't nodding at all, but shaking.

"You actually want me to jump to you?"

"Look at me," said Glen, giving Lauren's shoulder a squeeze. "We're going to be fine. We've got this. We're doing this. I'm going to catch you nice and easy, help keep the movement to a minimum when you're coming down that pipe, speed things up so you won't have to come all the way down on your own."

She closed her eyes and sucked a long, hard breath.

"We're going to move fast, understand?"

Lauren nodded, opening her eyes. "Okay."

"We have to. I'll be right there to catch you, help you ease into the water. Right there," Glen pointed. "Jesse comes down next." Glen glanced at Jesse, seeking confirmation of his understanding. "Jesse," he repeated.

The man was shifting back and forth, alternating feet as if about to void his bladder.

"Hey!"

Jesse's eyes snapped free of whatever sights or thoughts had held them captive. "What?"

"Christ, man. I need you in the moment," said Glen. "I go first, then Lauren, then you. Understand?"

Jesse nodded. He wiped a palm across his face, covertly striking out the tears that gathered just beneath his eyes, not yet fallen. "Yeah," he sniffed. "Yeah, I got it, man."

"All right." Glen turned Lauren by the shoulder, then moved the pack up on her back and adjusted the straps. "All right," he repeated, looking past the edge one final time. "Keep it high, keep it dry. We don't want to get any of this wet. It's all we have."

The final rays of twilight came down through the trees and stained the misty air, coloring it the orange-gray tinge of spaghetti dish suds, as if the pond that stretched across the lot were but a kitchen sink, and they the ants along its rim attempting passage. Glen adjusted the rig that dangled at the middle of his back and scoped the range of water one last time in search of movement.

The mist seemed thinner now, and through the sheerness of its cover he could see no signs of life. The water was so still its physicality appeared more solid than liquid, as if one could merely step across its pristine surface to the other side. But Glen knew its stillness only proved more dangerous, and would only serve to amplify their presence when they stepped into its midst, with every movement broadcast like a spider's web disturbed.

Glen wrapped the rag rope's end around the drainpipe's upper bend, just above the bracket plunging deep into the brick by two large lag bolts. When he'd knotted it sufficiently, he pulled against it, drawing out the sections one at a time to double down on every knotted segment in advance of their descent. He dropped it down the building's side a few feet at a time, careful not to make the same mistake that Tony had in his misjudgment of its length. But as he neared its end he saw that it was safe, the length of rope suspended nearly two feet up above the water's touch. Glen took a long and leveling breath and turned to face his daughter, repeating his instructions.

"I go first, then wait for you in the shallows of the loading dock. When you're close enough, shove yourself off to me, I'll talk you through it then, gently bringing you down."

Lauren's breaths came fast. Too fast. She closed her eyes.

"Take it easy, take your time."

She opened her eyes, nodding again, the motion somewhat slower now, falling into sync with her father's agreeable lead. Her words seeped from her throat. "Be careful, Daddy."

Glen kissed her forehead. He pressed his brow to hers and closed his eyes. He then stepped back and lifted several feet of rope. He sat down on the building's ledge, straddling it so that his right leg dangled down along the length of pipe.

"We got this," said Glen. "We've been through worse already. We're gonna make it."

Lauren drew a breath, attempting a smile that seemed to short out well before it started.

Glen fit his toe into an edge of bracket and laid his weight against the knotted string of rags that ran down through his hands and swept the air above the water like a tail.

The cloth snapped taut. Glen hung there for a moment as he felt for slippage. A hard breeze touched his left. The seeming absence of the blood within him, throttled out by stress, gave its bite a helping hand.

For the moment it was holding, and while it remained agreeable, he went ahead and started down the pipe. The battery clapped against his back with every move, and a corner of the cube repeatedly attacked the meaty space between his ribs. He winced and stayed the course, careful where he placed his feet upon the wall and downspout out of fear of knocking loose some stray debris, announcing his approach.

Reaching the final bracket, Glen paused, then pushed into its edge and shoved his body right and over to the loading dock. He lowered his booted toe into the two-inch depth of water laid across the concrete dock until his entire foot had settled flat. He stopped there for what seemed an endless moment, muscles tight and burning hot from strain. When his balance was secured, he pulled his left foot from its station, bringing it down into the water just beside the other. The slowness of the movement was excruciating in the most literal sense of the expression, and his entire body screamed in silence as it tightened in an act of reinforcement. He stabilized himself before he surrendered the makeshift rope and let it realign itself along the downspout.

Glen looked up at Lauren's face, peering down across the ledge. He gave her a nod, signaling with his hand.

Lauren hesitated, working her hands against her chest, knotting and unfurling.

"Come on," he mouthed, gesturing again.

She drew a fractured breath and closed her eyes, a long and lingering blink. Lauren sat down on the ledge and lifted one leg over. She pulled the rope into her lap and wrapped it twice around her right wrist. A scab of paint jumped from the pipe and fluttered downward.

Glen's eyes followed its descent. He watched it hit the water, sink beneath the surface, then spin away without a trace. His breath went into remission as he waited. The surrounding body held its flawless sheen beneath the dying light. He exhaled, then reeled her downward with another gesture of his hand.

Jesse stood beside her. His face was a conspicuous mask of false bravado, poorly fitted over one of utter terror just beneath it as he helped Lauren cross the edge. He gripped her wrists until she'd found her footing on the pipe, then let her go and held his breath as Lauren's head sank down below the ledge.

Her arms were trembling from the strain of her position, and in short time her upper body strength had drained away and left her dangling outright on the rope. Her feet, her legs, attacked the metal pipe, notes dully sung with every strike, prompting Glen to clench his teeth and hush her from his post below. He motioned to her, pumping his palm upright against the open air as if to somehow bring her to a standstill with the powers of his mind. Glen turned and looked about, still spotting zero signs of movement on the water from his vantage point. He looked back up at Jesse, who shook his head in negative report.

Despite the cold that fell across them, beads of sweat were gathering on Glen's brow, stinging where they touched some secret cut he'd not yet come to know until that moment. He felt beneath his sternum such a bump and twist that made him tighten up to thwart the ruckus of his heart, to still the birth of ripples on the water he was sure were soon to follow.

Glen's mind was racing now. He couldn't shake the visions roiling to the surface, reminding him of what existed somewhere in the water at his feet, to what his child would also be exposed in just a moment, and all the secret doubts that circled in his mind surrounding just how little faith he had in the efficacy of their makeshift weapon in that vast expanse of water. Within the diner, the threat was localized to that small space, a minor congregation of the microscopic organism, wiped out with ease. But out here, it would be a different story. The quantity of water and the population of the threat within were relatively boundless. What would be killed off or thwarted by the shock would no doubt be overrun in droves to follow, all others rushing in to take their prey.

Lauren dangled several feet from termination of the rope, stilled there at the final bracket. Glen braced his shoulder at the building's edge and with an outstretched hand he beckoned to her, hanging there not three feet out, her face the color of the ashen sky that covered them above, its lifeless tone still backlit by the sloping grade of twilight.

"That's it," whispered Glen. "Now ease yourself this way. Do it easy, take your time, pass me your foot, your leg."

"Don't let go," she pleaded. "Please." The words came dry and frightened, catching in her throat like rusted hinges. "I'll fall."

"I'm not letting go. Not going anywhere. I've got you. Come on. I've got you, sweetheart." Glen's shoulder shifted on the brick, scrubbing loose small crumbs of mortar. He leaned in her direction just the slightest bit, trying not to move the water at his feet as Lauren's weight came down against his palms. The backpack shifted, slipping several inches down her arm. Her body trembled as she tilted left again, fighting to counter its descent. Glen's hands rocked beneath her foot. He firmed his grip and nodded. "Go on, I've got you."

She clenched her eyes. Chills stirred to life and crawled across her outstretched limbs like baby spiders. Lauren removed her right hand from the rope and leaned for Glen, stretching, reaching for his neck. And then she let go altogether, falling forward into his chest and arms and for a moment they just stood there, risking not a single movement as they held their breaths, stilted on the water as a single mass. Glen looked down and caught the faintest glimpse of ripples fleeing from his soles. A wicked fear rose up and dangled off the backside of his tongue, nearly gagging him. Several feet from their origination, the ripples smoothed and disappeared completely. He closed his eyes and let the tension out. He breathed again, feeling the terror slide back down his throat.

"Okay," he whispered. "Okay. Time to step down."

"Dad." She shuddered, the word dissolving like a ghost that passed between them. "Not yet. Just give me a—"

"I can't hold you here, Lauren. I'm going have to set you down, and I need you to hold on to my shoulders, my neck, okay? Hold on tight, take your time."

Lauren made a quiet sound.

"You got the bag?"

"Yeah."

"Both hands," he whispered. "Both of them. Tight. Do not let go until I tell you to."

She did as she was told, fingers hooked into his deltoids like the talons of a hawk. Her nails dug through the fabric into flesh, and Glen was certain she was drawing blood yet didn't say a word. He'd take her grip as tight as she could give it.

"Now bring your right foot down." His voice shuddered like a leaf, all breath and strain beneath her weight. "Slowly."

Again, she did as she was told.

"Slowly." Glen closed his eyes, fighting the exhaustion in his muscles. He tried his best to reign the tremors in.

Her toe made contact with the water with such subtlety that its surface puckered up to meet the rubber of her boots. The remainder of her foot descended, laid against the concrete slab below.

The water rested undisturbed.

"Okay, good. Perfect," whispered Glen. "The left now. Go on. Same thing. Keep your hands on me."

Lauren carried out the action, conducting efforts with the same precision as the last.

"Okay. Now, carefully, slowly," whispered Glen. "Come next to me, one foot at a time. Easy moves. Slow, careful steps, straight up, straight down. Lift and lower, careful not to sweep the water. Take your time."

Slowly, Lauren pulled her feet from where they lay. She moved with all the slow precision of a hunting egret tracking fish among her feet, eyes locked onto the glossy surface down below. One foot at a time, she relocated parallel to her father's left, now facing outward toward the downspout. Glen and Lauren turned their eyes back up the wall to Jesse, now straddling the ledge and pulling free beyond its lip to drop into his first steps of descent.

Glen stood and nodded as he watched the man step down along the stretch of pipe. He spoke silent words of reassurance to himself, words that only he could hear, twitching as he moved his head in gestures of encouragement. He kept his eyes on every movement Jesse made, pursuing every grasp of hand, step of foot along the way.

"That's it, Jesse. You got it, man," whispered Glen. "Step at a time. That's it. Keep it coming."

Jesse cut a glance across his right, down, then over toward the man and girl who watched him. He forced a smile and took another step, courage building as his movements came more quickly, more steadfast in his descent.

Glen smiled. "You got it."

And then the rope broke free.

CHAPTER
THIRTY-SIX

Jesse struck the edge of the loading dock and plunged beneath the water's surface. The crack of ribs was audible. The numbing cold delayed the pain enough to let the fear take hold and drive him upright with a sucking breath. The breath transitioned to an agonizing wail as Jesse's lungs inflated underneath the shattered cage of bone, prying them outward. The cry cut out across the falling night, exchanged among the shadowed regiment of trees along the range of hills.

Glen and Lauren stood in horror as they watched the swell from Jesse's impact lift and move across the water, and then another when he surfaced from the blackness, thrashing in the icy depths for traction. Jesse looked around the lot, fighting the sudden urge to vomit from the violent cocktail coursing through his system, equal parts of pain and terror. He saw no signs of life, but it would be there soon enough, slipping through the mist to greet them.

Their time was up.

"In the water!" yelled Glen. He turned to Lauren. "Now!"

Lauren froze and eyed her father like he'd lost his mind. She pulled the pack up high upon her back and drew the straps up in her fists.

"Get in the water!" Glen grabbed her by the arm and snatched her from the edge into the depths beside him. The water wrapped its jaws around them, sinking its icy teeth into their muscles. It seemed to snatch their souls out through their legs, instantaneously numbed and firmed with splints of muscle gripping bone. Glen pulled Jesse upright by the arm and grabbed his sputtering face between his hands, forcing his eyes to meet his own, to understand the urgency of what he had to say.

"Move!"

The three set off, churning their way across the lot.

Glen helped Jesse fight his way through stomach-high water as the agony of every breath attacked his torso with expansion and contraction of his lungs. Jesse's breath emerged in shallow chops that dashed the air with steam. His vision melted down beneath a flood of tears that rushed to meet the open air, and he whimpered fiercely as he moved.

"Come on, buddy." Glen grunted beneath the weight of Jesse's outstretched arm. "Getting out of here now. Come on. I know, I know. Push through it. Save the pain for later."

Lauren moved out front, swiveling back to watch the men behind her. They were trudging through the pond at half speed now as Jesse fought a losing battle with the pain that filled his body, his already shorted mind.

Something seemed to move out behind them, out beyond the spill of gray.

Lauren squinted, straining through the static haze of falling night. That was when she saw the small swell of water moving toward them through the mist, the rippled body of the liquid trailing out behind it like a fleet of chills.

"Oh my God. Dad."

Glen turned, then Jesse, choking on the pain. They saw the shape approach, wide and deep, closing in at twice their speed some forty feet behind, the closest edge of rocky shore another seventy feet ahead.

"Shit. Come on, man," Glen was virtually dragging Jesse now, and the wounded man blew threads of froth across his lips. It dangled like a fringe of Christmas tinsel, and a sound like angry sirens squalled from in between the rigid narrows of his throat. His body plowed the water where his feet refused to reach. And where they did he shuffled over asphalt like a toddler learning how to stay upright on unlearned legs, soft as bread. The ruins of his ribs collapsed and shifted over one another at the prompt of every step, every agonizing breath.

Lauren slowed her stride and reached for Jesse's other arm.

"Keep moving!" snapped Glen. He struck his arm across the air between them, waving Lauren onward. "Don't slow down. No matter what, you keep moving. We're coming."

The mass that moved behind them stayed its course, plowing toward them at a steady clip. Out to their left, more movement captured their attention as something passed among the brush and reeds that sprung up from the limestone outcrop, spilling out between the cracks and flowing down into the larger body. Another joined it at its side, and together as a single living unit, it set out toward them, even closer than the inbound body at their rear.

Lauren felt a tickle at her hand and whipped her arm away, throwing free a beetle that had found its refuge from the water. Beneath collapsing nerves, the tears began to come again. Lauren spun in place and ran her fingers through her hair.

"Dad, it's all around us!" She moved backward as she watched the thing close in behind the men, then turned to catch the one that came in from the side. "They're coming!"

Out beyond the shape, the building was no longer visible, devoured whole beneath the fog and night that swarmed them. Their only means of sight now rested in the fragile yellow spill from lamps that watched them with disinterest from above.

Jesse slowed his stride, then stopped completely. Glen tugged his arm, then yanked him forward several feet. Jesse cried out at the crushing pain that chewed the right side of his back. He grabbed Glen's hand and threw it away, lashing him forward with a burst of voice and pain, mined from someplace deep, almost inhuman.

"Leave me!"

Saliva ruptured from his mouth, dangling from his lips, tinged with blood.

Glen stared back, then looked past the man and saw the massive sheet of living death that skated toward them through the water.

"Y'all ain't gonna make it. Not with me you ain't." Jesse

folded over, dropping a wad of bloody spit down to the water on a ruby thread. "Go. Just go. You gotta move."

"Jesse, cut the shit." Glen reached for his arm again and Jesse fell away two steps, wrenching it out of reach—an agonizing move that made him cry out loud, staggering backward yet another step.

"Go, goddammit!" He let out a lingering howl, fighting to right himself, locked forward into a fetal posture from the pain. Jesse turned away and started back the way they'd come. "Just promise me." He paused for another agonizing breath. "You tell my baby girl her daddy did some good here."

Glen stared after him. He knew the man was right. They wouldn't make it with him. He felt a rush of shame rise up beneath that revelation, but he knew that it was true.

Lauren stood behind her father, her hands wrapped in the excess fabric of his sleeves like handles. She pulled him onward. "Dad," she pleaded.

"You tell her that, Glen," repeated Jesse, walking farther out into the haze. "Now go before you fuck this up and it was all for nothing. Go, you stupid bastard! Go!"

Glen was nodding, backing through the water with a look of disbelief, struggling to pull his eyes from Jesse. Finally, he turned and grabbed Lauren by the hand. "Come on. Fast. Move!"

They'd only made it fifteen feet or so before they heard it strike, taking Jesse where he stood. Glen cast a final look back at the man who'd offered up his life for theirs. He saw the water lashing up across the top of Jesse's head, extending down his back like straps of liquid muscle. The ropes snapped taut, drawing his head back on his neck completely. The move came fast and violent, the breaking of his spine a final snap that clapped across the open void. Jesse dropped down to his knees, then fell forward on his face, completely disappearing underneath the raging water.

"Keep going," urged Glen. "Keep moving. Don't look back. Don't look. Just go. Go, go, go."

"Oh God," whimpered Lauren. "It got him. It's right behind us, isn't it? Where is it now?" The girl plowed forward, thrashing through the water, what was previously at the low point of her chest now at her waist in gradual ascension of the land beneath. "Dad?"

Glen didn't answer, turning once again for confirmation. The water billowed where the man had fallen, busied with the plunder of his moisture. The independent clusters crossed each other as they feasted, turning the desiccated casing down below, dueling over last remains.

"They're still back there. They're busy," Glen pushed onward. His muscles burned and felt as if they'd gone to liquid with the water all around them. "I haven't moved yet." Between the cold and panic, his voice felt threadbare under stress, thin and weak.

The collision of the currents lashed and scored the surface of the water, still well enough behind, though on Glen's second glance it made him falter in his path. The water once again was calm beneath the milky sheath, and the chaos rippling out across the surface now was gone. All was smooth and still beneath the night and distant glow of lamplights overhead.

The only movement was the slightest breeze that came in from the trees and rushed the mist across the water. In the void between the roving mats of gray, a placid surface showed itself like some horrible game of peek-a-boo, moving only with the slightest shimmer in the touch of mountain air.

But then Glen saw the range of water shiver, set in motion, cutting perpendicular to influence of the crossing wind. It quickly picked up speed enough to drive the smallest swell out front and aimed itself directly for them. With a reborn sense of horror, they watched the mass divide three ways, narrow strips that peeled off the parent body, slithering out across the water. The liquid things had picked up speed in their reduction, thin and slick like eels, independent streams, self-contained and gliding toward Glen and Lauren now at double rate. Threads of yellow caught their movement from the sodium bulbs above, the glance of light passed out along their lengths and jolting outward from their borders like some kind of spectral heat.

"They're coming again." Glen grabbed Lauren's arm and pulled her forward. "Everything you've got. Move! Go!"

From the shoreline, the thinnest notes of water shaped themselves to form two words.

Over here.

Glen continued, unsure if the words were only in his head. The headaches had returned, and the thump of blood began to fill his ears again.

Lauren turned, slowing down. She looked toward the shore, to Glen, then back again, confused.

"Did you hear—"

"Don't stop, Lauren! Keep going! It's just a decoy! A distraction! Don't stop! Keep on moving!"

Over here.

Lauren's breaths were short, halved by the tears and fear that robbed her lungs, and she stumbled forward on legs she now could hardly feel, the shoreline closer yet before them. She slipped and fell beneath the surface, pulling down the backpack when she did. She came up blind and frantic, bleeding from her knee, hoisted to her feet by Glen. Lauren lunged across the underwater asphalt, making up for lost time with long and taxing strides. She forced her eyes ahead, keeping them from drifting back to Jesse, or the thing that used to be him. Beneath the water, a trail of blood stretched out behind them like a line of chum, the things behind them driven to a frenzy as they crossed it, picking up their speed.

"Push through it, Lauren!" Glen gasped. "We're almost there! We're going to make it. We will. I can see it. At least we know where it is. We can see it. We know we're ahead of it. Just go. Go."

It was then a chill broke out across the open gulf beyond the clouds above, disgruntled murmurs rolling out across the black expanse, enough to shake the ground beneath their feet, dusting the air with ozone.

The first few raindrops met their open flesh, and all around the water went to static as the clouds split wide and sent their bounty ripping toward the world below.

CHAPTER
THIRTY-SEVEN

Twenty feet ahead, higher ground awaited. Glen and Lauren were running now. Their legs were blind and dumb beneath the water, fumbling over potholes and debris that found their feet with every other step, their muscles burning hot and cold at once.

The things were speeding toward their backsides now, rubbed out beneath the stippling rain, swept from recognition. Glen had now abandoned any efforts toward the futile glances to their rear, exchanged with frantic lunges toward the safety of the shoreline just ahead.

"Come on, girl! Come on!"

Glen heaved Lauren back up to her feet, having caught them on the edge of something down below. Then he began to struggle on his own, toppling forward just the same. He slammed his shin against a wedge of granite. They'd met a bed of rocks beneath the water, and though the depths had lessened, the terrain began to test them in a different way, every step a blind and vicious gamble in their ascension toward the open earth ahead.

Thunder cracked the sky above, its sound a cattle prod against the night.

But as it sounded off again and again, they came to realize that it wasn't thunder, but the same horrific sound they'd heard so many times over the preceding days. Somewhere out beyond the forest, the hills ahead, something sharp and angry lashed out in the darkness, crawling toward them through the open sky.

The shore was ten feet out now, and Glen urged Lauren up ahead of him where she'd be there in his sights, to where he'd be the first in line if something hit them from behind, taking them in the chaos of the night that thrashed around them.

Five feet out now.

They slipped and fumbled forward through the rain and darkness, and at one point Glen had sunk the battery beneath the water, feeling its electric teeth plunge into his side before he hauled it up again, brushing the pain away. Lauren climbed onto the rocky exposure of the shoreline, scrambling up and over, then paused to wait for Glen.

"Keep going! Go!" He lashed his arm across the air. "Go!"

She turned and moved, tumbling on her hands and knees, climbing higher up the multilevel crags of stone that seemed to bare their teeth at her approach.

Glen had stepped up to the first rock, pushing his foot against it when he felt the tendrils bind his other leg, snatching it down between the blades of limestone. It seized his foot and calf, and when it did, he didn't waste a moment's thought. He gripped the cable's ends, clenched firmly in his fists.

The jolt ignited everything within him, and all surrounding night became alive and bright.

Vivid, numb, then painful.

He released his hold and through the mental haze he stumbled forward, letting his head spin to a halt. He felt the freedom of his leg now as the pressure vanished and the hold dissolved into the water. He moved his leg, pulling it from the depths. And then the other, again, again. He clamored up onto the rocks and hauled his weight across their surface to the soil, gripping maple saplings springing from the turf like helping hands. He dragged himself along the ground on newborn limbs, virtually boneless in that moment, the memory of the shock still ringing through exhausted muscles like some masochistic drug. His body was a sack of lead, and he crawled on all fours, away from the water down below, hearing now his daughter's screaming as she groped his arms and back with outstretched hands, inspecting him for safety.

"I'm fine. Go. Keep going," he slurred. He reached his hand up to her arm and squeezed, assuring her that he was fine, then slipped across the rocks, shaking free the forms that hummed and throbbed behind his eyes. Glen pulled himself upright and leaned into the body of a nearby pine.

Lauren tugged him forward, onward to the softer ground that started at the edge of thinning trees, and brought him up across a heavy mat of pine and leaves that dressed the ground beneath them.

They stepped again, and again, until the pond became a puddle far beneath them. They moved till they were well beneath the deeper canopy of largely naked trunks and limbs that offered them some slight reprieve from where they'd come, and hope for where they now were headed.

———

Despite the limitations of the water's touch, having somehow kept dry certain regions of their upper bodies in their journey, the rain had finished off the task in little time. It soaked them through to maximize the icy mountain night around them, much as gasoline excites the flames. Their bodies shook with all the fury of a useless furnace, and the two had bound themselves to one another as they journeyed farther up the mountain, through the blinding ink of wooded desolation. The ground was firmer now, drier than below despite the driving rain.

Amid the rain and wind the forest countered back, hushing the sky as if to pacify the bellows rolling out beyond the layer of soot that lined the low-slung ceiling. It wasn't long before the sky fell quiet and the hiss of rain died off to leave behind the lonesome tick of water as the trees wept in the aftermath.

They moved among the trees and underbrush, Lauren in a seeming state of endless panic, the thrum and strike of water all around like taunting whispers of an enemy that stalked them in the darkness, somewhere out of sight. Glen pulled her closer to his side. Her quaking body thrashed against the cold beneath his arm.

"Try to relax. We're okay," he said. "If it were here, around us, it would've already taken us. We're safe right now."

She didn't speak. He heard the spongy breaths beside him as they staggered through the darkness, and though he wasn't sure if they were born of tears or cold, he also didn't ask. He didn't blame her. It was nothing he was fit to judge or try and fix. He was scared, as well. And truth be told, had she not been walking next to him, he'd have likely broken down completely long before this point.

Glen and Lauren finally stopped, inspecting their surroundings as best they could inside such utter blackness. The forest seemed to cancel out the world around them, dialing it down to only several notes that played on loop: taps of water, snapping twigs beneath their feet, the cross of wind between the last remaining leaves.

They reached down and ran their hands along the earth. It was firm enough to rest, though wet, and there wasn't any sign of water at their ears, save for the recession of the constant tick of drops that fled the limbs and leaves around them as their cargo tapered off. They decided they should stay till morning, gain their strength, and share what warmth they had with one another while they could.

They made their way inside a nearby copse of oaks, seeking shelter from the wind and cold between the huddle of their massive trunks. They formed a wall of sorts, great enough to cut the wind and form a pocket of protection. It offered some degree of refuge from the Appalachian night, the driving October cold that flayed their bodies and forced their heads to bow, their minds to pray for day.

CHAPTER THIRTY-EIGHT

DAWN CAME FAST AND INCONSIDERATE. Glen's eyes winked open, still half steeped in sleep and night that somehow seemed to come and go in seconds more than hours, and his mind laid down and struggled with the speed at which the darkness had unnaturally moved to day.

Glen had dreamt of duneless skies again that night.

Of utter, helpless loss. Nothing but the endless swells and valleys all around as Claire had drifted farther out to sea. He dreamt of Lauren's hold, of Claire's, of salted air and screaming gulls and loss of hope with the disappearance of the shoreline, knowing that they'd ventured too far out for him to save both his daughter and his wife.

The disappearance of the dunes.

That single image. One nightmarish snapshot seared into his mind, standing representative of all the loss he suffered then and now. And that night the feeling somehow was the dream, the visuals of the memory merely fuzzy accents falling out into the background. The moment that he'd known for sure the total of his family wouldn't make it out alive.

Glen moved up on his elbows, blinking free the devastation of his sleep. He turned and witnessed Lauren on the forest floor beside him, still asleep and wadded tight against his side. Glen rose to his feet and stretched. He looked out across the mountainside, most wetness of preceding night already wicked and gone. The ground was split with dehydration fissures sprawling out like micro-canyons, the scattered leaves and needles only mildly damp and trees that birthed them dry and brittle up above.

All leaves and needles by and large had been discarded from the trees, the last of them devoured overnight. The desiccated towers thrust and scratched the blue sky overhead like starving hands. Their creaking motion chittered out across the forest, swaying on the wind that pulled and pushed and racked their ancient bones together in the morning light. It seemed as if some plug had been removed deep down beneath the sprawling network of their roots, leaving them to starve to death.

Glen knelt and rubbed his daughter's arm, prompting her to shift and mumble something to herself before her eyes sprung open and her arms shot out across the ground.

"Easy. Hey, we're fine," said Glen, his words delivered on a low and soothing frequency. "It's morning. We're okay."

Lauren pushed herself upright and looked around, leaves and needles dropping from her body, dangling from her hair.

"This place is pretty dry. More than it should be,

considering the rain we had last night," said Glen, looking over their surroundings as he spoke. He grabbed a wad of detritus and crushed it in his palm, letting bits of leaves and dirt slip in between his fingers, sprinkle to the ground. "A safer place, at least for now."

She swept the bits of forest from her arms, her chest. "Was it here? With us?"

Glen shook his head. "No telling. Left to guess, the water drained down low among the roots, went downslope toward lower ground. Plants, trees were probably mostly dead already. Thinking it's already finished here, hopefully won't be coming back." He knocked his hands against his legs, sweeping fragments from his palms. "Likely came through well before we showed, probably days ago. At least back when we first noticed their foliage had dropped so soon on our drive here." He looked around again, shaking his head. "Besides, if it were here with us at any point, we wouldn't be talking right now."

"I'm hungry. And cold." She worked her hands along her arms, bunching the fabric in her palms, damp and frigid. She stood and placed herself beneath a patch of sunlight spilling through the treetops.

"I know," said Glen. "Got some crackers in your bag. Go ahead and have some. I'll hold out. Far's the cold goes, the day will warm us as the temps come up a bit and we get moving again. We'll dry the rest of the way out then." Glen tugged loose the filthy bandage on his hand, the burn beneath a blackened patch of scab with blushing borders, though infection hadn't taken hold. He flexed his palm and grunted on a breath, and in the daylight also noted welts across the underside of both hands' fingers where the shock the night before had branded him.

"Dad," said Lauren, wincing. She stooped and took his hand in hers. "The battery?"

"It's okay." Glen nodded. "It's just a surface burn. Besides, it worked. Most important part." He pulled his hand away and wrapped it up again beneath the strip of cloth. "We should go now."

"Do we even know where we're going at this point?" asked Lauren, still raking free debris that nested in her hair, picking out the knots of bark that hung against her face. She bent and knocked her legs and jacket clean, coming up again with hands that worked against themselves. They were shaking, as was her voice, driven from her body, thin and fractured.

Glen didn't answer right away. He knelt down on his knees and feet and rummaged through the pack of dry goods, tossing out what had been ruined by the water. Fortunately, damage had been scant.

"Gonna do like the lady of the radio told us. Follow the sounds. Far's I can tell, they're coming from ahead, last we heard. And long as we're moving, we're heading up, never down." He threw a nod up the mountain where the dying foliage at their level offered greater visibility than average. The earth climbed through the thinned-out fauna till it disappeared inside a gray-white smear of far-off trunks, lined up like a distant beam of cigarette ash.

And somewhere out beyond that blur of dying forest, the

sound emerged again. It crawled through the space around them like some kind of cosmic spell, rolling toward and past, crackling like electric mortars on the wind.

CHAPTER THIRTY-NINE

THE MOUNTAINSIDE GREW STEEPER AS they climbed, the stony turf increasingly contorted such that on occasion they'd be forced to double back to seek out routes less treacherous. And as they climbed, the air took on a harder edge than what they'd felt at lower altitudes. Not so much colder, as the temperature had risen with the day, and their clothing now had mostly dried beneath the passing shots of sunlight winking down between the trees. It was a dry, serrated chill, without moisture. As if it somehow had been wicked from air as well as ground, the bounty carried off to someplace far away from where they were.

They'd been walking several hours when the smell had found them. A rancid odor, starting light at first, no doubt tamed by cold and thinned by wind, but as they closed in on the source, it seemed to stain the air around them, fixing itself inside their airways. And when the sound of rushing water joined its side, they made their way with greater caution, mindful of the moisture of the ground beneath their feet and signs of water run astray. Another twenty minutes later, the subtle lap of water had matured to a violent rush. The sound had grown to fill the air so much their very voices nearly drowned beneath it, and they'd pulled their shirts above their noses in a move to cut the acrid scent that wafted through the forest.

It was the odor of neglected death. One that should have moved them out along their way, as far as they could grow the void between them and the odor's source. But in a place where death resided, they might find life nearby, as well. Others like them, taking shelter, seeking help. The others that had led them out here, following the constant sounds.

Glen gestured toward an incline running upward roughly twenty feet. They made their way along its edge, carefully stepping over fallen logs and half-composted banks of leaves until they found their footing on a ledge of rock that jutted out and upward like a broken spine of something huge and ancient.

The climb came easily, stones laid out like steps along the route, but the mounting smell and rush of water just beyond the peak had slowed their stride, and every move was made as if a dare completed. They stepped, then listened, testing earth and rock beneath their feet with every upward push, the battery a biting thing that hacked Glen's back beneath its swinging edge, no doubt drawing blood by now. Lauren opened up her mouth to speak, but Glen signaled her to hush as both approached the ridge's peak, the call of water at full force now, as was the stench of death that rose to greet them.

"Keep quiet right now," whispered Glen, leaning close to Lauren's ear. "We don't know what we're coming up on here. Stay beneath the ridge, keep our scent back on the wind as much as possible."

Lauren nodded, mirroring the movement of her father, crouching low against the leaves as both came up and over. There, they laid out flat and stared in ruthless awe, a horrid fascination with the scene beyond.

What had likely started as a subtle stream had swollen up behind a wall of wildlife: deer, rabbits, squirrels, birds, foxes, raccoons, fish.

Humans.

From the middle of the dam a set of human legs kicked in the current. To their right an arm protruded from the heap and waved its salutations, the movement of the river bringing life to death within its flow. The carcasses were stacked up like an open burial mound, the pool of water behind the rotting dam a depth of ten to fifteen feet and spilling overhead to rush downhill and gouge its path across the forest floor. Flies swarmed above the corpses like a shadow brought to life. The smell was unbearable, and Glen and Lauren fought to still their turning stomachs as they slithered back and down behind the ridge.

"What happened?" Lauren leaked the question through the cotton of her jacket, nothing but the liquid of her eyes exposed. "So many animals. And the people. Why are they like that? How'd they all get there, that one spot?" She closed her eyes, sliding down to further shield herself from the odor spilling down from overhead. "Where'd they all come from? Somewhere upstream? Maybe there are others. Maybe we should—"

Glen shuffled down beside her, shaking his head, holding a finger to his lips. "I don't know," he whispered. "Maybe they came for water, were taken then. Washed downstream, maybe dragged downstream for all we know, dammed it up." Glen turned to hide his nausea, blowing a breath beneath the fabric shield. "And all that water coming down from the highlands added to the river, grew it even more."

He turned and squatted on the rocks, holding out his hand, bracing himself. "Could be right about others being upstream." Glen turned over, stretching flat and resting for a moment, weighing options in his mind. Finally, he shook his head, making a subtle noise of disagreement. "Too dangerous so close to the water, though. We need to keep a safer distance. Not worth the risk. Gonna follow the sounds. Betting that's where those folks washed down from. Others out there, to be sure." Glen sat up, repositioning the strap across chest, moving the battery behind him once again. "Come on. We don't want to stay up here. Let's keep moving."

CHAPTER FORTY

By the time the evening rolled around again, they'd moved continuously in the general direction of the electric bursts that hit the sky, and the source seemed closer now, yet all around them, with some still sounding off across the mountains far away. The surges ruled the void above and woods around, and Glen began to feel as if they may be in his head alone despite the fact that Lauren heard them too, conditions of some shared delusion.

"Maybe we shouldn't be heading toward that sound. Maybe we don't want to know what's going on out there. What if it's dangerous?"

"It's all we've got. It's where we were told to go. I know you're scared, Lauren."

"You're not?"

"I didn't say that. Of course I am."

"Then why are we going closer to those sounds, Dad? Let's

go our own way, someplace far away from whatever's making that awful noise." Lauren slowed her steps a bit, hoping he would do the same. "We don't have to go this way."

"What other way is there, Lauren?" said Glen. "That lady on the radio—"

"What if it's a trick?"

"Lauren," said Glen. "What motive would she have?"

"I don't know," she said helplessly. "Maybe—maybe they don't want us here. Maybe, for some reason, they want to make sure—"

"Our rations aren't much, and we're without shelter." He pulled her close and wrapped an arm around her. "That sound means there are others out there. That's all we know. Maybe someone who can help. Someone who could take us in. Let's give trust a shot, hope that lady was right."

Lauren hung her head and kicked the leaves beneath her feet. She didn't speak.

"I'm not going to let anything happen to you, Lauren." He leaned down, an attempt to catch her eyes. "Hear me? Not anything."

"Things happen, Dad. Things beyond our control," said Lauren. She leaned down and swept a stick up from the ground, slashed it through a mound of grass. "And sometimes there are choices, Dad. Ones we don't know we'll have to make, don't think we'll ever have to make, but then they're there. All of a sudden, things happen. They just do."

"What's that mean?"

Lauren shook her head and tugged the pack across her

shoulder. She swiped the stick across the ground before her, striking wilted knots of vegetation at her feet.

"No, stop. Stop." Glen stopped walking, turning her toward him. She flung the stick into the trees. "Hey, come on. Talk to me." He shifted the sling across his back, working the battery into a different stance. "I'm listening."

Lauren turned to face him, sweeping a lock of hair behind her ear. She looked into her father's eyes. "You had to make a choice once. A choice I'm sure you didn't want to make. Didn't plan on making at the time."

"Lauren," said Glen, "is this about what happened back—"

"At the beach," said Lauren. "That day. With Mom."

Glen shook his head. "No, sweetheart. We already talked about this earlier. I already told you it—"

"Was a choice," she finished.

Glen released a breath and clipped his hands against his waist, trying to find another point of focus somewhere in the forest's depths. For the first time in a long while, somewhere far away, he heard notes of birdsong threading through the trees. A hopeful sound.

"It was. It was a choice, yeah," said Glen. He cleared his throat, dropped his face. "I had to make a choice."

"So, that's all I'm saying, Dad. Just, you never know. You can't make promises, because you never know until the time is there in front of you. Until you're faced with something that you weren't prepared to face."

Glen didn't speak. He only breathed, listened. Tony's words crossed through his mind.

Power of the ear, my friend. Strength in listening, understanding. Don't underestimate the power of the simplest things.

"I'm not angry, Dad. I understand. I do. Maybe not so much before, but I do now. You couldn't help what happened and you did the best you could. Just like now. You're doing the best you can. It's all any of us can ever do."

Glen reached out and smoothed her hair, wiping a scuff of dirt from underneath her chin. "You know how much I love you?"

She smiled. "Love you too, Dad."

"I mean it," he said. "You're so grown now. So mature. When did that even happen? I feel like these past six years have been a blur. Where've I been, Lauren?" He shook his head and clipped his face between his thumb and forefinger, taking in a breath.

She tilted her head, smiled. "You've been here, Dad. In your own way, but you've been here."

"Why can't I remember all these years? It's all just been some comatose blur. Like the world just fast-forwarded us to now, this moment. Like I'm just now seeing you for the first time these past few days. This new you."

Lauren laughed. It was a good sound. It made him laugh too.

"You're not making a lot of sense right now, Dad." She smiled. "Maybe time for a break?"

He turned to hide the tears, holding his eyes up high to dry them in the crossing wind. "Mom would be so proud of you. Of the person you've become. So proud."

She'd formed her own tears now, and they shaved their downward tracks across her dirty cheeks, unashamed. She was smiling still, a subtle upturn of the lips.

"Just as proud as I am. You need to know that."

"I do, Daddy." She threw her body into his and wrapped her arms around him. They stood there like that for a moment. "I still see her, you know," she whispered. Her breath was hot against the center of his chest. "In my dreams, she's there. She's never really left us. Just crossed over."

Glen held her tighter, letting tears spill down across his face.

"I think that's when she's nearest," she whispered. "In our dreams. On the other side."

"Other side, huh?" Glen folded over, resting his face against her head. He kept his eyes closed, catching a smell like sunscreen, coconut, and salt, sweet and warm, the scent of sunlight held inside her hair. "I like the idea of that."

A tension that he'd never even known was there began to thaw and drain, and he held her there against him as his tears crossed to the fibers of her hair, wicked across their lengthy channels. They stayed there like that for a moment in the lonesome patience of the forest, nothing more than wind and distant breath of water somewhere not too far from where they stood. And out amid the cyclic hush and rush of water, the sound of seagulls could be heard, laced among the sheets of wind that found them through the trees. It swept past and fled into the shadows of the forest at their backs.

Glen rubbed his daughter's back, rising, falling underneath his hand. He shoved a dirty sleeve across his face to wick the sweat away before he let her go. "Let's keep walking. Can't be far now."

He took her hand and led her up and through the arid stalks

of pine and oak that cracked against the wind. The setting sun came through the trees in ways that set the cold ablaze and lifted shadows from the forest floor on sheets of orange and red and yellow. The air seemed warmer now despite the falling day, and his conscience felt unburdened somehow after their discussion.

She understood.

Maybe she always would have, though. Maybe he'd just made things worse by being too preoccupied with his own issues to notice. Too busy dodging what was real, content in selfish ignorance. Punishing himself for what he didn't do, couldn't do. Angry over things he couldn't change, believing that he'd failed them all.

And now he'd found he'd been alone in that belief, sickened by the time he'd spent consumed by that delusion. Sickened by the fact that in the course of all those false beliefs, he'd led Lauren to believe he'd actually regretted the choice he'd made. All those wasted years.

He looked down at Lauren, oblivious to observation, and he watched her as she walked.

Mouse-brown hair, olive skin, the long and graceful bridge of nose, the half-stepped, busied stride—her mother's clone.

Glen smiled and turned again to face the way ahead. He kept her hand inside his palm as both came up and moved between the fence of trees, crossing out into a narrow field of tall and desiccated grass that chattered in the wind, whipping horizontal to the earth beneath the ceaseless gust. Out beyond the open edge, a sound both soft and brutal came and went, somehow reminiscent of his youth, his old man rolling the radio dial across the AM stations on their way to Sunday service, bursting in and out of static. Glen's legs began to slow, his feet now stilled beneath him as he gazed across the open range ahead.

What lay ahead evaded comprehension, and the smile that played on his lips had softly lingered there on last remains of moments prior, sputtering on the waning fumes of hope and joy. And then it fell away, and he felt his daughter give his palm a squeeze, her search for words as fruitless as his own.

An ocean filled the valleys in between the mountains for as far as eyes could see, its currents rushing through in violent channels throwing whirlpools off like glittered vengeance, unfurling as they spun into the deep. The drowning sun set fire to the great and winking body as it sank beneath the liquid edge of day, riding massive swells that heaved and dipped and played the light like spectral eels.

Inside his ears, the pulse returned.

Hand in hand, they watched in utter silence, halfway steeped in awe, halfway in futility of their condition. The fury of the surf abrased the mountainsides, new shores cut where currents sheared away the vegetation, mangy strips of earth and rock now wrapping every hill like filthy cuffs, binding nature in its devastation. Where the breakers charged the mountainside beneath them, the hiss and rush came up to meet their ears, and both their minds swung back into that last day at the beach when they were still complete.

"The dunes," whispered Glen. "We haven't lost them yet."

Lauren turned her head to look at him, tears riding high and cradled in her eyes. He pulled her close, and the two sat down inside a nest of withered grass there at the mountain's peak, the world around them turned to water. The field of oats bowed to the inbound winds, flattened out to kiss the ground beneath them on repeat beneath the rise and fall of forces all around.

"No," answered Lauren. "They belong to us this time."

Glen cast a tired breath into the open air. "Maybe we'll just sit here for a little bit, enjoy the sunset." His voice came flatly, shock removing all inflection, all emotion, a distillation of the moment's inevitability as he eyed the sprawling sea that scrubbed existence from the earth.

"We can still do that," he said, words trailing off into the faintest breath. He pulled Lauren closer to his side.

The day was thinner now, bleeding out. The evening turned to yellow, to orange, to hints of red that stained the shadows in such ways that left them dark, yet still illuminated all the same. Lauren leaned into the alcove of Glen's chest and arm, tucked comfortably beneath its hold. Her breaths fell into cadence with his own, as if they shared a common set of lungs to suit them both.

Glen blinked to still his bustling mind, thoughts sliding through its corridors like bits of ice, his sense of consciousness caught in the slipstream as they all fled down into the plunging wells.

He felt as if the air had thinned by half, his equilibrium offset and tilting all the world around him. His body tingled as if crossing through a curtain crafted from the naked ends of live wires, kissing nerves and raising them from long and numbing slumber. Lauren's voice disintegrated at his ear, words unknown and swept up in the rushing sound that filled his head. He reached for Lauren, felt her hand slip into his. He squeezed, held it tight.

"Stay with me."

Glen closed his eyes again, so tired now, and beneath their lids the darkness flickered, bloomed, then opened up to sudden light.

CHAPTER
FORTY-ONE

STERILE, WHITE LIGHT.

Voices came in on the wind. They spoke his name, their echoes mingling with the screaming gulls that seemed to hover at the farthest reaches of his mind.

"Glen," a woman said. "His eyes are open." Again, his name. "Glen."

It took a moment for the brilliance of his sight to calm, diluted just enough to let the details trickle through, slowly inking themselves across the empty page.

He was lying down. The bare earth was gone. A bed stretched out beneath his back and head. His mind felt like a bowl of static, turning over like a restless ghost inside his skull. Understanding of the world around him broke apart like deconstruction of a jigsaw puzzle, thrown back into its box, shaken hard, its picture irrevocably dismembered. The artificial glow bled out and filled his thoughts, and swimming in its alabaster pool the shapes of his environment began to come together.

A person. No, two people. On one side was a woman, by the sound of her voice alone. The other, indistinguishable. Glen was at a loss for where he was, *when* he was, sense of place and time abolished from his mind. He forced a swallow, going down like shards of glass, and tried to make out details of the space around him.

There seemed to be a door ahead, nothing but a vague rectangularity, its boundary but a dash of black sketched out across the powder coat of white that bloomed around it.

Other objects hinted at their presence. Smaller forms against a wall. Tables, carts. A square of light caught fire at the backside of his eyes, causing him to wince on contact. He closed his eyes to cool the white-hot irons laid against his optic nerves.

"Glen." The woman's voice was in his ears, his head. Someone touched his face, his hair, tending it in rows across his scalp with long and gentle nails.

"Give him time" came another voice. A man's voice, emanating from the hazy form out to his left. "His reality has shifted. There's always an adjustment."

A resonation swarmed the air around him, the slightest oscillation at its core, a baritone vibrato threaded down the middle like an auditory trunk. The electric chirp of some unknown device called out beyond the reach of sight, then another, alternating tones that spoke to one another every several seconds, conversation never deviating.

As if caught between two worlds, calling out from some

bizarre and distant past of only minutes prior, he heard the distant skies split wide again beneath a heady charge, then felt a touch within his brain like static needles. He brought his fingers to his temple, feeling wires sprung about the round patch of adhesive where the hair had been removed, cleanly sheared beneath it. And then he heard the crack again, sizzling out beyond the boundaries of perception. He felt the tingle at his temple cross paths with his brain again with subtle stabs like sleeping limbs. He winced and pulled his features inward till the strange and raw discomfort passed him by.

"It's okay. That's just your suspension equalizer" came the voice of the man. "We'll get those wires off you here soon."

"Where," started Glen. The word was dry and shapeless in his throat. He tried again. "Lauren," he mumbled. His throat was utter sand, walls seeming to adhere to one another between swallows, dragging long and arduous.

"Shhh." The woman touched his arm. "No, Glen. It's me."

"What? No," Glen said as he reached up to wipe his eyes, to remove the haze that held them like a skin of drying glue. "Lauren," he repeated. "Where's Lauren?" Glen pushed into the mattress, rising on his elbows. His mind felt like a lagging load that fell against the front side of his skull, its inside lined with pins and nails that ran it through on contact. He winced and came back down again, huffing through the pain.

The woman hushed him again, gave his arm a squeeze. "Take it easy." He saw her hazy form glance upward at the man across from her. "Is this normal?" she asked.

"You've been away a bit, Glen" came the man. His voice was

firm, authoritative, expert in his given role, whatever that may be. "You're at the institution now. Do you remember?"

Glen shook his head. "What day..." He tried to calm his vision, rid it of the ghosts that swarmed and smeared the world before him. "Who are you? Where is Lauren?"

"I am Dr. Warren Baxter, your treating physician. Today is Wednesday, October 10th. It's 12:00 p.m., your appointed extraction time." The man produced a light and passed the beam from one eye to the next as he continued. "Your wife is here as well." He disengaged the slender unit with a single click, returning it to his pocket.

Glen's face fell in confusion. "My wife is dead. Six years."

There was a brief silence. The two forms turned to one another.

"I want to see my daughter. Tell me where Lauren is."

"Oh, God," said the woman. "I... Glen, I'm not dead. I'm right here." And then she hushed him softly as his eyes adjusted fully to the world around him, to the balding doctor standing at his left, his mouth a pensive line. "Lauren isn't with us." The woman's tear-struck face above him now came into focus: Claire, weeping through the fingers of her left hand, splayed across her open lips.

CHAPTER
FORTY-TWO

CLAIRE MASTERS PUSHED HER THUMBNAIL down the pencil's edge, breaking free the school bus yellow flecks of paint that flickered down across the corporate knit of charcoal carpet at her feet. The floor became an abstract piece beneath the spots of yellow, painted like an inverse leopard. She'd been waiting in the adjacent office for roughly thirty minutes while Dr. Baxter tended to Glen, coaxing him back into the world outside the medically induced coma that had held him captive for the past six hours.

She could almost see him break inside. Something in his face, his eyes, as Baxter dosed him with the lengthy explanation of his circumstances. She saw his mind resist the words, kicked away in self-defense. He'd tried to physically remove himself, clawing at the wires trailing from his head, tubes running from his nose, from his arms like vines of fluid. A dose of diazepam had lulled him back to rest. Not asleep, but more compliant, more receptive to the coming truth.

The door opened, and Dr. Baxter slipped into the office, pressing it shut behind him, before sinking into the leather chair behind his desk. He pulled the wire frames away and plied the rubied indentations on his bridge between his thumb and index finger, then gently laid them out across a sheaf of papers at his front.

Claire watched him with expectant eyes.

He cleared his throat, sniffed. "Well." He paused, clearing out the desktop laid before him. "I can't recall a more complex experience in the time I've been working in our grief immersion program."

"When is it enough?" demanded Claire. "Two weeks you're telling me you've been at this. Three times he's been under now. *Three*."

Baxter shook his head. "The program, it takes time."

Claire hung her head, giving herself a moment lest the words that begged escape come tumbling out. They wouldn't cater to the soft and socially acceptable.

"What is going on with my husband?" she said. "Because what just happened in there, Glen's reaction when he woke up, that doesn't seem normal to me. Frankly, it scares the shit out of me."

"You're here because you care," said Baxter. "And your support is appreciated. Not just by Glen, but—"

"I'm here because you *asked* me to be here. You told me it would anchor him in his reentry from the coma. That it would help to reestablish reality."

"That is true."

"And so I came. I came because, yes, I care about him, because I'm still his wife, *technically*. But I *never* thought this was a good idea. Let me be clear. I support my husband's desire to recover. Not this science project you call therapy."

"Of course," said Baxter. "And that support still makes a difference."

"Well, he didn't seem very fucking anchored to me, Doctor," said Claire. "He woke up asking for Lauren, for Chrissake." Claire leaned forward. "It's been six years since she *died*."

Baxter worked the glasses on his face and cleared his throat. He leaned back in his chair, dragging his fingers across his chin in contemplation.

"Claire, we talked about this. In grief immersion therapy, the mind's subconscious comes into the forefront. Reality, memories, emotions are reshaped, reinvented to suit the mind's agenda. It is designed to free the mind to reprogram its means of experiential learning, charting its own course back to health, back to safety when the real world pushes it too far and causes it to run off course."

Claire frowned. "I get the theory, but what does that mean for Glen now? Right now, post-procedure. Is he okay? He woke up asking for Lauren. My God, does he have to keep living this all over again?"

Baxter held a palm upright, stopping Claire. "No, not exactly. For the past six hours, Glen experienced an alternate reality. One which, in his mind, spanned days not hours. One in which your daughter did not die that day."

Claire's felt her insides squirm, rolling over.

"Because the mind is eager to confront its past, to reconcile the grief experienced, it generates a scenario that affords it an opportunity to do so. In Glen's case, this was done through reengagement with Lauren. But because his mind still contended with the grief of her passing, that grief had been displaced, transferred elsewhere. He couldn't logically grieve her death while simultaneously interacting with her in life, and he also couldn't simply dispose of the grief outright without some measure of resolution, of healing. As a result, in this alternate reality, his mind was forced to reassign it.

"Claire," he continued, "in Glen's reconfigured world, it wasn't Lauren who had drowned six years ago."

Claire's eyes opened, focusing directly on him. "Then who was it?" She squinted in delivery of the question, the sinking horror of its answer already bleeding through before he'd said the words.

"It was you."

Claire blinked several times in succession. She felt the wall of tears rise up beneath her eyes. Her expression melted down, reformed into a shape of contemplative disbelief, sorrow, and anger.

Baxter nodded once, slow in execution as Claire mined the logic of his words for understanding.

"And so Lauren had been the one to live."

"That…would seem to be the case."

Claire leaned forward, pitched her forehead on the fingertips of both her hands. "So now, today, he gets to learn for a second time that Lauren's gone." She huffed and gave the man a dry laugh.

Baxter moved his brow, studying Claire.

"And you're honestly going to sit here now and tell me that this somehow isn't worse? For six years, he's walled himself off, dealing with the grief of Lauren's passing on his own: the guilt, the anger, everything. Shutting me out, shutting the whole world out."

His hands went up like two flags. "Please, Claire. That's not what I'm saying at all. I think we've found success today. That's what I'm trying to explain."

"How so?" Claire glared back at Baxter, holding her position. "You're a pusher."

The comment took him back, forcing him to pause a beat.

"You sell false hope. You profit off grief, creating addicts of your patients who are desperate to be relieved of their pain."

"You don't understand," started Baxter.

"The man's already asking for his next session!" yelled Claire. "You tell me he's progressing, but that's not what I'm seeing. I'm seeing no more than a junkie, addicted to a false reality, jonesing for the chance to run back to a place where our daughter isn't dead! Preferring to live in a world in which I am the one who died, rather than face his grief and live with me. Do you know how that feels?"

"Please, Claire, hear me out," said Baxter calmly. "From what he's told me, I do see a healthier man emerging from these sessions."

Claire knit her arms together tightly and sat back in her chair, her disbelief laid bare.

Dr. Baxter leaned forward, returning the glasses to his face. He thumbed the first few pages from the stack of paperwork before him, finding his place among the text. "His subconscious took the circumstances surrounding Lauren's death and, combined with his knowledge of biology, invented a world in which water actually took a living form by some sort of microorganism that controlled it."

Baxter waved his palms as if to clear the clutter of his explanation, breaking it down to basics. "He's personified the water itself. His subconscious seems to have created a living entity from that which took your daughter's life. A means of assigning intent, purpose, a cognizant antagonist."

Claire was merely listening now, blinking on occasion, silent as the doctor filled her in.

"It gets more interesting," continued Baxter, working through the papers. "This body of water had surrounded him and Lauren in a building. A diner. But not only them. There were others trapped there with them, and each of those individuals were personifications of the various emotions and experiences he's encountered over the years and harbored deep inside."

Baxter wet his thumb and pulled a segment from the sheaf of papers. He peeled off several sheets and dealt them out across his desk. He uncapped a yellow highlighter, then made his way across the pages, striking through assorted blocks of text.

"This one character," said Baxter, circling back to reference notes within the first block, "Right here. Hank was his name. This Hank individual was representative of the anger, the rage your husband harbored all these years, manifested out of Glen's subconscious, raising these suppressed emotions to the surface as a living, breathing person he was forced to face." The doctor paused, looked up at Claire across the topside of his glasses, which were now lower on his nose. "Tell me," he said, "are you familiar with Freudian theory?"

"Referring to the id, ego, those things?"

"Correct."

"Vaguely," said Claire. "Only what I remember from grad school, which isn't much."

"But, you have a surface understanding," affirmed the doctor. "That's good. That's fine." A pleased expression crossed his face.

Claire uncrossed her arms and laid her hands in her lap, regarding Baxter blankly.

"What we're dealing with, in a manner of speaking, is something similar, at least as I interpret it. The id consists of primal, instinctive thoughts, behaviors, emotions. And such things are inherent to any major life event. Left to run amok, unacknowledged or perhaps dealt with in unhealthy ways, the effects can be quite damaging." Dr. Baxter stopped, offering Claire a moment.

Claire carved the pencil in her fingers, a blind and nervous action as she listened, littering her lap now with the flecks of yellow paint, down now to the grain of natural wood along much of its length. She didn't speak, waiting for the doctor to continue.

"Right," said Baxter, starting up again. "Well, the id can most easily be thought of as a horse, while its rider is representative of the ego. Essentially, the horse is the power, the motion, the force, be that behavior, emotion, or thought. The rider, the ego, provides direction and guidance."

Baxter leaned forward again on his elbows, pushing his hands together at their sprawling tips. "Glen's ego has created a more acceptable means of contending with these emotions, these thoughts, within the id. A means of confrontation and control not previously available in the conscious world. In his alternate reality, the one created in his comatose state, his thoughts, fears, emotions, became flesh and blood, living entities with which he interacted."

"And so you're telling me Glen's ego generated this Hank character as a means of dealing with his anger?"

"I believe so. Yes. That is my understanding." Baxter nodded. "But that's not it. It didn't end there. There were others." He brought his hands down to the papers on his desk again, transitioning to another block of yellow. "A second character, Tony, displayed traits of weakness, fearfulness, timidity, regret as predominant traits. This Tony was a manifestation of those emotions Glen's been dealing with. Self-perceptions birthed from Lauren's death. An incident for which Glen holds himself personally accountable, weak for his inability to stop it, having allowed it to happen."

Claire closed her eyes.

"As with Hank," continued Baxter, "this Tony persona was created as a means of dealing with those emotions, perceptions in the human form, in circumstances manifested by the ego."

Baxter moved the page aside, continuing on the next.

"There's Laj, the protector, a personification of strength. Helen, representing hopelessness. Fred, frustration, denial. Jesse, codependence." He reassembled the pages, racking the sheaf into a solid form once more against the desktop. "See, he contended with them all, interacting with them in various ways that put him up against each and every one, face to literal face until they'd all cleared out, left his psyche, laid him bare beyond their influence. Only then could Glen successfully address his issues without their interference."

Baxter laid the pages down, settling back into his chair again. "And then, of course, at the center of it all, there was Lauren."

Despite the best of efforts, the tears that surged behind Claire's eyes spilled over, emptied out across her cheeks.

She spoke through clenched teeth. "It sounds like a nightmare. That you've placed Glen inside a six-hour, hyperrealistic nightmare." She shook her head, struggling to maintain composure. "And at the end of the day, isn't that pretty much all it is? I have dreams, Dr. Baxter, but they're just dreams. I don't wake up a changed woman. None of it is real. None of it sticks."

Baxter pushed the stacks aside and laced his fingers on the desktop. Claire sat in silence.

"There are numerous accounts of patients who have emerged from comas having lived in, having experienced, alternate lives, alternate realities. Not dreams, fleeting manifestations, hallucinatory experiences, but true touch, visual, tactile interactions that stuck with them, clinging to their psyches, carried out like lasting keepsakes that yielded, in some cases," said Baxter, throwing up a hand to interject his disclaimer, "not *all* cases, mind you. But, in *some* cases, lasting psychological change. *Positive* change."

Claire pushed her tongue against the inside of her cheek. "Okay, but it still seems no more than a dream. I don't know." She took a breath and scratched her forehead, rippled under thought.

Dr. Baxter sat a moment, mulling something over, then leaned forward. He opened his mouth to speak, then stopped, recollecting his thoughts, reconsidering his words. "In these other cases, a major impetus in our pursuit of this research..." Again, he paused and raked the corner of his mouth, then continued. "I am not a spiritual man by any stretch of the imagination. I don't believe in the spectacular and the supernatural. I am a person of science, okay?"

Claire frowned. "What is it?"

Baxter worked the fingers of his right hand with his left, twisting one at a time. "Some comatose patients, some predating our research here, some I've had the pleasure of tending to here personally, their experiences went beyond the dream state, yielding other kinds of responses."

"Other responses?" repeated Claire, waiting for the rest.

"Bruises, cuts," said Baxter. "Physiological responses to the mental stimuli experienced during the coma. Odd as it may sound, even smells." He sat back in his chair and ran his tongue along his lower lip. "There are differences of thought on the matter. Some believe this suggests these individuals, in the depths of their conditions, their treatments, are able to cross between existential planes, experience alternate realities, other dimensions that run parallel to our own. Some have even gone so far as to hypothesize, at the furthermost extremes, that these existential planes weren't merely visited, but actually created. That perhaps by tapping into some uncharted portion of the mind, a sort of key to tangible manifestation had been turned. These individuals had seemed to physically live out these alternate realities while under, even bringing subtle elements back with them."

"Surely you're not suggesting his experience was real in any way," said Claire, almost laughing at how pathetic this sales effort was becoming.

"No, Ms. Masters," said Baxter as he shook his head, a jittery movement. "To be clear, this is not my personal belief. Personally, I find the belief absurd. My belief is that these changes came about because the mind, in its conviction of the given moment, whatever given event, simply made them so. Even the smells, the odors."

Claire began to speak, but Baxter cut her off before she had the opportunity.

"The instance I'm referencing had to do with a particular child, a seven-year-old boy, who dreamed, pardon..." said Baxter, correcting himself, "experienced an *alternate reality* in their comatose state, in which they'd escaped a burning house. His hospital room smelled like smoke. Not the smell of an extinguished match or candle, but full-blown ash and cinder. I would go so far as to describe it as not so much a smell but as a stench. It's incredible, certainly unbelievable, but I believe there are explanations for this. The human body is an incredibly complex system, still not completely understood today despite all efforts. One theory is perhaps the body produced the scent to match its perceived environment, supporting its perception of reality. I really couldn't tell you. There is still so much to learn."

He shook his palms before her. "All that to say, the oceans of our comatose psychologies differ vastly, *vastly* from the puddles of our everyday dreams."

Claire was on her elbows, pitched into her knees. She rolled the pencil in between her fingers. "And so, for Glen," she started, letting out an irritated laugh, "you don't believe he'll suffer from this? That you're causing him lasting psychological damage here?"

"To the contrary, I believe it was a therapeutic experience. In this other world, Glen and Lauren were able to share their thoughts and emotions, and he was able to save your daughter. And in that process they healed together, Claire," he said, coming forward again on elbows. "He has been given an opportunity to work his feelings, his emotions, to the surface, expressed directly to your daughter. I believe we're finding success in that. Don't you? In all of this, I believe he's achieving the closure he's been missing all these years."

"I want to see him," blurted Claire. "When can I see him?"

"Anytime you're ready," said Baxter, rising from his chair. "He's available now."

CHAPTER
FORTY-THREE

THROUGH THE WINDOW OF HIS suite, rain-specked in the early touches of the larger storm to follow, Glen mapped the geometric skyline over Norfolk, Virginia, from the elevated angle of his bed. Somewhere out beyond the endless gray, the sky seemed to expand, and throaty pains of its development fell out across the city, low and long. The pane of glass reverberated in its frame, a low-slung buzz that faded out as quickly as it came.

Claire stood there at the open door a moment, watched her husband watch the world outside. The only sound between them was the sonorous huff of air that spilled from two vents in the ceiling. The other tones of various machinery had left the room since he'd come out of hibernation, their sources laid to rest and sleeping in their server racks along the wall. If he'd suspected she was there, he hadn't made it known.

Claire walked the length of room and laid her purse down

on the bedside table, sat down on the vacant edge of mattress. She led a spill of hair back to its post behind her ear, then leaned toward her husband.

Glen rolled his head to face her. He examined her the way they did the first time that they'd met. His eyes glimmered vivid blue, enhanced beneath the tears that cloaked their surface.

Seeing Claire was bittersweet. Knowing she was here again, alive and well beside him, meant that Lauren wasn't.

"What are you doing here?" asked Glen.

"I don't know," said Claire. "Baxter thought it would help. Something…something with transitioning," she rattled. "Why didn't you reach out? Why didn't you tell me about this process sooner? About what they've been putting you through?"

Glen snuffed, rolling his head away. "When he took your info, I didn't think he'd actually use it."

"What're *you* still doing here, Glen?" whispered Claire.

"And that," said Glen, "is why I really hoped he wouldn't."

Claire stiffened. "Answer the question, Glen. I'm not here for my own health. We're separated, but that doesn't mean that I don't care. That I'm not still your wife."

Glen watched the city through the water-dappled window. "Just working out a few bugs," he murmured. "Probably wouldn't make a lot of sense to you."

"Dr. Baxter filled me in."

"Everything?" asked Glen. He turned his eyes back to her. She nodded.

"Then if I told you I was gutted," continued Glen, "I don't expect you'd ask why."

"I'm worried about you," said Claire. She leaned toward him, holding his attention. "I'd like you to leave this place today. With me."

Glen's eyes narrowed, his body stiffened.

"Let's get out of here. We can go anywhere," continued Claire. "Tell me how I can help."

"I'm not going anywhere. Not yet. Things are just a little patchy, a little vague, right now. What's real, what's not. It's normal." He squinted at the thought, eyes drifting through the narrows of his lids.

"Says Baxter," said Claire. "None of this is normal. You realize the conflict of interests there, don't you?"

"It's like I'm caught between two truths." Glen focused on the wall ahead, a combination of embarrassment and uncertainty coursing through him. Wariness of boundaries which seemed to shift between delusion and reality without warning. "I know how strange this all seems."

"It's not just strange," said Claire. "It's dangerous."

"It's therapy," said Glen impatiently. "Since when is therapy a bad thing?"

"Bullshit," hissed Claire. "This is *compulsion*."

Glen fell silent. He turned to face the window once again. The rain was coming harder now. Tracks of water striped the pane, droplets racing one another top to bottom, starting small and ending large, their abbreviated lifespans still more whole than Lauren's. He filled his chest with air, pushed it out into the room.

"You should go," said Glen finally.

Claire remained silent.

"I'm starting again in the morning."

"You're kidding me." Claire laughed. It was a hollow sound devoid of joy, filled with disbelief. "I'm...not just leaving you here."

"You don't have a choice," said Glen. Two men appeared in the doorway behind her, dressed in lab coats, neatly groomed. All business.

She stood up from the bed and stayed there for a moment. Her body was shaking. "Glen, just—"

Glen turned and looked at Claire, the strain of her emotions emanating from her body, vapor thin and anxious, fearful, spilling out into the room.

The two men moved into the room and stood on either side of her.

"Lauren told me that she understands. That she knows I did the best that I could do."

"Stop it. It's not real," hissed Claire. "*This* is real. Right here. *I'm* real, Glen. I miss Lauren too, every fucking day, Glen. But she is gone." She laid a hand against her chest. "But I'm still here. Please let me help you."

"She's waiting for me," said Glen. "We're not done yet. She needs me."

Tears rushed down Claire's cheeks.

"I'm just so tired," he whispered. "I'm going to get some rest."

"I...I can't," said Claire, shielding her open mouth behind her hand, choking back sobs. She turned and walked away, stealing one last glance before the two attendants blocked her view and gestured for her to leave.

The motion and the sound of Glen's breathing were the only signs of life remaining in the now-still room. A touch of dampness drifted through the space. A scent of leaves and pine, suddenly present.

As the minutes passed, sleep began to come down softly, filling him. As it did, Glen's consciousness began to flicker, memories changing like channels as his mind attempted separation of the manufactured from the real, one world dissolved into another, a great and shifting experiential mass. The hiss and pat of rain on glass became a distant sound, a quiet rhythm playing out along the borders of his waning thoughts. Ghosts of smell and touch and taste rushed through him, bringing the moments back to life, the painful and the precious, a hypnagogic churn that towed him through the void of here nor there, along the borders of his two conflicting worlds.

A rush of ocean filled his ears, a patter of the rain laced in between. He felt Lauren at his side, just beneath his arm, a subtle weight that hinted at her presence on some hidden level of perception.

The scent of forest found him, a rush of wind across his face. Lauren's voice came through, circling in his head.

Never really left. Just crossed over.

A single tear descended, slowing to a standstill on his cheek. Its surface glimmered, driven by a rhythmic pulse emitted from the stir of life within, an organism of a single cell that fluttered at its core.

EPILOGUE

IT WAS 2:47 P.M. WHEN hospital security received a call. It came on the tail end of another call about an incident unfolding on the fourth floor in experimental therapeutics. All hands on deck had been summoned, leaving this second call to a lone new hire left to occupy the desk.

A female, aged somewhere between thirteen and fifteen years old, dark brown hair, slight build, Caucasian, had been discovered in the tree line just outside of the Kaufman and emergency wings of Sentara Norfolk General. All indications pointed to shock. She'd been unable to speak, and her core temperature rested at 95.5, her body on the verge of hypothermia. She'd been cowering beneath a grove of cypress trees, terrified, disoriented, seeking shelter from the rain, when a woman and her son had spotted her. The girl had seemed to calm, only slightly, once she realized they hadn't come to any harm beneath the rain, the bizarre apparent source of her terror.

Once inside and under care, no form of identification had been discovered on her person. Her voice still hadn't found her, nor had any sense of situational awareness. Her eyes, a muted shade of gray, didn't seem to register her whereabouts or any of the doctors' efforts to engage her. Her body tingled, as if this were the first time her nerves had met the world around her. Physical examination revealed the presence of a clover-shaped birthmark, situated just behind her left ear.

Outside, the thunder rolled. With the darkening sky, everything had taken on the surreal colors of a premature and richly amber twilight. The rain now lashed the building without mercy, punishing the walls and windows with a low-grade roar. It nearly washed away the voices calling through the intercom, panicked yet professional. Their composure hadn't left them yet. That would take some time. Somewhere in the building, a security alarm could now be heard.

In the room, Lauren did as she was told. She waited for the doctors to return. Waited for them to work out what had happened, to tell her where she was. To see her father, to know that he was safe. But she knew that wasn't going to happen. She had been disabled by the numbing weight of inevitability.

Wherever this place was, a storm had followed her, and it was only getting started.

Consciousness determines existence.

—Michio Kaku,
*Parallel Worlds: A Journey Through Creation,
Higher Dimensions, and the Future of the Cosmos*

READING GROUP GUIDE

1. Why do you think it's so common for teens to be ambivalent to their parents? Did you feel this when you were a teenager?

2. If you noticed someone acting strange or aggressive in a public area, what would you do?

3. If you saw something that was acting against the laws of nature or physics as you know them, how do you think you would react?

4. Glen's memory is frequently triggered by scents and images throughout the story. Is this something you can relate to? What are some specific sights, smells, sounds, or textures that are often tied to certain memories of yours?

5. How prepared are you for emergency situations?

6. Should parents lie to their kids under certain circumstances? Is it the job of parents to "make it better," even if that comes at the expense of always being honest with them?

7. Did you find Glen suspicious throughout the read? Did you have any theories as to what was really going on?

8. Lauren tells her dad: "It's okay for everything to not be okay." What does that statement mean to you?

9. When Glen's reality is finally revealed to the reader, how did you react? Do you think this unconventional approach to treating grief could ever work from someone in his position?

A CONVERSATION WITH THE AUTHOR

Where did the inspiration for this story come from?

The concept was inspired by the near-drowning of my wife while vacationing in the Outer Banks region of Ocracoke, North Carolina, some years back. She was trapped in an aggressive rip current that swept her far away from shore. By the time I swam out to her while our kids watched from the shore, she was going under and sucking water into her lungs. With luck, I was able to shove her up onto a boogie board and get her to safety without being caught in it myself. I came close.

Afterward, I was kind of rhetorically thinking about what could possibly be more horrific, and the only thing that flashed into my mind was if the water was actually alive. A predatorial, living thing that pursued its prey. That was the genesis of the concept behind *Body of Water*.

What is your writing process like?

My best ideas come when I'm not overthinking them. This is the reason I do better not outlining the entire book at once, because it's so restrictive and binding to the creative process. I'll roughly outline little sections here and there to offer some general direction, but beyond that, the most fun is flying by the seat of my pants and just enjoying wherever the ride decides to take me. That way, the end product isn't so prescriptive and vanilla. If I'm not writing with a formulaic approach, and not even I see the end coming from a distance, odds are the reader won't either.

What kind of research did you do for this book?

Some of the research I conducted for the novel was related to real-world water-harvesting microorganisms, as well as suspension states/long-term preservation and reanimation of microorganisms in nature. The latter topic led me to the discovery of an anthrax outbreak in the Yamal Peninsula back in 2016, which was an event that is referenced in the book. That event helped shape the protagonist's theory of where the water-manipulating microorganism might have come from, potentially being a prehistoric organism that's survived millions of years via cryogenic permafrost suspension, suddenly reanimated. In other areas, being the son of a high-school biology teacher who's kind of always grown up in a constant state of education where those things are concerned kind of provided a general knowledge base from which a number of other details were drawn.

Do you have a favorite character?

While I really loved writing all of the characters, I think Laj stands out as my favorite. Likely because he represents the strong, calm, cool, and collected individual we all really need to be in the middle of the chaos taking place in the world today, both for ourselves as well as for our loved ones.

How did you decide how to end the book the way it does?

At the end of it all, I didn't want to leave things on a purely tragic note. I wanted there to be a spark of hope, though born out of an equally terrifying situation. I wanted to leave the readers not only pondering the possibilities of what comes next but also eager to reread the book to recognize all those hidden elements that ultimately were right there in plain sight, though their significance hadn't yet been realized.

ACKNOWLEDGMENTS

My first debt of gratitude goes to my wife, Heather, for enduring this grueling publication journey at my side. For the many years of being my sounding board through countless highs and lows, new paths and dead ends, impossible deadlines, innumerable revisions, and providing such unwavering support and understanding across so many days and evenings when the future of this book required me to sit at the computer instead of spending time with family.

Thank you to my three daughters, McKenna, Elise, and Teagan, not only for always being my personal cheer squad but also never failing to remind me when it's time to come up for air from time to time.

Forever grateful to my parents, who encouraged me to pursue my writing dreams since day one and who never let me forget about my talents.

Thank you to my literary agents, Christy Fletcher and Kelly

Karczewski, and my film/TV agents, Geoff Morley and Olivia Fanaro, for your invaluable industry expertise and guidance along the way. You're the best, and I couldn't have done any of it without you.

A special thanks to my editor, Shana Drehs, for your belief in this book and keen editorial eye, which helped shape this book into the greatest version of itself. Lastly, thank you to the entire Sourcebooks team, to include those in marketing and publicity, art and design, editorial, and any others who have had a stake in bringing this book to life.

ABOUT THE AUTHOR

Adam Godfrey has published numerous short stories spanning genres of horror, thriller, and science fiction and is the author of the horror novella *Narcissus*. He holds a BA in marketing, MS in cybersecurity, and has worked for the United States Department of Defense as a cybersecurity risk management professional for over twenty-five years. Adam and his family live in Chesapeake, Virginia.